Airstreaming

A Novel

Ray & Jeanean,

*I hope you enjoy this
novel and have many
happy travels ahead!*

Tom Sch

9/19

Tom Schabarum

This book is a work of fiction. The characters, incidents, and dialogue are drawn from the writer's imagination and are not to be construed as real in any way. Any resemblance to actual events or persons, living or dead, is entirely fictional.

AIRSTREAMING

Cover photograph © by Richard Charpentier

ISBN-13: 978-0-615-60304-9

For Grandmother

Airstreaming

A young girl of ten watches her mother as she sits in front of a vanity mirror. On this particular morning, the dawn light reflects from the mirror and casts a warm glow around the room. The girl laughs as she bounces a bit on the bed. The bed-sheets billow and envelop her. As her mother fixes her hair and applies makeup, she catches her daughter's reflection and smiles back at her. A pair of strong arms, her father's, catches the girl mid-bounce and she is lifted into the air and swung like an airplane, back and forth, over the bed. Then her father lets her go and she lands, softly and swiftly, among the bed-sheets, laughing.

Home

Now sixteen, older, she comes home. Here are the things she doesn't see:

Her grandparents' Ansonia clock (chiming just now).

The dining room table pushed against the wall.

The darkened kitchen, the open door to her parent's bedroom, the bright dining room, a small mud-room off the kitchen with the door open, the living room in disarray.

Assorted lamps and burning candles.

A lit-up TV.

An upturned TV tray—the contents listed will be spaghetti with meat sauce, kernels of corn, milk, a broken glass, knife, fork, spoon, and a napkin.

A soiled daily prayer guide from Cambridge Baptist Church.

Her frantic mother.

Her dead father.

Linda sneaks into her room from her bedroom window and removes her white dress. The sleeve is torn. There are sprays of dirt where the fabric was folded against earth. She goes into the bathroom and wipes away the signs of him: the white chalk of scratched skin, dirty palm prints from her forehead, dried semen from her shoulder. As the water runs, she hears her mother's footsteps in the hall. Her bedroom door bursts open.

"You're home. Follow me." Her mother hasn't noticed her daughter in her slip, held lopsided by a broken strap, the top of one large nipple exposed. Linda removes the day-old underwear and shoulders on her robe. She looks in the mirror to see if there are any scratches; her hair, thin as thread, lies flat over her forehead. Holding the leaves of her robe together, she goes down the hallway to her parents' bedroom. She sees long, dark stains running like skid marks along the wood floor. Her breath runs fast. She can hear her mother pacing around the room and when she enters she sees her father lying on his back, eyes closed, mouth open. Blood soaks the sheets from a wide gash on his temple. The beginnings of a swollen eye puff the skin of his eyelid. She goes over to the bed. Her hand clutches the folds of her robe. She puts her cheek down to his mouth, hoping to feel some sort of life-breath, some sort of heat, because she knows that he wouldn't be able to look at her, see the scratches where she fought the boy, see the panic in her eyes. He'd make it right; she was counting on it, but her father lies on the bed, quiet as church.

"Daddy," she says.

"One minute he's standing there talking to me," her mother's voice quavers like dry leaves, "the next he's on the floor."

"Daddy, wake up." She touches him. There's a mossy dampness to his skin. He doesn't move.

"I've called the doctor. I don't know what else to do." Mother is behind her. Her nightdress falls over Linda's robe. When she pulls away to the other side of the bed, her mother's dress lingers, blood-sticky to Linda's arm, and then pulls away.

"How long has he been here? I mean like this?" A way-off siren steals the quiet.

"We were waiting up in the living room for you to come home. Then he said he was going to bed. When he got up, he turned around and collapsed." Her mother absently put her hand to her stomach.

"How long, Mother?"

"Fifteen, maybe twenty minutes ago."

"You stay here; I'll see to the ambulance."

"Linda?" her mother calls after her.

"What?"

"Would you pick up a little? Your father made a mess of the living room when he fell." Linda's mind turns pinwheels. She picks up a tray, a bowl, and an empty glass. She goes to the kitchen and deposits them in the sink and catches a night reflection of herself in the window. The lights from the hallway give her hair a slight halo as she begins to cry.

Outside, the ambulance pulls to the curb. Neighbors come to their porches. There is every odd assortment of them, and they do not worry about the weather because it's coming on summer and the heat is still on the bricks.

These are war-built houses, strung together on street after street, built fast, mortar spilling over the bricks in some places. The wiring and plumbing is what's strongest, copper everywhere, but each house resembles the other and the years have aged the neighborhood and given it beauty as the maple trees have grown to line the streets, and the hedges, once low and sun-starved, have grown against the houses. Most of the early families have moved farther from town, into the low hills. Their fathers went to work for new corporations and moved up. The mothers stayed home, had children so that they quickly outgrew the tiny houses.

Linda's family moved in to one of the few remaining the day it was available. Her daddy said of that day: "There were colored ribbons and balloons, moving vans lined the sidewalks and were in the driveways, gleaming furniture and toys littered the lawns. Everything was new. I felt along each thing and it had that store-bought smoothness to it. And it smelled good, too." He'd go on. "All that new earth overturned. It was like waking up to find yourself in the Garden of Eden."

Her daddy had purchased one of these houses on a VA deal after the war like everyone else, but with special circumstance. The payments were kept low enough to afford a night out every so often at the movie house in town. Mother made popcorn and stowed it in her purse, making her smell buttery and fried, and Linda could tell that the ticket-taker knew they were sneaking in food.

She'd avert her eyes from his as she passed through the cold, metal turnstile. Her father brought black licorice vines and handed them, one by one, to Linda throughout the movie so that by the time it was finished, her mouth and tongue were black.

She wondered if he felt the flicker of light on his eyelids.

He sat on the porch for hours, keeping his hands busy sewing buttons onto tattered clothes, fortifying elbows on sweaters. "You don't need eyes for this kind of work." But then he'd call out when he needed a needle changed or new thread. Most times it was Linda who'd come, thread the needle, then go back inside to her things. He knew the distance between buttons by measuring the spaces with his fingers. The neighbors admired his work and announced themselves from the sidewalk, though he'd know from their gait who it was. He'd wave to them every time, looking way over their heads as if looking for a plane just off the horizon, tiny threaded needle slicing the air, button between forefinger and thumb against the fabric.

Sometimes Linda stayed, watched her father work. He pretended to reach over and sew through her body, then through his in exaggerated gestures, tightening up the string, binding them together. "This way," he said, "you'll always know where I am."

Two men come from the ambulance. One comes up the stairs, thick-chested, short legs, and each step a heavy, hard thud on the wood. The other stays to collect things from the back. Linda shows him the way down the hall. She sees that he notices the living room and probably wonders if there had been a fight. When they enter her parents' room, Linda is surprised to find her mother changed, hair brushed, standing by her father. She expected the last thing, but the blue print dress makes her believe that her daddy might still be alive to at least smell the soapy fabric of it, feel the starch.

The medic holds her daddy's wrist, counts seconds on his watch. During that time the other comes into the room with a large kit and sets it heavy on the ground.

"Nothing there, ma'am." He puts Linda's father's arm down over his chest, listens at his heart. "Here, either.

Was there some sort of trouble, ma'am? I have to ask." The attendant looks at her mother, too finely made up at this moment. Linda sees his face change slightly to accusation.

"Of course not." Her mother stares directly at him as if he didn't know anything about the world at all. "Of course there wasn't. One minute he's up, the next he fell over and caught the edge of the table with his head. We were waiting up for our daughter, watching all the Saturday shows."

"I'm not accusing you. Just trying to determine the cause. The wound here isn't very deep; more messy than troublesome." The medic has already examined the gash, determining that it wasn't the cause. He shakes his head as if he can't figure what was, but he relaxes his pace, is more methodical about things. The other sees this and goes about the paperwork.

Linda backs away from the bed. She can feel the stitches pulling away one at a time.

Two days later, the autopsy report will come. Typed crooked under Cause of Death will be "Brain Aneurysm (FATAL)." Three words that mark the end of her daddy's life, giving meaning to it. Her mother covers the piano with a dark tablecloth so the people coming over to pay their respects won't play it.

In addition to the monthly government check, he had played piano for money down at the beer parlor Friday and Saturday nights, the Baptist church on Sundays. People hired him to play at weddings, parties. Her mother dropped them off and Linda led him to where the piano was, gently lifted the keyboard cover, guided her father to the stool, and then disappeared among the guests until he was through.

He played by memory. If a tune were requested for the event, he'd figure it out from listening to the record over and over again off the phonograph. He'd do it while his wife was at work and Linda was at school. He'd play it and then finger the keys until they sounded right and, in an afternoon, he'd have the whole song.

Linda made regular stops at Clifton's Music after school for the records. Her father would have already called, and they'd be waiting for her, in brown paper, flat as pizza. On Saturdays they'd go together, pay the bill, and collect record albums from the sale bin at ten cents apiece.

Her father is lifted onto the gurney. His head has been bandaged temporarily, more for the mess it is making than to help. The medics mechanically unfold a sheet up from his feet and over his head. Linda is in the corner watching her mother work the room, gathering the soiled sheets, taking the entire pillow and placing it on top of them. She passes Linda and goes into the hall to the closet where she keeps the linen and pulls down fresh sheets, a new pillow. She comes back and begins to make the bed. She sees Linda staring at her; the medics stop what they're doing. "I have to do something," she says, bitterness being held in check by sadness.

Mother had wondered aloud many times over the years that "how come the man she loved had been taken away from her little by little?"

Linda heard the same story told in mother's exasperated way, to anyone who asked, "You know, he was blinded in the war, unable to support our family, give me more than one child. I married him whole, complete, but bits of him disappeared, or were forgotten about and never found."

She looked at the medics as if to explain, "He had simply fallen, or rather slumped to the floor, knocking his tray of food over, hitting his head against the glass table. I cradled him in my lap, pressed my palm over his forehead where the blood seeped between my fingers. Then finally, in panic, I pulled him shoulder-first down the hallway to our bed, and with all of my strength, and some that came from God, I lifted him onto the bed. I dialed you all and went back to my husband and held his hand until I heard my daughter come home."

When the medics leave with her daddy, the house goes silent. Blue smoke from spent candles folds and turns through the living room. Linda wets her fingers to put out every one save for the tall, thick candle near the clock, as if it could keep light on the time. Time is now memory, she thinks, staring at the wavering flame.

Later, she will take her torn dress, her broken corded slip, fold them neatly, and steal out the back of the house to the trash and hide them among her daddy's ruined sheets.

The police come and take flash pictures, are upset that the medics have removed the body. Her mother sits with them in the dining room, makes coffee and offers angel food cake. The thin-as-paper officer keeps one eye on her, looking for signs of what Linda can't determine. They do their examinations of the scene, make notes and fill out forms, say their goodbyes, and look sideways at the living room again on their way out. Linda hears them talking at the car before they get in.

The skinny one says, "You think she did it?"

"Hard to tell. Sure made a mess, though. I expect she's got a bit of work to do."

This is the cue for Linda's mother to get busy.

"I'm going to change." She leaves her daughter at the window to watch the neighbors start back into their houses to discuss the night's events over their TV programs, their books and cards. Her mother is in the bedroom a long while and when she comes out, Linda is still at the window, not able to move.

"Come away from there, dear." Her mother touches her on the shoulder and Linda flinches. She sees her mother's swollen eyes, the red around their rims. She knows she's innocent, but she isn't ready to be touched again, not by anyone.

It is after two o'clock in the morning. Linda can hear her mother in the living room, the scrapings of the couch being moved across the floor, chairs being lifted and set down. She's lying in her bed with the sheets and blankets pulled up tight to her chin. It is the first time she's felt safe all night. She expects sounds from her mother, but hears none. She imagines her working things out through the sponges and rags that she uses from under the sink. It occurs to Linda that her mother has been cleaning since she got home.

It is not quite dark in her room. A nightlight, in the shape of a swimming turtle, glows, giving soft edges to the things in her room. She is waiting, fingering her soiled dress. Her mother is stubborn, working past exhaustion, through pain and disappointment.

Water sloshes, the brush scrubs, the kitchen faucet turns on, then off on the other side of Linda's wall. She keeps her eyes open, waits her mother out, and then goes to the back of the house where they keep the trashcans to dispose of her clothes.

What might she had told her father and kept from her mother? That she had wanted to be with that boy? That when he asked she'd said yes, and then no, but that it was too late and he was intent now, his hardness probing under her dress, finding nothing but shut legs tightened beyond breaking, then his quickened explosion over her dress, on her skin. Would she have told her father she was now disappointed that she hadn't let him inside her? She thinks of the boy falling off of her to one side, her delicate dress pulled and torn by his body's weight. His breath, liquor-laced; her eyes open, staring up through the birch trees, their spindly arms and leaves sheltering them from light; the wet earth seeping through her dress, touching her skin, and the boy, breathing hard, unsure of himself. Their eyes not meeting, getting up slowly, making adjustments and he reaching over to kiss her as an apology or a hope, and her turning away and running headlong through the trees, away, away, to home, to her father to repair her stitches with his thread.

It is the Monday after the funeral and summer's coming on. The lumbering garbage trucks work their way up the streets. Linda takes the trash barrels to the sidewalk, which daddy used to do. They are full of the leavings of neighbors, family, and friends, who had come that Saturday to gather. She stands by the barrels waiting for the rough men to come and take her dress away.

Airstreaming

Sounds

As the remaining school days dwindled, Linda stuck close to Barbara. They'd grown up together, and her family, or more specifically, Barbara and her mother, since Mr. Miller was gone for long stretches of time, spent several evenings in their home.

Linda was braver around Barbara, who was a constant source of energy.

Growing up with her was always interesting. They'd take off on Saturdays and be gone all day, wandering the streets, going to the pool in summer where'd they sit and make up stories and lives as they spied on the people lying about. When Mr. Miller was gone, Mrs. Miller took them into Kansas City every chance she had, asking Linda's own mother to go with them, but she always declined because of her own daddy because it was she who had to work, and time on the weekends was precious to her to spend with her husband.

When asked to leave for weekend trips with the Millers, her daddy didn't allow her to go, which Linda didn't understand. He always made some excuse even though their family never went anywhere.

On the day Linda returned to school, Barbara came over, her red hair up - strands like electricity bunched at the back of her head - and her dress accentuating her curves so that Linda's mother almost said something like she always did like: "Did your daddy see you leave the house?" or "You know, Barbara, when it turns cold later today, and I know because I heard the weather report, you might want to take something to cover yourself up." But these days, it seemed mother's energy had dwindled and she not only let Barbara slide, but her own appearance she'd let go; her trips to Woolworth's stopped, and she wore less make-up and didn't seem to care whether one item of clothes matched the other.

Linda's own daddy would not have let her leave the house like Barbara did. Not ever, so sometimes Linda snuck out jeans to the back and changed before going to school, and then changed back into the dress again when she got home. When daddy was alive, mother had already gone to work for the day, but now she lingered until Linda was out the door and gone on the bus.

Worried that the first day back might be all stares and whispers, sad looks from teachers and her classmates, Linda stayed with Barbara during the breaks, and at lunch, because Barbara was never one for sympathy.

And out in the circle at lunchtime, kids swirling by with tater tots, slices of pizza, and bottles of Coke, Barbara swung into Linda suddenly.

"There's Perry!"

Linda had seen him across the quad too, and had turned quickly away, but not before he'd seen her. Perry, in a shaft of light through the trees, who looked that day all angular and awkward in his jeans and converse sneakers, lowered his eyes.

Perry was a surprise. She'd felt him stalking her beginning in second period a few months ago and continuing through fourth, and then the last, sixth period with Mrs. Reedy whose name matched her voice as she conjugated verbs in French so fast that it was impossible to follow. Her kids attention drifted off one by one, eyes lifting towards the clock, eyes on the window with a view outside which beckoned even on the worst weather days, or, in the case of Perry Jones, his eyes towards Linda, which would not have been so obvious if he had ever blinked.

But, to be stared at! That was the thing. Linda combed her hair at lunch then, did away with her dad's old cardigan, still leaving it hung in her bedroom, but opting for the smarter wool coat given to her at Christmas. When she decided to return his look about a week later, he was so caught off guard that he lapsed into a fit of coughing and disrupted the elegance of Mrs. Reedy's ephemeral French.

Then, of course, there was the pressure of the spring dance. Barbara was set to go with Sam, who Linda thought was all grunts and crew cut, unintelligible mutterings, hands the size of cantaloupes that were not lost on Barbara when she backed into his chest as the three of them met in the hall, or sidled up to him along the banks of trees outside, budding in bright green clumps at the ends of their branches. Sam could do nothing else but reach his arms around Barbara as Linda watched. It was not long before she mimicked Barbara's behavior with Perry who took Sam's cue, though his hands seemed much smaller than cantaloupes and roamed around her body delicately as if he were pointing directions out on a map.

In those weeks, Linda held to her fascination with the boy, what it was like to feel the warmth of him, his heat rising because of her, her causing someone to need her close. She wondered if her mother missed it, if her father's absence she felt in the same way, but of course it couldn't be in the same way. Perry and her had never fully made love, but they'd come close, as close to being in love that Linda could imagine. She'd seen it – her mom and dad when she was younger, Mr. Adderley and his wife, the way he bent to kiss her on the sidewalk when she waited for him to come home everyday after his daily walks in spring.

She was close to it, but the weeks seemed to have stretched into a decade.

"He looks different," Barbara said, mocking, "like he's all grown-up."

"Stop." Linda said. She had not divulged everything to Barbara, and had only told up to the point of them kissing under the trees outside the dance.

"He looks lonely." Barbara nudged Linda, who now just had to look again and caught Perry's eyes. He looked around him, and then came walking across the quad without the swagger that she thought Barbara was expecting.

"You should leave," Linda said to Barbara, her eyes still on Perry.

"What? Are you kidding?"

"No."

"I practically threw you two together."

"I know. Give me a sec," Linda said and nudged her up and away from her.

Barbara stood up indignantly and sashayed past Perry, who was now breaking a sweat and was plainly nervous. He gave Barbara some distance as a dog does a mean cat and then straightened his line toward Linda, sitting there, sun-soaked, the humidity sparkling her skin, her eyes, deep-set and darkened from so much rubbing and crying for days, it seemed. She was glad of Perry's approach, was trembling slightly.

"Hey Linda," he said, "I heard about your dad and I just wanted to say…"

Linda cut him off, "I know."

An awkward silence ensued, and then Perry finally said, "And I'm sorry about what happened," his voice dropping to nearly a whisper.

Barbara was surprised he'd brought it up so soon, and waited for him to look back up at her. "My dad made that dress for me," she said, then paused, waited for a response and when nothing came from Perry, said, "I don't know what you want me to say."

"I didn't try to, you know. I just couldn't stop."

"Perry."

"I wanted you to know that. I didn't hurt you did I?"

"No." Linda, who felt she'd aged overnight, added, "I just wasn't ready. It was a bad night all around."

"Not all of it." Perry said and smiled. Then he finally looked at her, absolved of his wrong, but made to know that he was wrong all at the same time, relief across his face that Linda registered as an apology. "I hope we might, you know, go to a movie or something."

Sure of herself, Linda said, "No." As she rose, now seemingly towering over Perry, she said, "I have to go now," leaving him watching her join Barbara without saying anything to her friend. They just disappeared down the walk and around one of the circular classroom buildings.

Coming home that afternoon, Barbara and her walking up the drive, Linda was surprised to see mother's car in the driveway. She shouldn't have been home for a few more hours. Barbara stopped short of her driveway, hesitated, and then took Linda's arm, but Linda was staring off at the car, which really shouldn't have been there.

"See, that wasn't so bad today, now was it?"

"Um, no, I guess not."

"I still want the full story on Perry."

"I wonder why mom's home," Linda said, and nodded toward the car.

"Maybe she couldn't, I mean, didn't feel right at work just yet." Mr. Miller's black Olds was in the Miller's drive. "Look, my Dad's home, too." Barbara said, and drew Linda's attention to her and then said, with some urgency, "I have to go."

Just like that, Linda was left alone between the drives, wondering which way to go: into the Miller's home, where Mr. Miller now was or home, to where an oppressive silence had overtaken the house.

On the Saturday before her daddy died, Linda and he had sat in their usual spot on the front porch; mosquitoes were just beginning to buzz for the season as heat came sudden after a last cold snap. Linda anticipated the end of school, and the long days she'd get to spend with him. He'd taught her many things, and had made sure of her knowledge of people, had told her about what he called his "Blind Trust."

"You need to trust all of your other senses," he said, "smells, hearing, touching, and most of all, feeling, which is different from touching." He slapped his heart, "You need to trust your instincts of things, know what the meanings are behind the façade. Maybe façade isn't the right word here. It's the front that people show the world, but in reality, there might be something darker, not sinister, mind you, but everything from their past that makes up who they are."

Her daddy reached for his beer; his fingers knew exactly where it was.

"But how do you know if a car is a Chevrolet or a Ford?"

"I used to work on a lot of cars before I lost my sight. My father and I sometimes worked all night. You get to know their sounds, how their engines rev and idle," he paused, "Plus, I've asked all the neighbors sitting here over the years…" and then laughed again.

They sat on the porch for a bit longer and after awhile another car turned onto their street. Linda tried to listen like he did with her eyes closed.

"What kind of engine is that?" He asked.

"A straight six" Linda said.

"Good." When the car passed and it was quiet again, her daddy said, "can you hear the Adderley's murmuring to each other out in the front yard? It's amazing how they go on, talking about nothing. That's real love," he said.

Linda tried as hard as she could. She never did hear the Adderleys, but for the next hour she tried to know the knocks and whines of different engines going up the street, and identified whom they belonged to just as her father blurted out the car's owners.

"That's the Hanford's Mercury," he said, as he swung his head to the car noise going up the street. "I'm right, aren't I?"

"Of course."

"It's not the engine on that car, I hear," he said, "It's the slap of the wheels, how they are going bald and out of alignment," He laughed and drew her into him, "Linda, I want you to learn how to see things differently."

A couple of hours later the onslaught of bugs came, and Linda and her daddy were relegated to the screened porch in back.

Linda entered the house to find her mother sitting straight up on the couch. She did not move until Linda closed the front door, and didn't register her or call out. It struck Linda as an odd thing since her mother had moved from one task to the other in such an expressionless and controlled way since her daddy died. To see her now, stopped, still and unresponsive, was something new. But the most extraordinary thing was that there was music from the stereo in the living room, where before, there was silence save for the sounds of dishes, cooking and cleaning.

"Mother?" There was no answer. She went around the couch and saw tears etched on her mother's cheeks. It was as if she were catatonic with grief; her eyes were distant, full, and hurt. "Mother?" Linda repeated and when no answer came again, she went over to the turntable and lifted the arm, stopping the music.

"Don't do that." Mother said.

"What's wrong?"

"I miss the noises your father made," she said, "all his music, the shuffle of his feet, how he slid his fingers along the wall so he could trace his steps." She swept her fingers through the air like flicking on a light switch sideways, "turn the music on again. I want the music on."

Linda was alarmed at her mother pleading with her, so she placed the needle back on the vinyl, finding a groove just after the smooth line indicating a new song. Out came Abbey Lincoln's clear and authoritative voice again, up and high over the melody, singing about why she loves a man. Linda lifted her head from the turntable to see her mother lower her eyes and get lost in it. Linda went to the couch and sat with her mother thinking she'd draw her into her, but she didn't.

Later, when the house was silent, the dishes cleared and put away, Linda stood at the large picture window. The streetlights were just now turning on, glowing yellow against the cobalt sky. The neighbors' porch lights, too, snapped on and light spilled from identical windows down the street.

Mrs. Miller, apron on, burst out and ran from her house next door trailed by Mr. Miller, who caught up with his wife, grabbed her arm and swung her around against a side door of the black Oldsmobile in their driveway. Linda heard muffled shouting, and then saw Mr. Miller swing his wife around again and press her head hard against the driver's side window.

"Mother, the Millers…" Linda called out.

Her mother ran to join her at the window, and the two stood transfixed at the sight of their neighbors.

"Stay put and don't leave the house for anything," her mother said, and then rushed around the couch, and was out the front door running across the lawn to the Miller's, and to Mrs. Miller, who'd dropped to the driveway when Mr. Miller took his hand from the back of his wife's head when he saw Linda's mother coming toward them. He quickly looked up and down the street, and then his hulking shape disappeared back into the Miller's home.

Linda watched her mother cradle Mrs. Miller's head in her arms, and hold her tight for a long while until only their shapes were seen in the darkening sky. She wished she knew what they were saying to each other, and Linda could only guess that her mother had offered their home as a refuge, but that Mrs. Miller shook her off, because the two women walked slowly up the drive to the front door and her mother saw Mrs. Miller back into her home.

When her mother returned, she said, "You are never to go into that house with Mr. Miller there."

"But why?"

"Never you mind, just don't do it."

"I always go over there, you know that." Linda knew her argument was over, but carried on a little bit more. She felt she needed to challenge her mother for the sake of Barbara, who was teetering between her old self and something new, as if she were frightened, which Linda had never seen in her before.

And since school was ending, she knew she'd be at the Miller's like she was every summer, probably more now that her daddy had died, so Linda suddenly stopped her challenge, thinking to let it rest, and that her mother would forget about the episode, and her daily visits would not be remarked upon or stopped altogether.

Still, seeing Mrs. Miller thrust hard against the car by Mr. Miller's physical force shook Linda, and all she wanted to do was call Barbara to make sure they both were okay, but she'd wait until morning, when they were safely on the bus, and around the corner, and ask about the night before. Linda's daddy might have told her earlier to steer clear of Mr. Miller, in fact, had stopped chatting him up across the yard a couple of years earlier, but Linda never saw anything wrong, or heard from Barbara whether Mr. Miller had misbehaved. Her daddy just felt things, and Linda knew that well enough.

On the bus, Linda leaned into Barbara, "So what happened last night? Is your mom okay?"

"She's fine."

"I saw your father with her last night."

"You didn't see anything." Barbara said, staring straight ahead.

"I did see it. My mother saw it. Your mom was hurt."

"I said she's fine. Can you drop it?" Barbara twisted her fingers together, clenching them into little knots.

"If you don't want to talk…"

"I don't. And it's none of your business."

"Well, my mother says I can't go over to your house anymore." Linda said, more accusatory now, and as a kind of threat to get more information from her.

"Maybe you shouldn't then." Barbara said and moved slightly away from Linda to the window, her voice rose above the bus' rumble, "You won't tell me about Perry."

Linda considered this, and then said, "Nothing happened."

"Well then, nothing happened last night. Case closed."

And for the first time, Linda felt distanced from Barbara, as if their two lives were diverging, that the final weeks of school would draw out and their junior year might end with neither of them talking, or making the effort to divulge secrets to each other that they were now keeping.

River

From the kitchen window, Martha could just about see the whole world. It was that flat. She saw restless clouds spiraling up during tornado season, or the mad onrush of snow in winter. She saw cars pass on the highway in the summer heat, and if she looked hard enough, the exhaust from their tailpipes.

They had planted row trees along the highway to hide the cars, but they were still new and whisper thin. She was afraid they'd bend and break in a strong wind. This was their second summer in Olathe, a place where you could have a patch of land for not a lot of money.

She watched Jack pull the hose from the side of the house out to the garden he'd planted. There were rows of cabbages and beets, okra, green beans, tomatoes and peppers. He grew corn last summer, and the stalks grew tall and thick by June and he harvested the ears in July. Jack made small mounds with their own little moats and pressed pumpkin seeds into them. He watered before work, before leaving for Kansas City, twenty-five minutes away, to the dealership where he sold Fords, where currently, the hot car was the new convertible Mustang with whitewall tires. He'd driven one home the evening before for Martha to see and got out and said, "It's big and metal and it's going to sell like hotcakes." He always remarked how much he liked to surround her with metal.

Jack only had the car for the weekend. They were swapping it around among the sales and service managers, so he packed up Martha who'd made sandwiches, and they drove for an hour past Merriam to the Missouri River. When they reached its banks, the sun was going down behind them making the barges and motorized boats seem like they were floating on the water rather than slicing through it.

Martha had loved that time of evening. She remembered how surprised she was eight years ago, when Jack had proposed to her at this very same spot, though the late afternoon then had been threatening rain. But Jack didn't pay any mind to it, and had pulled the ring out from his pocket and brought his own sort of shine to it and slipped it around her finger.

They'd talked of the future as if it was just across the river.

They were living in the city then, so the drive was shorter, and they were able to get back to their friends, broadcast the news and celebrate through the night. They talked of careers and children, where they might like to live. They fashioned their future history and when they sat in the mustang last evening, Martha reflected on how that history had altered and left them childless, and her worn from worry that she had somehow failed Jack.

Standing at the kitchen sink, and looking at herself in the window's reflection, she'd grown thin and her roundness had diminished. At first, Jack liked the softness, had even made a point to touch her in the places where she was most conscious of it: under her breasts and shoulder blades, below her navel above her pubic line, and down along her inner thigh that used to tremble, but now seems as if it has withered away like the corn stalks.

It is not so much the future they talk about now, but the present, and rarely the past.

"Would you look at those?" Jack said, in the car last night, when he'd spotted two riverboats coming towards them, their white and black details etched against the darkened banks. "I imagine people are having some fun tonight with the weather so warm."

"I suppose so." Martha felt far away again and tried to bring her husband into focus. She concentrated on the music. Roy Orbison's high falsetto lilted out of the AM radio, which gave her comfort and set the mood for the evening. She swung the rearview mirror her way and adjusted her hair after the drive. They'd driven with the rag-top down and her hair, though tied in a scarf, was wild about her face. She had watched Jack and how the open-air kind of driving made him happy. "I wonder if there's an orchestra on board? I wonder what they're playing?"

"Probably all those old river songs, "Shenandoah," Ole Man River." He started to sing to her. "The water is wide, I can't cross o'er, And neither have I wings to fly, build me a boat that can carry two and two shall row, my love and I." He reached over and touched her hand, then drew it into his.

A loud explosion ripped across the water. A warehouse along the opposite bank burst in flame. Debris floated in the air and broke the still river where a wave of orange and red rippled out towards Jack and Martha.

She took it as a sign for something. That maybe things were going to change in the fire's heat that they thought they could feel, but of course were too far from it to feel anything. Jack got out of the car to see. Martha raised herself up on the back of her seat and peered over the windshield. She felt helpless since the bridge would probably be closed off quickly. She felt exposed in the fire's glow.

Jack shouted, "Look how there's no smoke, just those flames. My they go high, don't they?" He was at the water's edge. She thought that if Jack had a mind to he'd swim across to see if he might help. Which is one of the things she loved about him – his willingness to help in a crisis. He told her he wasn't always like that, but never elaborated on it. "Do you think we could get across that bridge?"

"Honey, come back to the car."

"Look at all the stuff floating in the water. Those riverboats are coming to our side. I wonder if they should stop so those paddle wheels won't get broke." Just as he said it they did stop. The flaming debris flickered away into the dark water and the night quieted after the initial explosion and sharp hisses of steam.

"I hope there was no one inside that building. And here we are sitting here watching." She had felt this way before, sorry for a thing so completely out of her control. The real fear she had was that she'd latch on to the burning building for days, worry it through as if she might have saved it.

Jack knew he should go to her. But he stayed at the riverbank for one more moment that made them separate. A few years ago he might have, he'd probably have brought her down with him and they'd dip their toes in the water to feel what it might have felt like to be near the heat. Martha slid back down in her seat and stared at the flames.

The next morning Martha listened for news of the fire on the radio while she fixed breakfast. Sunday mornings were not news mornings. Her radio station was given over to church hymns and sermons so she spun the dial to find a preacher she liked.

Jack was already poking holes into the pumpkin mounds then tamping the earth down over the seeds. That morning, as he left their bed after they made love, he told her he wanted to get a start before the sun came up full. She stayed in bed and waited until he left the room to hold her legs up, hoping that his semen found its way.

"I can't find anything on the radio about that fire!" she called out to him.

"Can you hold breakfast a little longer? I've only got a few more to go."

He's insistent about growing things, she thought. What on earth he intended to do with all those pumpkins she didn't know. She kept the morning sermon on, hoping the preacher switched to a better topic than the Lord asking Abraham to sacrifice his son and what that meant to farmers and how necessary it was that their own sacrifices were petty in comparison, and that rain would surely come. It all came down to weather out here.

Martha set breakfast aside, the rasher of bacon went back into the Thermador and she turned the fire off under the frying pan. She'd already cracked the eggs, so she put them aside to let them sit until Jack came in.

She went into the bedroom and lay down in the heavy cotton sheets. Her husband's smell, their morning sweat and secretions, their sex like wet sycamore bark was still in the sheets. She liked the spongy feel of him, like touching the top of a wide, flat mushroom, and how his softness was disappearing from the summer work. As Jack dug trenches, sawed wood for fences, and made a trellis for the bean's vines to crawl through, the work restored his muscles as when he was younger.

They were now closer to forty. Martha viewed this summer season as her last to be able to get pregnant. There was no reason really, but a sense that they were moving into a different phase of their lives – slower, more methodical, chores became important. She felt the move out of town had precipitated their leap into middle age before she ever wanted to. The raking of leaves, the sweeping of floors, the cleaning of gutters took on a higher purpose. Jack had made the vegetable garden a primary source of satisfaction. As he hardened from the work, she lost her softness too, became more angular, and her breasts seemed to wither and fall flat against her body. She felt a sense of urgency, of a need to stop the process of her aging.

In bed, she stared at the ceiling and watched the dust motes float in the sun. She waved her hand through them as if to create chaos, but they settled back into their laziness as Martha waited.

While Martha was in bed, Jack forced order upon the chaos of dirt clods and topsoil. A truck-full of manure, a gift from a friend who worked at Samuelson's Dairy a few miles away, was dumped in a large pile in the front yard. If the wind shifted from the north just right, you could smell the acidic undertones of cow urine amidst the manure from their stables. He mulched it through the fine grains of topsoil dust to give it weight and texture. A texture that he enjoyed folding through his fingers.

He has made a study of seeds. Catalogues continued to come to the house at an alarming rate, even after the season of ordering was over. He supposed they were sent as a reminder that spring and summer were still in the picture though snowdrifts took over the view of the highway after a series of near blizzard storms. The tops of the row trees, with their tiny skeleton branches, poked above the white ice. The weatherman had not officially called them blizzards, but the wind was strong enough to seem as if the roof might rip away from the house. Jack had a vision in his sleep of the sky opening up one night into white, and of he and Martha being lifted violently from the bed and spun into the cloud's satin coolness. But that was all just movie memory working him over.

In late winter, when the packets of seeds arrived, he put them in one of Martha's narrow shoeboxes and arranged them alphabetically: beets to zucchini. They came with diagrams and instructions. He read the backs of each packet carefully, and made further notes and listed each vegetable by month as to when they needed to be planted.

On his way home from work he stopped at the hardware store and bought wooden marker stakes and red paint. He painted the tops of them over newspaper and they dried slowly in the wet air. He had Sundays and

Mondays off. At the beginning of a week in February, he dressed himself in his heavy coat and woolen cap to go outside. In brutal cold, he marked off his garden using the stakes and a tape measure. While he tamped the stakes down through the snow and into the ice-encrusted soil, a gathering of crows looked intently on from a neighbor's barn and the branches of naked poplar trees. He heard their cawing and imagined them plotting an assault on the seeds when he planted them, so he walked back into the house and designed the rest of his garden on paper.

He and Martha had chosen the house for the way it sat on the land. When they drove in to inspect it for the first time, having seen the FOR SALE sign as they passed, they saw over its flat roof to the distance beyond. Martha had remarked, "Why you can see almost all the way back to Kansas City from here, so it's not very far at all, is it?"

Jack had worried that he'd taken her too far from the city, the things she knew, her daily routine of errands and calling on friends. He worried that she'd be lonely while he worked back in town. But it seemed to him that Martha wasn't worried at all. That she was mentally preparing herself for a child, for the onslaught of symptoms and tiny spasms. She hadn't discussed it with Jack, but she seemed to have focused her energy on conceiving, and that he just had to go along with it for making her move so far away. It wasn't that he was reluctant about children, it was that he was going about it as if it were a thing he was putting off indefinitely. Martha had tried to get him to talk about it, but he'd change the subject or go silent. It was when he went silent that Martha did too.

Even after a year they weren't fully moved in. There were still boxes here and there in the corners of every room. Jack had come home one day and asked Martha, "What do you do all day?"

She responded tightly, "I really don't know where you want me to put things, Jack, if I knew I would. Instead, you go on about that garden, and about the dealership, and about how you want to do all these things, but you never settle down to the task at hand. How many times have I asked you to stay home a day, or take one day on the weekend to help me put these things away? I don't even notice the boxes anymore, do you?"

"Obviously I do, or I wouldn't have brought it up."

"Well, it's not worth getting upset over." Martha put her hands on her hips backwards as if to contain them. "We shouldn't fight over such a small thing."

"Do you have enough to do, hon?" Jack changed his tact and he saw that Martha knew it.

"Of course, I do." Jack knew that Martha fibbed here a little, because when she did lie, she always shifted a foot forward and re-balanced.

"In the spring we'll go for drives," he went to her and brought her into him, "We'll go for these impossibly long drives through the country and find places where no one thinks to go." He drew his finger over her forehead, "Maybe we'll buy one of those silver trailers I've seen on the highway going into town, Airstreams, I think they call them, and drive clear across country."

"I'd like that," she said, and did a thing she never tired of: she smelled the crook of his neck where all of him coalesced. All of this preparation on Martha's part made her drift into memory, caused her to think about her relationship with Jack, because it did matter to her that he'd want the baby, to be a part of it.

During the course of their years together, she was always regarding him, smelling him, looking at his eyes, for what, she didn't know.

She knew that he drank before they were married. He had told her. One night, shortly after they met, he wanted to lay it out on the table. Put it before her and see how she'd react. They had not made love just yet, but there were the signs that they were about to.

They had stopped for hamburgers at Dillon's Barbeque on one of the city's side streets. Gingham red-checkered curtains hung from wooden rods in the windows. The menus were printed on hard paper mats where etchings of horses and cowboys lined the food selections. They had ordered already and Jack was rolling his mat in tiny curves, a nervous habit he'd had since childhood. The sun was angled against the curtains.

By now Martha knew something was on his mind when he started in on any paper object, fiddling with it like he did. "What is it, Jack?

"Well," he took a long breath, "I need to tell you something, and I guess this is the right time for it, though I don't think any time is right. But I have this feeling for you, but I want to be straight, as straight as I'd expect you to be with me on matters."

"You can tell me most anything at this point," Martha said, "most anything at all."

"And I understand that, you see, I know it and so I have to tell you that I drank when I was younger."

"You drank," she paused, "You're a drinker."

"Yes." the paper mat was now so curled that a hot plate couldn't straighten it out. "I mean no. I quit a few years back, but I just wanted to lay it out here so you'd know, so we'd start from somewhere clean."

He told her that he got used to the taste of liquor in college, and that he liked it, and there were a few episodes that he didn't really want to go into.

Martha listened intently, but she still felt all those things she'd felt the first time she was going to make love with Martin Slager in high school. She still listened because now she was thirty and hadn't married yet, and was wondering while he was talking if she'd be passed over again for what amounted to such a small thing if he weren't drinking now. She thought that it couldn't possibly affect her after all this time.

But Martha, despite herself, kept waiting to smell something, the sweet odor of whiskey or rum, but she never did, not during the last eight years of their marriage.

That night, their breath scented with hickory smoke, molasses and vinegar, they made love for the first time.

As she lay in the cotton sheets, the summer wind picking up, her husband outside planting things and her with her legs up, holding what remained of him inside her, knowing how fragile a moment like this was, she remembered that first night, its intensity, and how it sustained her to this day.

When Jack came in, dust on his pants, streaks of dirt lining his forehead amid beads of sweat, he called out to his wife. When she didn't answer, he removed his shoes and pants in the mudroom and went down the hall toward the bedroom. She had fallen asleep. Her hair, the color of corn, encased her head on the pillow.

He went back to the kitchen, found the eggs in their bowl, lit the stove, heated the frying pan, took out the rasher of bacon, and began to make breakfast himself. It took a moment for him to realize that the radio was on, and that a Christian song was being sung by a determined voice followed by a chorus of them. They got to "Come to the river, bathe your feet in the water," before he reached over and switched the radio off.

The pumpkin plants spread their long, leafy tendrils across the garden. The large orange flowers dotted the green. Some of them fell from the vine and withered away while others gave way to tiny round beads that would become fall's large ornaments. Martha had stopped bleeding. It had been over a month since her last period, but she hadn't mentioned a word to anyone. The calls from her city friends had tapered off over the past year, so the temptation to say anything to them was tempered by whether their friendships would hold.

She spent her time preparing.

She dusted the high places that usually went unnoticed. She cleaned the cans and jars of dust. The pockets of gathered spider webs in the eaves were whisked away with her mop. She canned peaches and raspberries, blackberries and tomatoes. The silver sparkled from Brasso as did the faucets and fixtures throughout the house. Working her way from one room to the other, she cleaned the summer dust away to get ready for the long labor of fall and winter. She cleared the remaining boxes and found a place for everything.

Each night she wondered if she should tell her husband. Even when they walked outside along the road, the moon angling its light from the west, she still walked beside him and said nothing. Instinctually, she knew that she must be certain before she told him because if he knew maybe he would be more careful when they made love. She wanted the opportunity that summer promises before fall made a person settle in for a season of solitude. But she couldn't wait much longer so she made an appointment with a doctor and drove the twenty-five miles into Kansas City on route 56.

It was humid, but the day was cooler than usual. Under the sun ran a thin line of clouds stretching as far as the window shield allowed her to see. She'd made the appointment for eleven o'clock to be home before three. She didn't think it would take long. She knew what the results were going to be. She felt her body shifting, her weight returning. She was constantly warm now and ran ice cubes under her arms and down the middle of her back. After Jack had left in the mornings, she'd regard her belly in the mirror and watch for any sign of growth. Of course, there wasn't any, not just yet. But she knew.

After her appointment, Martha started home through the city where they had watched the warehouse burning across the Kansas River a year earlier. She stopped to see the remains of it. Sky shone through the rafters and they hadn't started the rebuilding process if they were going to do it at all. There were men around it, but attention wasn't being paid.

She looked at the river itself, so wide where it split the states, Kansas and Missouri, and Kansas City itself.

She watched the lines of barges and boats making their way up and downriver, saw the rails intersecting the buildings, the glint of sun shining off their worn surfaces. She wondered how far it was to where the Missouri River originated. She thought of how the river started, first a cloud, then a drop of rain or flake of snow, and how it made its way into something larger, where people made commerce and lived their lives upon it. She knew it emptied into the Mississippi, growing ever larger and then fanning out into the Gulf farther away.

She sat for an hour and decided to drive back into the city to the Ford dealership where Jack worked to tell him, because that was what she was supposed to do, for after all, he was part of it.

Adjustments

The summer passed and it was near the end of August. Linda stayed close to home while her mother worked. She lay in bed until she heard the car leave the driveway. The house seemed larger now that her mother had sold off the piano and used the money to pay funeral expenses. It was the last thing to go after her father's clothes and mementos were boxed and taken to the church to give away, or stored in the garage.

Her mother hadn't said anything until the night before the new owners came. It was just after dinner, and she was removing the plates from the table and putting them in the sink. Linda knew something was up because it was usually her job to clean the table, and each night her mother waited to get up until Linda had done so.

"You weren't planning to take piano lessons, were you?" her mother said, her voice muffled by the running tap water and the clink of dishes.

"No."

"It doesn't seem that you inherited your father's talent." The water stopped and her mother turned around. "I've sold it." She pushed a loose strand of hair from her face that had fallen down from the steam.

Linda stood up from the table and walked out of the kitchen. Passing the piano, she ran her hand down the keyboard, pushing at the keys hard so that the jumble of sounds increased and then died away as she went out on the porch.

Her mother followed her to the screen door, but stayed inside the house. "We owe a lot of money," she said.

The piano was the most expensive thing in the house and both Linda and her mother watched it being carted off, strapped down by rope, in the back of a pickup.

Two men and a Wonder Bread slice of a young boy, with long, delicate fingers, arrived at the house. One of the men was pushing a flat dolly up the drive while the boy's father (she assumed) counted out twenty-dollar bills in three stacks of five on the dining room table next to where the piano was. The boy was already fingering the keys, and Linda wanted to slap them away or slam the cover down, but her mother had caught her look.

"Linda, why don't you offer them something to drink?"

"We don't have anything cold."

"We have ice," and then Linda's mother said to the men to save face, "we have some nice water with ice."

The boy's father went to the piano and gently closed the lid. The last note he managed to get out rang through the house. It was an E flat and Linda listened to its discordant tone and a deep well of grief that she had managed to keep in check for most of the summer swept through her. She ran to her room and slammed the door behind her.

Clare gathered the stack of bills and put them in her pocket. "It was her father's piano," she said. "But he passed on early this summer."

"I'm sorry."

"Frankly, I'm glad to see it go. It just sits there as a reminder."

"Understood." The man gathered his son to him. The boy struggled to get free so he could go back to the piano, but his father tightened his grip on the boy's shoulder.

The other man made it to the door with the large metal dolly, and both of the men got to work and pushed the piano across the floor to the door.

From her bedroom window, Linda saw them load the piano into the back of their truck. It seemed to take a long time as they stood around it, trying to figure out how to lift it into the cargo area. Mr. Miller, who was outside in his driveway, finally came to help them. He stood at the back and lifted it entirely up and onto the lip of the opened gate practically by himself, and then they slid it into place, regarded their work, and then surrounded the piano's bulk with rope. The boy's father shook Mr. Miller's big, fleshy hand and waved up to Linda's mother, who sat on the porch landing, her hands tightly folded in her lap, watching the piano being carried away.

When Linda came out of her room, her mother and Mrs. Miller were rearranging the furniture. Gone were the small lamp and pictures that had been set atop the upright, the small rug placed under the bench. They had turned the couch now toward the picture window, and the two large chairs with floral prints, hopelessly outdated and worn, were placed a foot from the wall. A large, empty space was left under the front window.

"Now you have the view of the street to enjoy," Mrs. Miller said, ever cheerful, standing and surveying the still tiny living room. It was less cluttered, yes, but still their furniture commanded the room like armies dressed in unmatched cloth and color. "Maybe we can find you a bench or another couch for that window."

"It'll be fine, for now," her mother said. Linda took a step forward into the living room and her mother turned toward her. "Well, it's not too bad, is it?"

"It's different."

Mrs. Miller sat on the couch. "Look at how you can see the whole street from here. All the way across to Mr. Adderley's and down to the corner." Mrs. Miller stood up and regarded Linda, who looked back at her with swollen eyes, her face that remained lined and crinkled from sleep, and said, "Barbara and I are going shopping; why don't you come?"

Before Linda left to join her neighbors, her mother took a twenty from her pocket and gave it to her daughter. "Buy something you'll need," she said, as if the guilt from the afternoon could be smoothed over by a sweater or blouse.

Linda thought that at least she'd make an effort. She'd buy something that was linked somehow to the piano – perhaps a stack of records because they still had the phonograph, or a cardigan that might have matched the one her father wore when he played.

Mrs. Miller had sent Barbara to fetch her and when she came to the door, Barbara wore loose jeans and a smart, white top. Underneath the button overlays, Linda saw the outlines of her bra and knew her own mother would have something to say, was probably biting her lip, so she hurried out the door before Mother had the chance to see Barbara.

On the way across the lawn to the opposing driveway where Mrs. Miller waited, idling the car, Barbara said, "Mom wants to buy me respectable clothes for school. She thinks that everything I buy is too 'show-offy.'" She stopped suddenly. "As if she knows what everyone is wearing nowadays. I don't think she keeps up despite all those magazines she reads."

Linda laughed with Barbara because she knew her mother was different and always managed to look just right — to dress, despite their lack of money, in nice-looking clothes. For the first time that day she felt light, and she bounced her way to Mrs. Miller's waiting car to escape into the city.

As they drove, Barbara and Linda in the back seat, Mrs. Miller said, "I don't know why I have to feel like a chauffeur for you girls – and stop all that giggling you're doing. I'm trying to concentrate on the road."

Linda caught her eyes in the rearview mirror. What did she think? Did she know what went through Linda's mind? She had that way of seeing right through you that made Linda uncomfortable, which is why, when she went to their house, she ran right up into Barbara's room, where the two of them shut the door and watched the black-and-white TV or thumbed through magazines. They no longer cut them up, but they'd linger on the likes of Shaun Cassidy, Bobby Sherman, or any of the Monkees, except for maybe Mickey.

Riding in the car, they saw the low skyline of Kansas City, knew just where they were going – to Lamont's department store. It had gleaming linoleum that looked almost like marble. Linda pictured hundreds of janitors armed with mops, cleaning and shining it every night after the thousands of customers. Every time she'd gone into the store she'd had to stop and marvel at how large it was, how the floor reflected the light, how bright the displays of clothes and shoes, pocket books, and jewelry were in their glass cases. Most likely she and Barbara would see other kids from school, but the two of them would pay them no mind.

They pulled into the newly built shopping garage, from where they were able to walk directly from their car inside. Music thrummed over the speakers, all violins and reeds. It might have been a notch above Lawrence Welk, whom her father had dismissed as a hack. He wouldn't allow it on in the house. Instead, he'd have her read to him, or they'd spin Chet Baker or Bill Evans on the phonograph to pass the time.

"Let's spin some music," he'd say, "some mighty music."

"Linda, c'mon!" Barbara took her hand and pulled her down one of the aisles toward the store's back corner.

They left Mrs. Miller to fend for herself among the racks and displays of clothes who took her time admiring the woolen skirts in fall shades of blue, dark brown, and three shades of gray. She fingered the cotton blouses. She held combinations against her in the mirror. Another woman might have looked matronly in them, but Mrs. Miller thought they were just fine – they had order, and the fuss of choosing what went with what was not an issue. Simplicity. Order. Good.

She replaced the clothes exactly where she'd found them, resolving to come back another day without the girls because they wouldn't approve, not with what her daughter chose to wear – those tight-fitting blouses and pants, parading around the house with barely a stitch on. Maybe it was time to have that talk with her about privacy, that despite the fact they were family, it was important she understood decency.

The thought made her stop, look in the mirror hung from one of the large pillars and say, "God, I'm middle-aged." She turned just slightly in the mirror to her good side, and then turned to her bad side. There was an enormous difference; her stomach seemed larger, her breasts drooped distinctly downward. How is it that one side looks better than the other? Wouldn't you think that no matter what side one looked from it'd match the other? She sighed and picked up her purse from the floor and meandered her way back to where the girls were.

She saw Barbara hold up a nearly see-through blouse, the blue cotton as sheer as nylon stockings.. "Put that back. I'm not paying good money to buy clothes like that," Mrs. Miller said. Barbara dismissed her with a look. "And if you look at me that way again, we'll go home right now."

Barbara turned away to another rack of clothes. A series of mothers and daughters tugged little boys after them. Mrs. Miller sat in a chair, suddenly tired. She leaned her head back against the wall, closed her eyes, and the store's sounds quickly diminished.

Linda worked her way through the sweaters. Their prices seemed high, even though signs declared SALE! More than once she fingered the twenty in her pocket. Barbara had split off when she became impatient with Linda's taste for the drab, oversized garments. Feeling the heavy cotton and fingering the large buttons, Linda tried one on. She wore it as she continued looking around the circular, even though the store was warm.

She had moved sufficiently around so that her back was to Mrs. Miller, who, when she brushed by, awoke, a little startled. Mrs. Miller smiled at Linda approvingly,. "Would you like that?" she asked.

"What?"

"Do you like that sweater?" Mrs. Miller sat up and touched its edge, felt the silky cotton. "I'll get it for you if that's what you want."

"I have money," Linda said, not fully turning around.

"Let me see you in it." Mrs. Miller reached for Linda to turn her toward her. Linda stepped back, but then faced the woman. "It looks nice on you. Perhaps a little large."

"I like my clothes big." Linda removed the sweater and hastily put it back among the others. She went to find Barbara.

A small crowd had gathered around the cashier as Mrs. Miller went to retrieve the cardigan Linda had picked out. She tucked it under her arm and went to the men's department where the line was smaller, waited, and paid for the sweater.

Barbara worked her fingers through the different colors and styles of blouses. She had chosen several and disappeared into a changing room, motioning for Linda to join her. Inside the cubicle she slipped each one on, turned in the mirror, and then looked for Linda's approval.

"Don't you think that one's too small?" Linda asked democratically. "I mean, it looks good, but –"

During changes, Linda mentally compared their bodies. Barbara's had natural definition; her ribs showed when she lifted her arms, where hers were covered by a thick, layer of flesh. And Barbara's hair fell in long strands to her shoulders while Linda's lay flat, short, and lifeless over her forehead and barely touched her neck.

"You sound like my mother."

"I could never wear something like that."

"You could if you stopped hanging out on your porch all day.".

Frustratingly, tears filled Linda's eyes and a fire rose to her throat. It was suddenly too hot in the dressing room and she turned to leave.

"Stay. I didn't mean it." Barbara's voice was soft, sorry.

Linda slowly turned toward Barbara. "I like it there."

Barbara pulled at the long sleeves of a shirt to stretch them beyond her palms. "Listen," she said. "You gotta get out."

"School starts in a week."

"That's not what I mean." She checked herself in the dressing mirror. The sweater was tight under her breasts, but it was dark brown and looked warm for fall.

Linda wondered if Mrs. Miller would reject that sweater, but gave Barbara a little confidence when she saw her reflection. "That looks good."

"It's something Mom would buy. I should be shopping with Dad, but she'd never allow it. He'd let me buy whatever I want." Barbara pulled the sweater off over her head so that these last words came out muffled.

"Really?"

Barbara sat on the small bench and folded the sweater neatly and placed it on her lap. She ran her hand over the material. "It's so soft," she said quietly.

On the drive home, the weather changed. Gone was the bright blue sky, and in its place were dark, fast-moving gray clouds. They were low over the horizon. Linda felt the car engine revving faster as Mrs. Miller sped through town toward the clusters of homes across the river near Shawnee Mission.

What had been a languorous afternoon became a race to get home to beat the summer storm. Linda braced herself against the front leather seat. She'd decided to ride up with Mrs. Miller, as Barbara's mood had darkened when her mother had only let her buy the one sweater.

Once again, Linda became a bridge between the two of them as she had when Mrs. Miller had caught Barbara taking a ten-dollar bill from her father's wallet while he showered. Barbara, lying in her bed one morning, heard them shouting at each other across the few feet between their houses until suddenly it was quiet and the only thing that emerged was the low murmur of Mr. Miller's voice.

That whole house had a carnival ride tilt that day; all of its inhabitants were at odds with each other when Barbara went over when her own mother had left for work. Barbara came out and flashed the ten at Linda like a trophy she'd won.

When they pulled into the driveway, Linda's mother was in the front yard raking the leaves that blew from the trees in great clumps. They got out of the car and Mrs. Miller walked quickly over to the edge of the lawn.

"Clare, I'm so glad I caught you!" Mrs. Miller shouted over the noisy clatter of raked branches and leaves. "I forgot to ask you something this morning."

Not hearing exactly what she said, Clare called back, "Fine, Anne, just fine," and smiled at the woman, but kept at her work.

"It sure got chilly in a hurry, didn't it?" Mrs. Miller moved in closer and headed up the small slope from the street's edge. There was a pause as she looked up at the house, and then said, "Michael can help you with the storm windows when the time comes."

"Linda and I have done it for years."

"That's right," Mrs. Miller said, "of course you have."

Clare dropped the edge of her sack. "How was the shopping?"

"Can you believe our two girls will both be seniors this year?" Linda's mother didn't answer, so Mrs. Miller added, "They are growing up too fast. Time just slips by."

"What is it that you wanted to ask, Anne?" Clare grew impatient. The wind steadily increased. If there was rain behind the storm, the leaves would be twice as heavy and harder to clean up.

"I thought perhaps we might share rides."

Clare picked up her sack and walked across the grass, scooping up the large sycamore leaves. Linda came from the car carrying a shopping bag.

Mrs. Miller looked at Linda and said, "Wouldn't you like to share rides with Barbara?"

"For what?" Linda stopped next to Mrs. Miller.

"To school."

"Sure, I guess. Mom, is that okay?" Linda stopped before stepping onto the sidewalk, looked at her mother who didn't look up. "Mom?"

"What's in the bag, Linda? What did you buy?"

"Mrs. Miller bought me a sweater." Linda made no move to show her mother.

Linda's mother put the lid on the trashcan and said to Mrs. Miller. "You don't have to buy Linda clothes. She had money with her."

"I wanted to."

"We're doing just fine without charity." She dropped the sack to the ground.

Mrs. Miller said, "I'm only trying to help." And then she turned, shook her head and went back to her house.

Clare studied her daughter. It might as well be now, before Linda got used to the idea of school coming. "There's a couple, honey, I met," she said, "They need your help." She inched closer to Linda, but her daughter stepped back. "I went out to talk with them yesterday. The woman's sick and has been put to bed."

"What are you talking about, Mom?" Linda stopped at the edge of the grass.

"I found you a job, honey. It's a good job and we need the money." Clare tried to be matter of fact about it, but a moment later she began to cry. Linda stood there as if her feet had rooted.

Inside, the school registration papers remained unsigned. The steam pipes came on for the first time and began to rattle and hiss. Out on the lawn, the two stared at each other. Linda, confused, hurt, her own furious heart beating, and feeling that her life was about to change, removed the sweater from the bag.

"This is what Mrs. Miller bought me." She left her mother and ran over to the Miller's house.

When Linda came in Barbara had her new blouse on and was showing it off, strutting for Mr. Miller who sat on the couch watching her. Mrs. Miller held her purse at her waist, her fingers dug into the leather.

Mrs. Miller said to Barbara, "Don't you think you can change upstairs and then come down and show your father?"

Barbara tugged the shirt down over her breasts and then let the fabric snap into place underneath.

"I think your father has seen quite enough."

Mr. Miller shifted on the couch and put his paper down. He looked up at Barbara, who stood there waiting. Linda thought Barbara was waiting for some kind of reaction from him. She looked at all three of the Millers one at a time.

"That's a nice sweater there," he said. "Fits you snug though."

"Do you really like it?"

"Sure I do. Did Mom buy it for you?"

"Yes."

Linda focused on Mrs. Miller, who's gaze was bearing down on her daughter.

Mr. Miller turned to his wife. "Then what's all the fuss for, Anne. I assumed you approved of this sweater before she bought it."

"That's not the point."

"Then I'm not sure what the point is."

"I'm going to wear it on the first day." Barbara looked at Linda who had halted at the front door and not moved. Then she faced her mother and turned her back to her father and removed the shirt, her bra still in place. "Thanks, Mom," she said and walked up the stairs to her room leaving the other three standing in the diminishing light.

Linda didn't return home because her own mother was still home, but she didn't really want to stay at the Millers, but had no other place to go. She followed Barbara up the stairs, where she watched Barbara put on an old blouse and sweater. They didn't talk and soon dinner was called up to them by Mrs. Miller, to which Barbara pleaded with Linda to stay.

It was a quiet, tense affair.

Mrs. Miller ate furiously, and dished out the string beans and potatoes onto her plate. Barbara was self-possessed and oddly sullen. Mr. Miller acted as if nothing had happened and engaged in idle conversation with Linda. He repeated the stories he'd just read in the evening paper and added his own spin on them.

Suddenly, Mrs. Miller stood up from the table and announced, "I'm going to get ice cream."

"What kind are you going to get?" Mr. Miller asked.

Mrs. Miller snatched her purse from the hall table. "It doesn't really matter, does it?"

The weather had cleared after the storm's false alarm. On the way home, her blousy skirt hid the stiffness in her walk as she came from the corner store in the warm evening carrying the ice cream. Linda was sitting alone on the Miller's stoop.

The neighborhood homes were awash in streetlight.

The heat brought all of the neighbors to their porches to sit. Their silhouettes loomed against the lamps that had been moved up to the windows to provide light on their evening reading.

Linda heard the Adderley's call out a "Good Evening!" to Mrs. Miller as she passed, the cement deadend clicks of her heels could be heard in the deadened night air. She didn't acknowledge them as she passed, which signaled to Linda that she was still upset.

Linda tugged on a loose strand of hair, itching a fresh mosquito bite. She thumbed through a magazine she usually read secondhand from Mrs. Miller who subscribed to most every periodical there was. Linda saw their mastheads poking out of the Miller's mailbox: LOOK and LIFE in bold bright letters, Ladies Home Journal in a kind of elegant cursive, and The Saturday Evening Post, Linda waited a week until she found them on her stoop tied with string, but now that she was at their house, she was getting an early peek.

Mrs. Miller arrived at the end of the walk. "Where's Barbara?"

"Talking with Mr. Miller, I think."

"Oh?" Mrs. Miller went quickly up the walk and stairs.

Linda felt the whoosh of air her skirt made. She heard Barbara's unmistakable steps rush down the stairs inside the house.

Breathless, Barbara said, "Did you get the ice cream?" as she slipped by her mother through the front door.

"Where's your father?" Mrs. Miller asked, her voice up a notch.

Barbara sat next to Linda on the top step. "Upstairs, I guess." She took the magazine from Linda and began to go through its pages like flash cards.

Linda turned to see Mrs. Miller go to the stair's landing through the screen door.

Mrs. Miller stood there, her back ramrod straight, the bag crackling under pressure. Then she called up, her voice flat and disembodied, "Harold, I have ice cream."

She went to the kitchen. Through the screen door, Linda heard the bag tear and then a loud thud. Mrs. Miller's voice broke in a strangled word. She looked through the screen and saw the solid square box of ice cream on the floor. Linda remembered her father then, the warnings about her being alone at the Miller's, but now she was trapped by her anger at her own mother.

Barbara glanced at Linda and then pretended reading.

"What's wrong with your Mom?"

"Nothing." Barbara closed the magazine and handed it back to Linda. "Here, I better go help."

"I'll go." Linda stood and disappeared inside. She picked up the ice cream block and took it into the kitchen where Mrs. Miller stood, her back against a counter and her eyes staring off into nothing.

"Here's the ice cream," Linda said, breaking the momentary silence. "I can help you with it."

Mrs. Miller turned to her and took the chocolate block in her hands.

The ice cream was still frozen hard so Mrs. Miller pulled a long knife from the drawer to cut it. After each slice, she ran the blade under warm water. Linda watched her touch the silver before cutting the chunk of chocolate as if through butter.

Mrs. Miller, her face flushed, placed a slice of ice cream in a bowl.

"My hands are dirty," she said, and turned, staring absently past Linda and into the rest of the house, chocolate dripping from the knife to the floor. After a moment, she straightened up and gestured towards the white porcelain bowls lining the counter and said, "Two of those are for you and Barbara."

Airstreaming

A New Job

On the Monday that school began, Linda stood at the front window and watched the yellow bus pick up the neighborhood boys and girls. She saw that the kids were shy with each other. First day apprehension required them to keep their heads down and navigate the bus aisles to choose their seats at least two benches apart from each other. Their corner had always been one of the first bus stops along its meandering route toward school.

It was mid-September. The days cooled and the leaves made brittle clicks against each other in the wind. They had started to turn slightly, but summer was lingering in her neighborhood where, in the early morning, the houses across the street had a golden rising-sun shine to them. But, the bus's black exhaust marred the morning as it pulled heavily away from the curb.

Linda's mother called to her, her voice grew louder as she came into the living room from the back of the house.

"Come away from the window. You are always at that damn window. Go finish getting ready, we've got to get going. You don't want to be late, do you?" Linda was used to her rattling off these admonishments, but she was surprised that the ring to them was no different than if she were actually heading off to school. So she didn't answer her, or offer anything of a reply as she went past her mother to the bathroom. There, she combed her hair with her father's black, fine-tooth comb. She brushed her teeth, and regarded herself in the mirror. She didn't really mind missing school that day. Seeing Perry again in the new school year would have been awkward, but she'd miss the daily time with Barbara.

Linda and her mother were ten miles from their home on the outskirts of Olathe. The last reminders of the city had fallen away; Gas stations, stores and apartment buildings were replaced by single homes that stood farther apart as they drove. The car engine's low rumble vibrated through the car. Smoke from Clare's cigarette found the autumn's cool air current through the cracked window. Linda was lost in her own thoughts, looking with new eyes at a landscape she'd rarely seen. She was at once nervous and calm. Only her mother seemed more ill at ease with her quick tugs on her cigarette and her uneasy exhalations.

Clare tried her hand at conversation, but her daughter was having none of it so she started in on the first of her daily two packs, which came handily bound together from the store. She saw the row of small, squat trees just losing their leaves up ahead that the lady told her to look for.

"What's the number of the house, hon?

"734" Linda handed over the piece of scratch paper, "You can see for yourself."

"There's no need to be smart."

"You're the one who arranged this, not me." Linda looked out her window as if to avoid her curiosity at what the house was like, but she wanted to make the point to her mother that she was uninterested and upset.

From her kitchen window, Martha saw the old Mercury pull in, its rounded fenders and black and white exterior worn and faded. It came to a stop at the top of their driveway and remained on the main road. Jack was out in the front yard tending to the remains of the garden, the late corn and squash. He had turned over the rest of it on Sunday to let the broad leafy plants mulch through winter.

When the car pulled away, a young girl was left standing, as if deposited, at the side of the road. She wore a printed blouse and plain brown skirt, but Martha couldn't make out her features from such a distance. She turned the faucet handle down, which stopped the water, and she shook out her hands and wiped them on the dishtowel. The girl started down the gravel drive kicking up the gray dust as she walked. She was not thin, but not fat either - just a girl about to go one way or the other. What was striking was how her hair lay flat against her head. It appeared wet, and she wondered if hair tonic or some other sort of spray held it in place. The girl walked with a heaviness that seemed to have more to do with her predicament than weight. The trail of dust she left grew, and the angled sun caught it and formed a white halo behind her.

Martha went around to the kitchen door. She waited a moment to open it, smoothed her dress down and tied the loose strands of her blond hair up into the bun she'd formed with colored hair clips. Then she went out to welcome the girl who had found the front door and was heading toward it.

"Hello?" Martha called to her and then turned to her husband who had stopped his work and was looking at the young girl. "Jack come here for a moment and meet…" She stopped, flustered. "My mind isn't right these days. Your name just slipped right out of my head."

"It's Linda."

"Yes, of course. And I'm Martha." She looked out to the road. "Was that your mother?"

"Yes."

"I wish she had stayed a minute. I would have liked to have met her."

"She was late for work." Linda said, "It was my fault. I wasn't ready."

"I'm sure you had to make some adjustments this morning. But we're glad you're here."

Jack came from the garden, still holding his shovel, wearing thick work gloves. "I'm Mr. Pearson. But I'd like you to call me Jack." He removed a glove and held his hand out to Linda. Linda shook it and saw him look at Martha and chuckle. "She's strong."

"I'm not supposed to lift anything," Martha patted her swollen belly. "In fact, I'm not supposed to be out of bed, which is why you're here."

Linda smiled at her and waited a moment for her thoughts to take hold. She'd been wondering why she was needed, but that was answered. She was surprised at how welcoming they were, and how frail the woman looked despite the oncoming baby. She wanted to take the woman back to bed. She talked quickly and sharp, and her hands constantly moved. Her husband was slow and careful with his words.

Linda offered, "Maybe I can go sit with you while you rest and you can tell me what it is you want me to do."

"Oh, there's nothing specific, nothing right away. I thought we'd spend the morning getting acquainted. Jack has to go off to work. He wanted to wait until you showed up to meet you." She turned to her husband. "Why don't you go clean up and change your boots and let me have those." She gestured to his gloves. He removed them and handed them to her. She led Linda into the kitchen. "I'm in the middle of a project, maybe you can help me finish up."

Inside, the kitchen counter was strewn with glass mason jars. Sunlight filtered through them and left bright prisms of light across the counter. There were boxes of glass jars, every size and shape, and their gold metal tops shone like large coins. Most of the cupboards were open; their contents haphazardly piled on top of each other.

Warm vinegar tickled Linda's nose and pickling spices, mostly of clove, came in behind the vinegar to soothe. There were strips of cheesecloth to gather the spices in, sugar and a basketful of small, smooth-skinned cucumbers.

It was warm and wet inside the kitchen. A large pot of boiling water steamed the windows. Glass jars sterilized in the heat. During the time Martha had been outside, the water had dissipated and the jars lay half exposed so she went to the sink and filled a teakettle.

Linda noted that she struggled to lift the kettle out of the sink and over to the stove. She went to lend a hand, but was too late.

"Just in time," Martha said eyeing the pot as she poured the water into it. "I shouldn't be so careless."

"You should let me do things like that."

"It's just automatic." Martha set the kettle behind the pot on another burner, turned and leaned back against the counter. Beads of perspiration had formed on her forehead. She had a thin S-shaped body with a belly that slightly filled in the lower curve. "I don't think before I act." She laughed a little. "You'll see."

Regarding her, Linda wondered how Jack had let her start on such a project.

In the early afternoon, while Martha slept, Linda went into the kitchen and cleaned up as best she could. She made herself familiar with where things were kept. She opened each drawer and drew a mental picture of what was there. She went into the service porch and found the cleaning supplies and where the brooms and mops were kept. She was surprised at herself for taking such care, but the woman's delicacy touched her.

Suddenly, she was back in the role she held for her daddy. Though both had an independence and protected it fiercely, they plainly needed help, and for her, it had become a natural thing to step forward though she wasn't nearly as attached to Martha yet.

They filled close to thirty jars that morning and from sheer exhaustion, Martha finally sat down and guided Linda as she went. From the banquette, Martha waved her hands and nodded to drawers and cupboards.

She rose briefly to show her how thin to slice the cucumbers and measure out the sugar for each batch of pickling juice, then slump back into the bench to direct

Linda to change ingredients slightly, and to make adjustments to the sugar content every ten jars or so for different tastes. By lunchtime, Linda's hands were irretrievably lost to pickling's sweet and sour smell, while the tartness lingered on her tongue.

The remaining jars lined the counter.

"Can you collect the unused jars? There's a box somewhere back there."

Linda gathered a few in her hands and turned it one way, and then another.

"Check in the service porch."

Linda found a box with like jars and began moving back and forth to refill it.

When she saw that Martha had closed her eyes and her head dropped, she took the ends of the cucumbers outside and looked for the mulching pile Martha spoke of. She walked for a moment among the remaining rows of late summer vegetables and corn. There was precision to the garden; the spaces between rows were exact. Even the pumpkins she stooped to thump had a similarity of size. She saw the difference between her two employers in the work they did.

She took time to wander around the perimeter of the house. A thin layer of cloud blocked the sun's heat and softened the shadows under the house's eaves and trees. The house was built in the newer style: longer, with garage and carport and fencing that added to its length and stature on the property. It was rather plain in appearance; the color was a light tan and the windowsills were painted white.

The trees had not reached their full height, and the shrubs were starting to weave together forming hedges along the house's lower exterior. What was not a summer garden, was not fully landscaped. It seemed the couple were slowly working their way around the house, so that there were large areas of unbroken soil and weeds that had browned from lack of water.

But what they'd done, they had completed with care. Linda looked across the rolling converted farmland to see many houses in the same sort of completion, and all of them were different in size and shape.

It was quiet out here. She stopped to try and pick out noises unfamiliar to her. Black birds in the low valley silently swooped from branch to branch. Cars rarely drove past on the highway, and just now the wind was resting in its mid-day laziness. Every now and then a pocket of breeze swept past Linda, but it quickly dissipated.

She went back around to the front of the house and stood under the carport, which was simply a flat, low-slung roof jutting out from the house covering a concrete slab. She shivered a little from suddenly being out of the sun.

Later, back in the kitchen, Linda was putting the last things from the morning's project away when Martha came in.

"Oh, look at all the work you've done." She sat on a high stool and leaned against the counter.

"It wasn't much, really," Linda said, folding the dishrag over the top of a lower cabinet drawer.

"I left you with a mess, I know that, but you are a dear to have cleaned up."

"Are you feeling better? Can I get you something?"

Martha got up off the stool and went to the refrigerator. "No, here, you sit. I'll pour us some lemonade." She pulled a pitcher out and Linda set two glasses on the counter. "I have a feeling we're going to make a good team."

After they sat and talked awhile, Martha went back to bed to read and rest. Linda was left in the kitchen with the television. She fidgeted mostly, not knowing what she should do. Finally, she turned the television on and Mike Douglas had Red Skelton on. Every once in awhile the phone rang and it was always Jack.

He came home early to check on things. Linda by then had turned the TV off, had checked on Martha, who was sleeping, and had now gone outside again. Jack turned the car into the driveway and pulled into the carport. When he got out, she noticed how tall he was, how a full third of his body towered over the hood of the car. His face was all angles and his eyes a bright hazel, rimmed by dark eyelashes that matched the thickness of his hair.

"She's sleeping," Linda said.

"Has she been up all day?"

"A good part of the morning, but then she sort of lost her energy and slept a good part of the early afternoon." Linda wondered if she'd be giving this man daily reports on his wife. She didn't know if she would like that or not, so she changed the subject.

"I walked around your garden. It must have been amazing this summer."

He smiled. "It was. We had squash, three kinds of beans, okra, bell pepper, watermelon - you name it. Now the pumpkins are coming in. It was quite a project, but it turned out."

"I've never had a garden."

"Well, maybe you'll help me with this when I go away for business next month."

Linda looked at him. "You're going away?"

"For a few days. Training in Detroit. Have you ever been to Detroit?"

"I've never even been out of Kansas, except for Kentucky when I was little. The only thing I remember were these caves we saw. We went on this tour and kept going down and down and they had these lights along the way. There were all these shapes like cones that came to a point."

"Stalagmites. I think I've heard of those caves. I wouldn't mind traveling some. We plan to, anyway, after the baby comes." Jack looked away and walked towards the garden. Linda followed him, matching two steps for every one of his. "I'll tell you, when summer comes, you've got to stay on top of the watering."

"I could do that."

The day was ending. As they walked, Linda shivered as she moved in and out of the day's remaining heat and the pockets of cold air that drifted up from the depression where their house sat among the low hills.

"So how was your first day?" Jack and Linda had wandered to the edge of the property before it sloped further down. Their bodies were silhouetted against the darkening cloudless blue.

"It was okay, I guess."

"I'm hoping that you'll be able to help Martha out in these coming months. Keep her from getting up too much. She's a willful woman." Jack smiled. "You might think she looks as if she might break in two from a whisper, but she's tough."

"We made thirty jars of pickles!"

"Did you now?" He broke out in a laugh. "Seems I'll be taking a bunch of those to work. You take a couple of jars with you tonight."

"Are you sure?"

"We're just two people with not a lot of neighbors." He suddenly got quiet. The sky darkened still and the sounds of the country began to change. The whirring of crickets rose among the dry weeds. Fireflies sparked in the black under the horizon.

Jack was entirely preoccupied by something that Linda wasn't sure of, but she knew her mother would be picking her up soon. "I have to get my things." She waited for him to say something, but he simply nodded, so she turned and went back to the house.

Martha was sitting in the banquette, staring out the window. "Did my husband show you the garden?"

"Yes."

"It's a nice garden, isn't it?"

"Yes, ma'am."

Martha turned to look at her. She too seemed lost for a moment, she pointed to a couple of the jars. "Take some home to your mother. You've been an awfully big help today."

"I feel like I've hardly done a thing." Linda tied her sweater around her and put two jars in a paper sack.

"Oh, you have." Martha was too tired to get up, but she smiled at the girl. A pair of headlights turned into the drive by the road. "Your mother's here. Now go, we'll see you tomorrow."

When Linda got to the car, she silently slid into her seat.

Her mother pulled the car back onto the highway and headed for home. "Don't you have anything to say about how your day went, a small incident that you might share? I'm curious to know what those people are like."

"They're okay."

"Is that all?" Her mother reached over to pull her daughter's sweater over the rest of her shoulder, but Linda pulled away.

"The woman is pregnant. Did she tell you that, because I didn't know?"

"Wasn't my place to ask. Does this mean more work for you?"

"I guess."

"Are they going to pay you more money?"

"I don't know." Linda looked out her window and saw the distant lights of Kansas City.

She didn't know how to ask for more money, and was irritated that her mother hadn't found out about Martha, but she liked the couple, and was intrigued that Martha was so much like her daddy in a way that made her feel needed again.

"Well, you better ask them before it arrives or you'll never get what's coming to you. I know how this stuff works."

Linda turned to her mother and angrily asked, "Do you?"

Clare tightened her grip on the steering wheel and then sighed heavily.

"It's just temporary. You'll be able to get a better job soon."

"With an eighth grade diploma?"

"It's not so bad. I've been working all my life."

Linda reached over and turned on the radio louder than she thought she should. Her mother, who otherwise would have turned it down, let it play.

The car's headlights picked out things along the way: a billboard, a roadside produce stand, reflections in the glass and mirrors of houses and cars. For the first time since her daddy died, Linda noticed their details, not just with her sight, so she could explain them to him, but how they fit into the landscape because it was so new to her.

Airstreaming

Water

Her doctor put Martha to bed after she'd found her sheets blood-spotted. They had rushed to the hospital. Martha shook during the whole drive despite being wrapped in blankets. Jack kept looking over his shoulder at her, "Just hold on," he said, "try to relax 'til we get there."

Jack not being able to reach the doctor heightened her panic. He called the hospital and there the nurse told them to hurry in.

When they arrived they put her in a room, her doctor appeared shortly afterwards, examined her, saw the bleeding had stopped, and sent them home later in the afternoon with instructions for strict bed rest.

Now, a couple of weeks later, Martha's belly had grown in fits; her weight shifted forward, the elastic of her husband's pajama pants stretched tight around her belly. She remained in bed most days for hours on end, but still made the effort to send Jack off in the morning and welcome him home in the evenings. Linda came and went during the days, and Martha was glad of it, for the help, and her company while Jack was gone, but she still counted down the hours when he'd return each night.

The black and white TV hummed most of the day with tinny voices and game show music. When she turned it off at night, the gray images seemed to ghost on the screen's curved surface a little longer than they had before the pregnancy.

She felt trapped and watched the constantly shifting weather through the window. She woke to find Jack gone from bed, then heard the shovel and rake ping when they hit a rock in the garden and the rain bird's incessant beating.

Everyday, Jack watered or weeded for an hour before work, and he'd carry in the late harvest, wash the vegetables in the sink, or bring the tomatoes in for Martha to see. It gave her some sense of involvement, if not the enjoyment.

He came in to shower and change, always with the same routine. He moved around the room, put his old clothes away, took out his work clothes and laid them flat on the bed's edge before he went into the bathroom. His back was browned and defined from the summer work, though his buttocks and legs were white from the long pants he wore. She waited to see him turn around and go towards the shower. She ached for him since she became pregnant because they'd stopped making love.

When he came out of the bathroom, she said, "Come here a minute."

"I'm late for work."

"Just for a minute." She held her hand out. He went to her and lightly kissed her and then went to the dresser and took out underwear and socks.

When he sat on the bed to pull his pants on and tie his shoes she reached for him, stroked his back. On some mornings he'd lean against her hand. Others, he'd lie just underneath her belly, his head on her thighs and feel her find the curves of his chest and then run her hand up over the crown of his head and pull his wet hair back, smooth it down and let her fingers trail through its thickness. The bathroom steam reminded her of when they made love. But, this morning, he simply got up to finish dressing, gave her a slight kiss again and left.

September 25th. Her daddy's birthday. Her mother had made no mention of it in the early morning as they ate, or as they moved around each other through the house getting ready for work. Linda opened her bedroom closet door and marked her calendar drawing an X across each box with the precise stroke of her pen. She counted the days of work and now there were exactly fourteen X's filling up the month. Like her father, she kept track of things: he with his little boxes of buttons separated by colors and shape, she by marking her calendar, which was the very last thing she did before she left the house to join her mother, who was accustomed to waiting for her in the car while it idled in the driveway.

When Linda arrived at the couple's house, Martha was usually napping. She cleaned the breakfast dishes and set the table for lunch. If Martha stirred, she'd take her a glass of milk, some hard candy, and sit on the bed until she was finished.

Today, there was a morning breeze. Linda opened a window and then another, which drew the wind across the top of the blankets and made the drapes flutter.

Martha lifted the bed sheet and let it float down over her body. "That feels nice."

"There were lightning strikes in town last night. I saw a burned tree branch on the roadside on the way out here," Linda said.

"The wind must have been very strong, but out here it was quiet, or maybe I slept through it."

Linda took the cup of milk from her and gave her a peppermint.

"Thank you." Martha said, and slipped the swirled candy into her mouth. "These sort of chill the milk. It's a wonderful sensation." She motioned for the cup of milk again.

"My daddy taught me that," Linda said.

"What else did he teach you?"

Linda folded the tiny cellophane wrapper in a square, as she always did. "Lots of things," she said.

Martha was tired from a restless night and settled deeper into the cotton sheets. They were the only kind she liked and the only kind that kept her warm; she replaced them long before they became threadbare.

Linda left her after she drew the drapes. Martha watched her pull them together with a snap and then she fell asleep and dreamt of home.

She dreamed of her family living on the lake in upper Minnesota. In summer, where people escaped the cities of Chicago and Detroit and filled the lake houses, but her family lived there year-round with a handful of people who spent the winters mending the things that had been broken in summer: boats, fishing nets, rods and reels.

They made coffee tables and lamps from deer antlers, and fixed the cars that people left behind for repair.

Snow fell incessantly, which forced them to work in barns fitted with furnaces. They did everything there – celebrations, religious services, schooling, Saturday night gatherings.

Martha loved those days, but she was lonely as there were few kids, and her parents were older. She waited for the short summer months when everything changed: when the boy she grew to love returned with his family. As the two of them grew older, their families only allowed them together in groups, but Martha and the boy snuck from their houses at night, and met on a dock hidden by Bayberry willows and honeysuckle.

In the dream, there was always a storm: the snow piled high around their home, and blanketed the ground in four-foot drifts. Her mother was at the window waving at her, holding a baby swaddled in white as snow inched up the house's siding. Great flurries came down as Martha stared her mother and the baby from a hill across from the house. Her father always joined her mother in the window, but then he lifted the baby from her arms and moved back into the house's dark.

Smoke from their chimney died out. Snow gathered higher and higher, covering their door, and the window where her mother stood. She'd begin running to the house, her feet finding their way as more snow fell. But she could never reach it in time before the snow blanketed its entirety and the house disappeared in it's shimmering curtain.

From behind her a boy called after her. "Martha!" he shouted. She turned. It was Morgan, the one lost in the lake, risen up from it, yards from the dock, where he fell through the ice while fishing with his dad. The one time Morgan had come in the winter.

And all the people from the scattered cabins had gathered lakeside, some with binoculars, watching Morgan's father lay on the ice next to where he fell in, looking down into the dark water for him. He lay there for hours until the Staley brothers and Ivan Stroot, walking arm in arm in case the ice cracked again, went out to him and coaxed Morgan's father in.

The following weekend the old barn filled with people. Summer folks drove up for the service. Morgan's stricken parents sat with their heads bowed. The Saturday night gathering had been canceled out of respect, but people came anyway to ready the barn for the next day's memorial. For two days the enclave of cabins bustled with people and she remembered her parents, down at the lakeside later that afternoon, in the gloaming, watching for signs of the boy.

When she reached the spot where the house must have stood, there was nothing but white and she woke in the sea of her white sheets, her face flushed, staring up at the ceiling, wondering how her parents could have abandoned her.

Linda finished the morning dishes. She wandered down the windowless hall, dotted by framed pictures, which caught the light from either end so that she felt as if she were walking down a hall of a blue checkerboard. In the darkness, she barely made out the photographs of Martha and Jack's family, but some had the faded sepia-tones of aged pictures, some bore cracks, but were flattened in their frames. It seemed as if the checkerboard was unfinished as the blue squares stopped midway down the hall.

There was Martha, younger, with the delicate, but strong hand of a mother on her shoulder. A serious man, with glasses and full moustache stood stiffly beside them. They were like those old western stills she'd seen in picture books, because the picture was taken outside in front of a wooded cabin, pine trees surrounding them and a shimmering lake behind, but she saw beyond all that and noticed there were no mountains, no steep rising cliffs.

Martha was seated on a chair on a bed of pine needles and leaves. Even in the billowy gown she wore she looked frail, a trait seemingly passed from mother to daughter. Linda stared at the picture a long time and might have turned on the light to look at the true details of it, but it seemed as if the artificial incandescence would have changed its formal mood.

She went into the sitting room. Two over-stuffed chairs faced a television set. Lamps hung their necks like giraffes over each chair. The drapes in this room were constantly pulled and kept it dark and cool even on the hottest days. The afternoon light filtered through the fabric as if it were made of tiny fiber slats.

Along the back wall were books. On one shelf there were a series of large, black bound journals. Gold lettering gave the year for each starting with 1952. Linda ran her fingers along their spines wanting to look inside, but she had seen Jack writing in one of them a couple of times, the lamp brightening his lap and the white pages. She liked their order.

She imagined he wrote down the day's events or kept a record of what he'd harvested from the garden, the progress of their baby. She went to the drapes and pulled them open. Silver morning light flooded the room.

"Oh, that's nice." Martha was at the door.

"I didn't think you were awake." Linda went to close the drapes again, "I thought I'd air the room a bit, but if you'd rather I didn't..."

"No, let's open it up. It's a wonderful idea. Jack always keeps this room so dark." Martha joined Linda at the window. "Those hills need some rain. Look how brown they are." Martha slid the glass door open. A light rush of wind blew through.

"Can I get you something?" Linda tied the drapes back.

"Oh, no. Let's just stand here a moment." Martha's face was softly lit, its angles and curves blended into each other. She had let her hair go, not caring how it looked, but to Linda, it had a natural beauty, sweeping back over her forehead.

"Those are Jack's journals."

"I wasn't looking." Linda lowered her head.

Martha touched Linda's arm. "I know. I saw you looking at them on the shelf. They're just a bunch of collected memories, but he's meticulous about them. Every day he writes. We have an understanding that I won't look in them until we're old. Then, he said, 'We'll look at them and see all that we've done.' It's an interesting notion, isn't it? A sort of casual history from one point of view."

"But aren't you interested in what he writes?

"Of course! Wouldn't you be?"

"I suppose. But how come he keeps them in plain sight like that. Anyone can look at them." Linda glanced over at the books' black edges. The gold lettering sparkled.

"I think he likes to see how many he has. I hope that after several years these shelves will be full of them." Martha chuckled and left the room.

Linda stared at the journals, wondered what secrets they contained. It was like never knowing what her father was looking at, that mystery contained beyond his feeling, beyond what she thought she knew of him.

Throughout the morning they worked side-by-side, cleaning one thing and then another. Linda admonished Martha to go back to bed, but Martha pulled up a high stool and sat, her hands covered in soap, cleaning jars and cans. Linda dried them and wrapped each in newspaper and placed them in boxes with pre-made lids. It was a mindless chore, but necessary for the next season's canning.

"Do you miss school?" Martha held up a jar and turned it in her hands. The light refracted in prisms through the shapes of letters.

"In a way, I guess." Linda kept working the bottles.

"I didn't go my last year, either."

"Really?"

"I didn't like where I lived." Martha said evenly. "I was so lonely there. The winters were long and there were hardly any people once they closed up their houses in the fall. All my friends left. But there was a boy named Morgan that I loved who came every summer," Martha laughed at the memory. "I wanted to find him."

"Where did you live?"

"Minnesota. A little town called Gran Marais." Martha spun a gold, metal top down on a jar. "He told me he lived in Kansas City, so I looked for it on a map and trailed the waterways all the way up to where we lived. It didn't seem so far to me then, but it was." She motioned for another jar to dry. "I would have taken a bunch of buses and then a train from Minneapolis into Kansas City." She said and laughed. "I was bored out of my mind in that little town and when Morgan came, everything changed."

"Were you going to leave?" Linda said.

"I was one night when it was bitter cold. The arctic winds were down out of Canada and would have chased me all the way to Kansas."

Linda struck a match and lit the stove, filled a kettle full of water and placed it over the fire. She took two mugs from the cupboard. "Would you have tried to find Morgan?"

Martha stopped what she was doing and smiled. "Absolutely, but he came up later that winter, and we spent time together, but then drowned in the lake. I never saw him again. I did leave Gran Marais soon after." Martha held back a little, and stopped short of the truth.

"But what about your parents? Weren't they upset?"

"They didn't speak to me for years." Martha shifted on the stool. "I sent them letters, called them, but they returned the letters undelivered and wouldn't answer the phone or hung up when they heard my voice."

"I'm sorry." Linda shook out loose tea into an infuser and closed it.

"I wanted to stay. It was my own fault. They'd spent their whole lives wandering from place to place, coming over from Scotland to New Hampshire, and making their way slowly across country, hearing about one job here and another there. Minnesota was their last stop. My father ended up guiding fishermen in the summer. He'd be gone all day, so I hardly saw him. In the winter he was home, but he'd be fixing tackle or working on the boat. I helped him build a skiff once."

"Did you ever see them again?"

The women stopped working and settled against the kitchen counter.

Martha continued, "The summer after Jack and I were married we drove up to their cabin. I sat outside their door until they came out. Jack sat in the car the whole time smoking, listening to the radio very loud, which I think is what finally drove them out of the house because they couldn't stand the interruption."

Martha went to the kitchenette and sat down. "We were a sight, the three of us. I think we embarrassed Jack. But here came my Mother down the steps, stopping at the last one, her hands on her hips backwards like this," Martha demonstrated so that her elbows flung out to her sides, "and she just stood there sobbing. That got me going, and then my father. We stood for the longest time just looking at each other, not knowing what to do next. Finally, Jack switched off the radio."

The kettle steamed. Linda took it from the stove. She poured the hot water into the teapot and dropped the infuser in. She gathered the mugs, a jar of honey and took them to the table where Martha was. She had a far off look about her. "Didn't they put out a search for you?"

"No. I kept sending those letters. I imagine they kept track of me through the postmarks. I broke their hearts."

Linda lowered her eyes. "I'm thinking about leaving." Then she looked up to see if Martha heard her, "If I have to work, I might as well live on my own."

Martha opened the morning newspaper. "I wouldn't have done it if I'd known what was going to happen. All those years are gone now." Martha went on, "I wrote the silliest note. I drew a picture of me on a bus, my hand waving out the window. And past the bus was this cartoon of Morgan. I had no experience of large cities. Even Kansas City worried me trying to get around in it. But I wrote, 'Don't worry about me' and signed it." Martha lifted the teapot. "May I pour you some?"

"Yes." Linda slid a cup along the Formica towards her.

Martha stole a look at her. "I miss the summers back home. They were so short, but we packed every day with stuff. The sun didn't even set until ten at night. We never went to bed before then."

"But we have winter here. It's not as if you came that far."

"No. But physical distance is not as far as mental distance." Martha sipped her tea and let the warmth swirl about the inside of her mouth.

"Oh." Linda paused.

"I didn't run away. I loved my parents. They were good parents." Martha laughed. "It was just me. I thought I would go crazy up there in all that white." She rested her elbows on the table and brought her cup back to her lips. The steam from the hot tea flushed her cheeks. "If I had to do it over I wouldn't have left when I did."

They sat for a while listening to birds skitter from tree to tree. The morning had been successfully frittered away. Linda wondered what it would be like to hop on a bus and just take off to somewhere unknown. She hadn't spent much time near water or even away from Kansas City. Martha must have seen so much coming all that way.

One time her mother drove her and dad to the Missouri River which seemed like some wide, dirty highway where boats coursed back and forth simply for commerce. She hadn't seen pleasure boats on the water, except the big paddle wheelers carrying tourists. The notion of what it must have been like, to be Martha, at the age that she herself was now, running away. It seemed exciting.

"Shall we finish the jars?" Martha got up slowly.

Linda saw she was tired. "I'll finish them up. Why don't you go lie down and I'll bring in some lunch after awhile."

"Are you sure?"

"Yes. Jack won't be happy with you up so much."

"Oh, we won't tell him." Martha said, as she went down the hallway towards the bedroom.

Linda was surprised at the last, but she turned to the sink and worked to clean the rest of the jars.

Martha settled exhausted into bed and fell asleep to dreams of water. Lake water. She saw small, curved wakes as her father's oars coursed through its black glassy plane, the colors of late-afternoon clouds reflected on its surface, diamonds of light exploding in a breeze. She had never been frightened leaving as she did, though a girl of sixteen had every right to be. Instead, every day opened up into propitious opportunity. There were days on end of unimaginable beauty.

Linda squandered the afternoon away while Martha slept. She swept the back porch, read a Life magazine, and replaced some flowers with blue cornflowers that grew wild off the side of the house. Her mind was filled, however, with winter and adventure - and the idea of boarding a bus because, when it came right down to it, she was afraid of water and heading off to anywhere, maybe St. Louis or St. Paul, on land seemed far more practical. She'd leave her mother - that wasn't an issue. Well, yes it was. They had to keep the house. But what, if finally, her mother decided that an apartment would be good enough? What if she met a man like Jack, who'd take them in and they left the house? All afternoon she thought of means of escape.

At five o'clock, as he had done every day since Linda started working, Jack pulled in off the highway and came down the long drive to the house. The Ford wagon bumped along the gravel drive and kicked off small stones.

Linda leaned over the sink counter and peered out the window to watch him pull into the garage. She dried her hands, went down the hall to check on Martha who was still sleeping and collected her lunch tray. As she came back into the kitchen Jack came in from the service porch.

"Is she asleep?"

Linda nodded.

Jack went to the refrigerator and pulled out a pop. "Watch this," he said, lifting the bottle for Linda to see. In a flash of his hands, the metal top popped off and sailed across the room. "Damn."

Linda laughed.

"It's supposed to go straight up and then I catch it in one hand. I can do it at work, no problem." Jack retrieved the errant cap and tossed it in the trash. His face grew dark a moment and then he smiled again.

"I believe you." Linda was struck at how such a small thing could change his mood, but he was good at changing it back.

"How'd the day go?" Jack leaned against a tall cupboard that contained the water heater. There was a grid at the top for ventilation that was always warm to the touch. "Did she rest?"

"Just barely." Linda walked to the edge of the sink. Jars were lined up in formation along the counter, turned upside down on dishtowels to dry. "She's been in bed most of the afternoon, but this morning she was in here with me. We didn't do anything too hard."

"That's good. She's not supposed to be up at all, but I'm sure you can't stop her too well."

"I try to, but..."

"I'll look in on her." Jack abruptly left. He had a ragged walk. A foot shuffled slightly before hitting the linoleum, and then the next foot would do the same. It was as if they were burdened by weight, and it was a long, tired effort to the next step.

Linda began loading the last jars into the boxes. She heard him open the door to their room and then there was a soft click as it closed behind him.

"I like these shorter hours. I like that you don't have to drive home in the dark." Martha had heard him in the kitchen. She did her best to scoot up in bed. The pillows were new and had not found their shape, but with all this time in bed, she knew that they'd form themselves to her quickly.

"Me too," Jack said, removing his shirt and work pants. He went to the bed and leaned in to kiss her. "You've been a bad mother."

"Have I?" She smiled.

"Linda tells me you've been working in the kitchen with her."

"Just a little." Martha would have to strike a deal with Linda. "Really, we just sat and talked."

"That you can do, but none of this work. That's why she's here." Jack worked his boots off with his heels.

"Come here," Martha lifted the sheet, "lie down for awhile."

"You know we're not supposed to."

"Just for a bit. Ten minutes, tops."

"I've got work to do. The squash is in –."

Martha's mood deflated. "Then go ahead. You barely look at me now."

"How can you say that?" He threw his work shirt in the corner just missing the hamper and sat on the bed.

"I am so afraid every morning, did you know that? I'm so afraid lying here alone because you are out there in that garden, and I'm waking, wondering if I'll make it through the day with this baby intact."

"I can't have this baby for you," Jack said, admonishing her a little, "You know what the doctor said."

"I have to lie here everyday."

"Apparently, you don't."

"That's not fair. I hardly do a thing." Martha pulled the sheet in around her. She closed her eyes and slid down in the bed. She was petulant at that moment, which she didn't like. It had never occurred to her before to act that way, and, so far, they had never had this friction between them, but his lack of attention to her was a growing irritation to her in the past week, which now had taken hold.

"I don't know what I can say or do. I'm working all day and our life was settling into this routine, this country routine that I've been trying to get to all my life." He stood up and moved away from the bed.

"I know you aren't necessarily wanting this baby." She watched Jack recoil slightly, turn away from her and then swing back to where he faced her.

"I never said that."

Martha continued, "And I accept that. I don't understand it, but I accept it. I worked so hard for this baby."

"We both worked hard." Jack let a small sigh go. He went to the bed. "However I feel about the baby is how I feel at any given moment. I want the baby because you want it. I want the baby because I want it. I want the baby because, without it, I think I might lose you."

"That's ridiculous." They stared at each other a moment. Martha looked for something in him: a confirmation? A need?

"Is it?" He stood up from the edge of the bed and went to find a shirt to work in. "I have to work it out. I'd like to tell you why, but I can't right now."

"Will you tell me when you have it figured out? I need to know." The morning had taken its toll on Martha. She was weak.

Jack nodded.

"Will you at least stay a few moments until I fall asleep?" Her voice trailed off inexplicably. She might have been calling after him from another room.

Jack came to the edge of the bed. He put his hand on her belly and then trailed it down her thigh. "I only have a little bit of light to work in." He put on his t-shirt. "I'll be outside. I'll have Linda bring you in some warm milk."

Martha wondered how they were going to get through the winter, with the garden under snow, the wind too cold, the pressure of all that white.

Linda sat at the kitchenette trying to keep busy, but really trying to understand what was going on down the hallway. She was also thinking of up North, from where Martha came.

She heard the door to the bedroom open. She got up and went to the refrigerator and opened it. She heard Jack behind her. "Does she need anything?" She asked.

"Could you heat some milk?" Jack said going past her to the kitchen door, which led to the front yard. "I'll be outside."

Outside, he thought of the guys at the shop, some of whom worked now on Saturdays for him, and had worked hard to humor Jack while his wife was going through her pregnancy and he tried to be all smiles there, using the shop as a refuge from the trials of keeping Martha in bed and rested after Linda left everyday.

They put a small party on for him with some of the others at the dealership, the women who ran the office and some of the salesmen. It was a Friday after they shut the doors. Beers were passed, pizza delivered, a cake lit as they needled Jack about diaper changing, sleep deprivation and how, instead of lingering after hours, he'd be running home to the family.

Carl, who Jack hired and relied on more than the others, was there and was watching him during the party move around the room and take on the friendly provocations. Jack kept his eye on the clock above the cashier desk, distracted and aloof. As the groups formed after the initial toast, Jack went from group to group and tried to enter their conversations gracefully, but failed. The clock ticked on and he became more falsely animated and overcompensated his happiness.

Carl pulled him away from Stan and Terry. "I've got to borrow Jack. Excuse me guys. I'll bring him back in a sec." He took Jack's arm and led him out of the conference room leaving the party in full swing and into the alley behind the building. "You looked about as comfortable as a cornered dog."

"They go on, those two."

"I see a man who's got something under his skin." Carl slid a cigarette out of its pack and placed it on his lip. "You've got something, alright, so I want you to tell 'ole Carl what's up."

"I'm good. These things just make me nervous. I don't like attention thrown at me." Jack stepped away from the cigarette cloud.

"There's something else." Carl waved the cigarette in the air and its spark brightened as he talked. "You've not said much about your baby, just Martha this and Martha that and how she needs this or wants that." Carl eyed Jack. "Never about how you can't wait to be a papa or, like most of us whimpering fools, how we're going to spoil them silly, take them to ball games, teach them stuff."

"That's not true."

"Hell it isn't. I know I drove these guys crazy with that talk. Still do! And hardly a word from you." Carl drew on the cigarette; its smoke drifted slowly between his parted lips. Jack offered nothing. Carl said, "It's like you're willing this thing away, Jack, willing it out of existence."

Jack glared at Carl. "You done? Have you said all you're going to say, because that's enough isn't it?" Jack was angry and up into Carl's face, the cigarette holding the space between them. "You think you got it down?" Jack held Carl's eyes until Carl looked away. "You don't know shit, Carl."

Jack left Carl standing at the back door and walked the entire way around the building and got in his car and left the party. On the way home, he heard Carl's voice in his head and wondered if he was willing the baby out of existence neither thinking the thoughts he did nor acknowledging his impending fatherhood. He thought that by focusing all his at-home energy on Martha that he was welcoming the future.

The next day Carl tried to apologize several times, but Jack just listened to him and never gave him any indication that he'd accepted it.

Linda had put a pan of milk on the stove, cut a slice of bread and buttered it. When the milk was ready she gathered it all on a tray and took it down the hall. She knocked at the door with her elbow.

"Come in, Linda." Martha's voice was shallow. She sounded more out of sorts than usual.

"Are you okay?" Martha was sunk down low in the bed, her face flush and beads of perspiration dotted her forehead. She took the napkin she had for the food and wiped her brow, then handed the plate to her.

Martha took the bread. "This is good, thank you. You really are a help." She took a bite from the slice of bread and looked out the window. She moved up slightly and nodded to the window. "I wish that were lower so I could see outside better if I have to lie here in bed all day. I really would like to see what goes on outside, even if I can't actually be there."

"I'll give you full reports."

"Then do me a favor and go out to see if you can help Jack. I want to know what's coming in, what's done, what else we have to look forward to before the weather turns. Make sure he brings in the things that are ripe." Martha took another bite and the cup of milk from Linda. "I'll be okay. You go."

"Are you sure?"

"Yes." She placed the dish with the bread on the bed and set the cup on the nightstand.

Outside, Jack turned the soil with a pitchfork. He jabbed at it with such force Linda thought the tines might break. The sun had since gone down and Jack worked in the twilight. He muttered to himself. Linda was afraid to break his concentration because his back was to her. He had not heard her come up behind him, but she heard fragments of what he was saying. It was a sort of repetition and with each plunge of the pitchfork he'd murmur. And he'd lift the soil, flip the pitchfork over and the wet earth would fall in clumps back on the ground.

Linda stood with her hand to her mouth wondering whether to interrupt him or go back to the house before he realized she was there. She walked backwards, tried to be quiet, but then Jack turned around to start on another patch of ground. He saw her and stopped, a little embarrassed. He was sweating and his face had a hurt look on it. Linda thought that he might have been angry, but his face was knotted up, which confused her.

"This is hard work." Jack wiped his forehead. "Would you do me a favor and go get the rake so I can smooth this all out? It's in the garage."

Again, the change, she thought. "Sure."

"Maybe you might want to help with this, keep it going." Jack leaned on the pitchfork's handle. "I have to leave in a few weeks and I could sure use some help in minding it to keep the weeds down while I'm gone."

"I can do it."

"Remind me to show you what to do then."

"I'll go get the rake." She walked quickly away. She went to the garage to search for the rake. The light was going fast.

Inside the garage two small windows allowed a little bit of light, but at this time of day it was not enough to see clearly. She hadn't been out to the garage yet, and didn't know where things were kept. She searched for a light switch along the wall, but couldn't find one. She stood a moment to let her eyes adjust. Maybe a string hung down from a bulb somewhere, so she looked up above the Ford.

"Couldn't you find the rake?" Jack stood at the open door, peering in.

He had frightened her. "No, there's no light."

"Oh, I should have told you where it was." He came in and switched on the bare bulb from a place over the workbench. "I keep the tools in the corner there."

Linda saw all of the wooden handles leaning together. They were all put away so neatly, like his journals. There was fastidiousness to him that she wanted to know about. She wanted to ask him about the journals, and why he spent so much time on the garden. What was he avoiding? Was he angry? Did he really want an outsider like her intruding in their privacy? Where Martha was plain about everything, Jack was a locked closet.

"Is there something wrong?" Jack started to move further into the garage.

"No, I think I found it." She grabbed the rake and pulled it out from among the other tools. She handed it to him.

"Thanks," he said, and looked at her for a moment. "Are you okay?"

Linda nodded. Behind Jack, the familiar headlights of her mother's car swung into the driveway. "My mom's here."

Jack turned. "You should invite her in sometime." He walked out of the garage and Linda ran by him. When she was halfway up the drive, she turned and yelled back, "Please say goodbye to Martha for me," then ran the rest of the way to the car.

On the way home Linda was silent. She was trying to figure out the people she'd been forced with, whether Martha's stories were true and whether Jack's feelings toward his wife were true as well. She was confused, and found it all far more complicated than going to school. Her mother tried to talk to her as well, but she finally lit a Pall Mall, cracked the window, and drove.

Another Country

The last days of summer glimmered with heat. It wasn't so much that Linda wanted summer to end, but that she wanted change. She wanted to feel the first break of weather when the wind shifted and came down from the north. She wanted to be able to close the windows, the front door and her mother and her to put in the storm windows for the winter. She wanted her daddy to do his annual inventory of the windows with them. She was tired of everything being open, voices carrying up from the street, car horns bleating near and far. Maybe then she'd put her father's memory in her back pocket, or that it might become a private thing, and the neighbors would move on and stop asking how she was, or looking at her with those faces full of pity.

The moment with Jack in the garden had convinced her of deeper things going on between he and his wife. She kept busy by cleaning their house, top to bottom.

Late Friday afternoon Jack handed her a twenty and a five in crisp, once-folded bills. In the car, she handed the twenty to her mother and put the five in the pocket of her skirt.

On Saturday morning, with the weekend ahead of her, Linda stood barefoot in the grass of their front lawn, wearing loose blue jeans and a print blouse watching her neighbors do their chores.

Across the street, Mr. Adderley arthritically pushed his lawnmower back and forth since the neighbor kid suddenly quit on him with no explanation. He leaned to the left and put his weight on one side causing the mower to constantly turn which made him stop several times to adjust its direction.

On the other side of their house, Mrs. Dempsey, her young husband wounded in the Vietnam War, wrestled her hose down the driveway to water the median of grass between the sidewalk and street. She had remarked to Linda's father once that the city should have thought about putting in sprinklers when they built the houses.

Linda watched Mrs. Dempsey as she did her work. Though the hose was hopelessly kinked, she looked over at Linda and smiled through her frustration. She had come by the morning after Linda's father had been taken away and left a plate of ginger cookies. They reminded Linda of Christmas, so she had tossed them out and returned the plate, thanking Mrs. Dempsey for thinking of them.

Mrs. Miller came quickly out of her house wearing a sleeveless dress, somewhat disheveled, which, Linda thought, was not like her. She carried a wooden tennis racket with broken strings. So far, she was unaware of Linda standing at the edge of the lawn. Barbara's mother backed away from the front door and went down the steps to the side of the house where she disappeared behind the hedges. Mr. Miller appeared at the screen door, dressed only in khaki work pants. Linda was surprised by the bulk of him. She'd always thought of him as just slightly larger than her father, but there he was, his mass blunting the interior of their house until he disappeared into its darkness.

Remember her father's admonition, Linda thought that maybe she shouldn't try and catch up with Barbara this morning on what was happening at school.

Mr. Miller and her father had shared bottles of Pabst in their backyard, but Mr. Miller was never invited inside the house. Her father always led him through the side gate, down the cement path into the small expanse of yard. They would sit in the metal lawn chairs, on the frayed yellow cushions, and talk for a couple of hours. Linda's mother stayed in the house during these visits, and gave Linda inside work to do as well.

"I don't like that man," Linda's mother had said as she snapped open a new dishtowel and looped it through the handle on the refrigerator. "And I don't like your father entertaining him like he does."

"He's just being friendly because he's our neighbor." Linda hooked a long bang of her hair under her top lip and wet it with her tongue.

"That still doesn't excuse it."

"Excuse what?" Linda knew that there had been shouts next door, loud crashes, and had seen Mrs. Miller dragging Barbara by the hand down the steps, and across the street to Mr. Adderley's one day last winter.

Her mother looked at her long bang hanging limp down the side of her face. "I wish you wouldn't do that."

"Do what?"

"Play with your hair. You have such beautiful hair and all you want to do is mess it up." Her mother looked out the window at her father and Mr. Miller. "Go see if they

need more to drink." Her daughter started to go outside.
"You can call from the screen door."

Linda hesitated a moment before defying her mother
and began opening the screen door.

Her father turned his head toward the sound. "Linda,
come outside a moment." He held his arm out for her to
join him. "Mr. Miller was just telling me about Russia."

Linda checked her mother through the kitchen
window, who now was angry and had her eyes narrowed
on Linda. She slid the door fully open. The slip of metal
scraped as the screen door was pushed back. Her father
wiggled his fingers beckoning her. Linda moved into the
crook of his arm and watched Mr. Miller watching her.
He was flat-featured, with a high forehead and soft
blonde hair. His nose, too, was flat; the nostrils flared out
like a bull. His cheeks sunk in and created shadows and
his eyes were dark and glassy, like a gopher.

"Mr. Miller was just traveling in Russia for his
company. They're planning electric power generators."
He squeezed her a little and then settled against the back
of his chair. "Go on, Harold."

"I was just talking about this valley, how in the
middle of nowhere it just falls away into nothing, but on
either side are these high, flat plains where they crossed
during the war to go into Europe. You can see the tracks
from the tanks for miles, and bones of horses and dogs.
Sometimes I thought that maybe they were human. We
heard these stories of men just stopping, huddling close
in winter, freezing together in great clumps. Their land is
not so different from ours except, where we were, there
weren't any trees to speak of."

Linda looked past Mr. Miller to the unadorned backyard and imagined white bones, shaped like beehives, grasses growing amidst their tangled forms. It scared her some to think of traveling along those rivers, seeing the carcasses of wild animals.

Her father shifted slightly from the weight of her, "I suppose it must have been a hard trip, seeing all of the devastation from the war."

"We drove two days from the nearest airport into the upper Ukraine. There were only villages here and there. We camped. The mosquitoes were thick enough so that we had to wear netting until the wind came. Can you imagine clouds of them?"

"No." her father said, and laughed, "I have trouble with the ones we have here."

Linda returned her gaze to Mr. Miller, whose white, collared shirt was stained yellow under the arms. She was surprised at how casually her father talked with him, given his stearn warnings to her and her mother. She couldn't bring herself to say anything, let alone stay there much longer. The conversation about bones and war, and Mr. Miller's embellishments to prop himself up, made her uncomfortable "I can get you another beer if you wish, Mr. Miller."

"I have to get back, the women of the house are probably waiting for me at home." He got out of his chair; his shadow fell over Linda and her father who felt the loss of the sun and stood up as well.

"Can you see yourself out?" Her father's hand squeezed her elbow holding her still. "I hope the rest of your work goes well."

"I'm home for awhile now. We'll have to have our families together for supper soon."

"I'm sure we will."

Mr. Miller nodded towards Linda, and then clapped her father on the shoulder. "Bye now," he said, and went down the side of the house, and back into his yard.

Her father's fingers relaxed around her elbow. "Can you take these bottles inside? I'm going to sit for awhile." When he sat down, he accidently knocked one of the empty bottles over. "I'm sorry, honey."

Linda reached under the chair as her daddy sat again in the chair and put his feet up.

"I'll get you something if you want." Linda retrieved pillows from the chair where Mr. Miller had sat and placed them behind her father.

"No, no. You go in and help your mother."

At dinner, her mother looked up from her plate and said to her father, "I wish you wouldn't talk to that man like you do. Not after the things I've heard coming from their house. He frightens me."

"I have to." Linda's father said and went on eating.

"You don't have to do anything." Clare set down her fork; the tines clinked on the plate's rim. The sound seemed louder than it should have been.

Linda stopped eating and watched her parents.

"It doesn't seem right that you humor him in front of his wife and child after the things he does."

"We don't know what goes on over there except for the shouting," he lowered his head slightly, "and it's my only way of protecting you." After that, there was no more discussion of Mr. Miller or anything else that night.

The family finished dinner; Linda cleaned the dishes, her mother wiped the table down, and they all ended up in front of the television to watch and listen.

Mrs. Miller came round the other side of the house, brandishing a tennis racket, hurrying past the rose bushes, past the creeping ivy, its leafy tips now sun-burnt and wilted, and into the front yard, her chest heaving. Linda, surprised to see her again, forced herself to move from her post at the lip of the grass at the beginning of the walk, and ran after Mrs. Miller to see if she needed help.

"Mrs. Miller," she called out.

The woman turned and saw Linda and turned again towards the house, pointing the tennis racket at the top floor. "He's got Barbara!" Mrs. Miller's voice cracked. "He's got my baby!"

Linda's mother came rushing out the screen door, which made a loud whack against the house. She ran by Linda and grabbed her arm. "We need to get her," she said. Linda, startled, blindly ran after her mother as they rounded the hedges and ran up the front steps, but the door had been locked. Her mother pounded on it.

Mr. Adderley let go of his lawnmower's clutch, which sputtered to a stop. He came hobbling across the street, his one leg dragging after him. He took the racket from Mrs. Miller and went to the large picture window in front and, with as much force as he had left in him, slammed the racket against the glass, which shattered and fell in large splinters on the porch.

The shattering glass caught everyone by surprise. They were momentarily stunned into complacency until Mrs. Miller climbed through the opening, catching the leg of her pants and tearing it down to her calf. Linda and her mother followed.

At the top of the stairs, Mr. Miller stood in his boxer shorts. Light from an open doorway threw his shadow against the flowered wallpaper over the banister. "What the hell!" he shouted as he came down the stairs.

"Where's Barbara?" Mrs. Miller shouted, going up the stairs trying to get past him. Linda and her mother stood at the landing. "Barbara!" She shouted. They heard the girl's muffled sobs. Linda reached behind her and unlocked the front door from the inside hoping that Mr. Adderley would hear it and come in so more of them were there.

The Millers met in the middle of the stairs.

"Let me by," Mrs. Miller shouted.

Mr. Miller shifted his weight around to block her.

Mrs. Miller pushed him hard against the wall and knocked him off balance for a moment. She'd pushed hard into his side and tried to hold him there and get by him.

Linda's mother started up the stairs, one by one, and shouted at Mr. Miller. "Harold, let her up the stairs. Now."

Mr. Adderley came through the front door, but was helpless to do anything and stood amid the chaos next to Linda far below the Millers.

Mr. Miller grunted as his wife tried to further knock him off balance, but then he shifted his weight, steadied himself and then the bulk of him picked up his wife and threw her over the railing as easy as tossing a large bag.

It was almost like slow motion, and yet it was over quickly.

Linda screamed. Her mother, who'd continued shouting at Mr. Miller was stunned into silence. Mr. Miller stared dumbly down at his wife who had landed, her arms and legs buckled under her, with her head tucked obscenely against her shoulder. It was such a horrific sight that years later, when they talked about what happened objectively, Linda and her mother couldn't recall the sound she made when she hit the wooden floor.

Linda spun around when Mrs. Dempsey came running over. Other neighbors came out of their houses.

Barbara emerged from the lit doorway and came to the top of the stairs. She looked over the banister and saw her mother below; the dress she had put on that day in front of her as they'd talked, now billowing out from her, a stain of blood ballooning out from under it as if underwater. She looked over and saw her father inert where he stood and their neighbors, all of them steadfastly holding the air in their bodies except Linda's mother.

It was moments before everything registered. Barbara clutched the railing and let out a long wail. In the instant before the robe hid her body, Linda saw that she was naked underneath. Barbara continued to lean over the railing and then sunk down against it, her red robe pushing against the white, molded wood.

Once the girl had settled, crouching on the top landing, Linda released the air she'd been holding and began breathing hard. She wanted to run out the door, but Mr. Adderley was blocking it just by standing there with a shocked look on his face.

Her mother went over to where Mrs. Miller lay, one leg twisted away from her body, the rest of it in repose, slumbering, safe. She leaned in close to see if there was an indication of life from the woman. She put her hand up against her cheek, then her mouth and felt for any sort of heat. Now, rising, her mother pushed Mr. Adderley out of the way and went down the porch stairs, the walk leading to the sidewalk and over to their house and then came back to the Miller's driveway where she stayed until the police came.

Linda was shocked at how quickly things had escalated, made themselves known, and then just as quickly settled. They all stood around not knowing what to do next. Mr. Adderley stood dumbstruck by the door. Mrs. Dempsey had stopped at the landing. Even Mr. Miller was somehow placated, as a baby is by food or something to suckle. He'd moved down to the second stair from the bottom, stood wide-eyed, and stared straight out the front door into the morning light's glare.

Here were Barbara and her father, their secret unions becoming a fact for her mother, for the neighborhood, and for Linda.

By early afternoon, the Millers house was empty. Mrs. Miller was taken away by ambulance, Mr. Miller by police car, and Barbara by friends of their family until her relatives could come take her to their home in Arizona.

The weekend, which had stretched out before Linda, now seemed compressed. When she returned home, having given an account of the afternoon's events to the police, and having taken Mr. Adderley back across the street to home, and him seemingly more frail than ever,

Linda found that she was hungry. It had been hours since she'd eaten.

"Do you want something to eat?" Her mother came into the kitchen.

"I can get it." Linda opened the refrigerator and looked inside. It was nearly empty save for some milk, butter, a loaf of bread and old jars of jelly, mayonnaise, and mustard.

"No, let me." Her mother opened a cupboard. "How's soup sound? You can cut some slices of bread." She pulled down a can of Campbell's. "That would be good." After her husband died, she'd taken to bringing home dinner every night, stopping quickly on the way home from picking up Linda. They alternated between a bucket of Fried Chicken from the new Colonel Sander's store, pizza, or quick food from the supermarket.

They moved around each other warily. The Millers still held a sort of grasp on them. Linda had read in a magazine that a dead person's presence stayed a bit, before fully leaving the area, and though she didn't quite believe that, she did feel that Mrs. Miller's death had entered their kitchen. A thin layer of clouds blocked the sun's full light. Linda cut the bread carefully and spread butter on it dramatically, covering every white inch with yellow.

Annoyed, her mother stopped turning the can opener, "What are you doing?"

"I'm buttering the bread."

"You're treating it like a science project."

"No, I'm not. I just want lots of butter." Linda said, and put the knife in the sink with the rest of the dishes that had been piling up for two days. She turned to her mother and asked, "Why did you leave the Miller's like that and not come back inside?"

"What are you talking about?" Her mother poured the contents of the can into a saucepan; noodles flaccidly floated in chicken broth. "Don't you think I've seen enough for one summer?"

After they ate, the two of them retreated to separate parts of the house. Linda to the front porch where she'd started her day and her mother to her bedroom. Since Linda never really watched TV at home, her mother had moved it in with her to watch it from her own bed.

When Johnny Carson came on at ten-thirty, his image silhouetted white against the dark curtains giving him a reverential halo that she liked; she called him her 'Angel of Sleep' and developed the habit of talking to him as if she were in the chair next to him. Sleep came in the middle of the program, but then she'd wake to a late night movie and watch until the test pattern came on at three a.m.

The streetlights slowly warmed: large, pod-shaped globes sat upon gothic, filigreed cement posts. The lights never just snapped on, but took their sweet time to heat, to signify the day passing into night, as if timed to the sun's rotation.

Linda sat on the porch as the sky darkened and the streets were illuminated. She wondered where Barbara might be, how she might feel. She thought of Martha and Jack, and resolved to sit with Martha as long as she needed her, to listen to her stories. She felt that Martha needed someone to tell them to.

In her bedroom's quiet dark, Linda listened for the television's sounds, the long monologues broken by laughter, and waited. After an hour, she slipped from bed, drew her pants on, shoes and a sweatshirt. She'd taken the flashlight from the kitchen drawer earlier when her mother was in her bedroom.

When she was outside, she looked around the neighborhood to see if anyone was coming up or down the street in their cars, or walking along the sidewalks. She stole over to the Miller's front porch, looked again and went over the window's transom that hadn't been repaired yet, and into the house. She was careful of the glass though the large pieces had been collected by Mr. Adderley and thrown out. Her eyes adjusted to the near dark, and she saw Mrs. Miller's stain still on the floor. After a few minutes, she made her way to the stairs, hesitated and then climbed toward Barbara's bedroom.

Until now, she did not think she was capable of stealing into someone's home, but the pull of Barbara's nakedness, and her father's desire, created questions that Linda wanted answers to. What interested her most was Barbara and how she had settled into a state of calm after the initial shock of her mother.

Turning from the windows facing the street, she switched on the flashlight, cupped its beam in her palm so that there was just enough to see and proceeded up the stairs. Each step groaned and creaked with her weight and echoed through the house. The gaping hole left by the broken window chilled the inside air. Linda reached the landing and peered over the banister just as Barbara had done. She felt a sort of vertigo due to the effort of climbing the stairs, which was harder on her legs than if she'd taken them casually. She looked first to where Mrs. Miller had landed and then to the step where Mr. Miller ended up.

The streetlamp's light angled in between cracks, doors and windows. It ran along the floor, over the furniture, the walls. It ran in harsh, straight lines. In the dark light, Linda lowered herself between the banister's arms, into the position that Barbara had been in. She wanted to see the afternoon's events from her point of view, to try and understand what she'd done.

From there she went into Barbara's room, which contained very little light so Linda removed her hand, and covered the flashlight's beam splashing across the ceiling. The room was a deep blue.

Barbara's collection of stuffed animals were strewn haphazardly across the floor close to the bed. Ruffled blankets lay in triangles over its side. The bed's pillows propped up oatmeal bears, ducks and the monkey with long limbs, bright red lips and elongated body that Linda always liked. The small dresser top contained brushes and combs that she and Barbara combed heir hair with, a vial of amber liquid, more golden in the flashlight's yellow. There were bobby pins, Barbara's red, canvas-covered journal with its small locket, curiously in plain view among an assortment of colored pencils that Barbara had drawn outdoor scenes with.

Above the dresser, the attached mirror reflected Linda in the dimness as she went toward it to pick up the journal.

"Why are you here?" said a voice from behind her. Linda was afraid to look, but in the mirror she saw

Barbara. Was she an apparition? Barbara moved out of the mirror's reflection. Linda turned.

Barbara sat on the bed.

Linda stammered, "I don't know."

"What are you looking for?" Barbara stood and walked towards Linda, which scared her, then reached behind her and switched off the flashlight. The room went dark. To Linda, the air seemed colder. Barbara was a foot away. "They might have tried to follow me."

"Who? Linda stepped back, frightened, saw a numbed Barbara, her eyes deep and swollen.

"The Shellings. They kept watching me all night thinking I might do something. I finally told them I was going to bed. It seemed like hours before I heard them go into their room. Then I snuck out of the house." Barbara came up to Linda again. "You haven't answered me yet. You shouldn't be here."

"I was just looking around. I'll go."

"What are you looking for?"

"I don't know," she said and went for the door.

Barbara stepped in front of her and said, "Follow me." She took Linda by the arm and guided her down the hallway to her parent's bedroom. Several feet separated two twin beds; between them was a small nightstand and lamp. Barbara let Linda go and walked over to her parent's dresser and opened the top drawer. She felt around underneath some white underclothes. She pulled something out that was long and looked brittle in the blue window light. Coming back to Linda, she held it in front of her and motioned for Linda to take it.

Linda lifted it up to inspect it. It was a bone of some sort, porous, but smooth. She turned it around in her hands; the shadows of her fingers fell across its whiteness.

"It's from the arm of a little girl." Barbara whispered.

Linda dropped it to the floor and it broke in two.

"You were always clumsy." Barbara stared angrily at Linda, which hurt. Then Barbara knelt down and collected the two pieces, put them back together, and held it up in the light.

"My father brought it back from Russia. My mother wouldn't allow him to show it to me, but he did when she wasn't home. He showed me where he kept it."

Linda didn't want to see or hear any more, was ashamed suddenly that she'd trespassed into the Miller's home and left their bedroom.

Barbara followed Linda out of the room and into the hall. She stopped where Linda had last seen her that afternoon and looked down. "We would do it when Mom was gone," she said, "But she knew it was going on. I sort of did things to let her know."

"I saw you once." Linda, wide-eyed and chilled, looked over the banister with Barbara.

"I know." Barbara said. "I wanted you to. I sat close to him that night on the couch with my knees up over his leg while we watched TV. Dad touched my knees and would see how far he could run his fingers up before Mom notice."

Barbara pulled her hair back and pointed the flashlight's beam at her neck. There were bruises. "This afternoon, when my mom found my dad and me together, she tried choking me. I had gone into their bedroom while Dad was in the shower. I think she was jealous of me or something." Barbara held the bone fragments up so Linda could see. "I took the bone from the drawer and I held it up to my mother's face like this. I said, 'Look here. Look at this. Look at how white and bare this bone is. Look at how small the arm of that little girl must have been. Look at how clean it is now. Can you imagine all of the birds and animals pecking at this bone – stripping away the meat to make it this clean? Can you imagine the bones of a little girl, my little girl, your granddaughter?"

Linda wanted to leave, run out of the house, but Barbara kept her there by her vacant stare.

"Dad came out of the shower and found Mom choking me right here on the floor. He tried to pull her off me, but she wouldn't let go. I pried her fingers open and ran into the bathroom and locked the door. I heard them fighting and then her running down the stairs and out of the house." Barbara looked at her and said bluntly, "that's what you wanted to know isn't it?"

"I guess so." Linda started to cry – more from being frightened than by anything else. She wanted to ask questions, but couldn't form them in her mind. She realized she had no inkling of who her friend was.

Barbara went into her bedroom and came back with the small red book. "This is what I came back for. You can go now if you want. I have to get back." Barbara left down the stairs and through the kitchen, out the back door, and slipped down the side of the house.

Linda listened to her leave from the top of the stairs and then came down into the living room. She had visions of Barbara, her father, them together, and a white tangle of bones. She imagined Mr. Miller stooping over to pick the bone from the mossy tundra and carry it secretly in his pocket as a souvenir, a possession to possess his daughter. All of it closed in on Linda: the view of the whole world as darkness, the trains, the Russian valley that would someday be lit by electric light, and all of the children without homes during the war, walking across tundra, collapsing in heaps, brought together for warmth for staving off cold. Here was Mr. Miller bringing a bone – that of a small girl to another girl – his daughter, carrying the cold with him.

Linda shuddered. All of her daddy's misgivings about Mr. Miller, her mother's too, and her own naiveté of the world coalesced in one afternoon.

She knelt at the place where Mrs. Miller had fallen and touched the spot. The wood had grown cold, the stain had dried, but there was still a sort of heavy presence that Linda felt or imagined as she stood up, opened the front door, and went home.

A Good Day

Late October. The Kansas sky was cobalt blue, cleansed by rain and strong winds. The threatening storms had dissipated, their cloud remnants moved over the plains like great sails - patterns of wind in them, their bellies ever-changing, and the caverns of light and dark amid wisps of gathering rain.

The leaves of sweet gum trees out by the road clung to their branches waiting for the first snap of cold. In the garden, the round, plump pumpkins waited to be cut from their vines and delivered to the neighbors who drove by and marveled at their size. On more than one occasion, someone had stopped while Jack worked, admired them, and before they pulled away had coaxed a promise from Jack that he would deliver a pumpkin to them.

Martha was given a slight reprieve by her doctor and was allowed outside to sit. Her features had softened, grown puffy. She had gained weight and was less frail than before. It was the weekend, and Jack was home all day. She felt good and was able to take in the sun, let it brown her arms and face.

Jack's garden, as she thought of it, had yielded tomatoes, carrots, lettuce, pickling cucumbers, okra, radishes (though she didn't favor those or the beets), watermelon, a slew of turnips, and an assortment of squash (scalloped and long-necked spaghetti being her favorites). Jack took bags of his harvest to work almost every day when they all seemed to ripen at the same time. It was a test season, he told her; he wanted to see what would grow and what wouldn't, and what was prone to bugs, rabbits, possums and the like. He built a fence to keep the animals out. All of the stalks and leaves had browned and withered, and Jack was turning it all under.

"That's about the last of it, I guess." Jack pointed to the fall corn and raised up off his knees, "except for the pumpkins, of course."

Martha laughed, "We'll have to buy a tractor sometime soon to save your back."

"I suppose so." He put his shovel down and came over to her.

"I guess now I'll get you back." Martha touched Jack on the arm where beads of sweat had formed and wet her fingertips.

Martha saw him look at her a moment in her loose sundress. Color had come to her cheeks again. Was she beautiful to him like this? Had he been afraid of her gray pallor before? Did he get too close to the idea of not having the baby? He seemed to her ashamed of how he'd behaved towards her. His remorse had been coming on for a week or two since her health had improved. Maybe her getting better was a sign from God that he had to put such notions away.

Jack reached over, touched Martha's belly and said, "I'm getting used to the idea of this baby."

"Good. I knew you'd come around." Martha had waited for this moment, for his public announcement.

She didn't quite know how to respond, so she did so perfunctorily. It had been a few weeks since he'd shown some bit of tenderness to the coming baby.

"I don't know if I'm there yet," he said, and propped his shovel against the house. "I had things to sort through, straighten out."

"Was it about the drinking?" she asked.

"Partly." He sat next to her on the lawn among the black walnut casings that had fallen from the thick-trunked tree. They had been shattered by birds and pried open by the small claws and teeth of ground squirrels. "I'm afraid of what might happen."

"When? Now?" Martha placed her hands over her belly.

"No, later."

Jack had the sensation of floating then, angling back into memory. "I'm afraid that we'll lose it someday from some inexplicable accident."

"You can't think like that." Martha treaded gently here.

Jack leaned into the chair. He felt the run of cotton from her dress against his neck. It made him want a drink somehow. Instead, he put his hand on her leg and held it there to steady him. He had tried to keep what was coming at bay, but in the full light, the future reaching out ahead of them, he couldn't keep what had happened from spilling forward.

Martha put a hand on the top of his head, "Tell me," she said, rising up.

"It had been a day just like this," he said, "bright, clear. I was living at the time in Iowa City, just existing really. I had some odd jobs doing handyman things. If someone wanted a wall built, I built it. I patched roofs, fixed plumbing, all that stuff. And when I collected my pay at the end of the job, I'd go to the bar and get tight."

"I know all that." Martha smoothed the dress down over her knees.

"I know, but that's only half."

"The point then –."

"I drank to forget." Jack said, "There were weekends I don't remember. Or I sat out in the fields or along a river with a bottle. I drank until there was nothing to think about."

Martha grew impatient. She took her hand away from Jack's shoulder, but felt his grip tighten around her leg.

"I remember every detail of that street – the white fences, the shadows between the houses, the morning light striking the car window. I remember turning to look at this one house, the gabled roof, and the curve of the arch over the front door; it was green, the door was a bright green where the rest of the house was white. Every house had some sort of arbor with vines or flowers. Oh, I was in awe of those large homes where people seemed to have no troubles."

Jack got on his knees in front of her and placed both his hands on her thighs. Martha brought her knees together. He looked up at her as if he was at a pew in church. "I wasn't even drunk at the time – I was on my way to a job just enjoying the morning ride and how new everything looked - but the thing I don't remember was seeing the child come into the street. And I'm barely able to recall the bump I felt when she went under the tire. It was almost like hitting a rabbit. But it was a child, and I can't keep her out of my mind."

Seconds stretched out like plains. The air stilled. Martha took a deep breath and sighed heavily. Then she took his hands from her knees and said, "Why haven't you said anything about this before?"

"Because you're pregnant."

"I wasn't a long time before now." Martha made a move to stand, but Jack lifted from the ground and put his hands on her thighs to hold her there.

"Let me up," Martha said.

The cool morning was taken over by the coming heat. Jack felt the air change and shivered.

"Did you go back and see the little girl?"

"Yes."

She kissed his forehead and then his mouth. He closed his eyes. She bent forward despite the fullness of her belly and lifted him up. He stood in front of her. She pulled his loosened shirt from his pants and began to unbutton it from the bottom. Martha sat up in her chair and let the rest of the buttons open and pulled his shirt from him. "And what did she look like?" She unbuckled his belt.

"She looked like she was asleep."

"Did her parents arrive?"

"Yes."

Martha opened his pants and pulled them down. She thought that if she could make him talk, keep him talking. "Did you touch the child?"

"The parents came running from the yard."

"Did you touch the child?" She said, more of a command now than a question. Jack's hands were on her, lifting her dress. "What did she feel like, Jack?"

"Warm and soft and then her parents told me to get away." Martha's skin was hot from the sun. He moved his hands over her hips.

"Touch me here, Jack." She took his hand and placed it on her belly. "Right here."

He felt its hardness, the contours, but he was too ashamed to look at her.

It was mid-day. People, if they drove by, might see them, though the details of their bodies would be lost in the shade from the walnut tree. He lifted Martha up.

Jack unbuttoned her shift at the back. He slid it down over her shoulders exposing her breasts. He leaned in and brought one nipple to his mouth. The shift fell down around her feet. He slipped a finger into her and her body buckled slightly. He caught her with his other arm and lowered her and bent her forward, her belly, and their child, hovered over the grass.

He entered her and was gentle. A walnut fell on her back and rolled off. They both laughed, but her body tensed.

"Does it hurt?" he asked.

"No, no." Martha whispered. "No."

He felt her body shudder again, and he brought her hips up and held himself inside her. Martha pushed against him thinking that this was the way they should have conceived - with this need, the unconsciousness of their bodies moving together, his face at the back of her neck, his fingers digging into her, holding her hard.

"Look how the wind has picked up," Martha said, a little sore, returning to herself, shivering from her cooling sweat. She wanted the feeling of what should have been and wasn't, particularly now.

They lay together in the grass. Jack brought the shift up and covered her body. He cradled her head in the crook of his arm. She didn't move for a long time. In the depths of her a crack seemed to form separating one existence to another. She couldn't place it as either a longing or a lost item – something of herself. She had wanted Jack to make love to her for so many weeks that now, after it had happened, and after so many refusals, the crack that had opened might have been one of grief from the time that had been lost.

Martha stroked his hair and thought for a moment. "We should go for a drive. Go get us some drinks and put them in a cooler." When she sat up, she felt a little dazed.

"Are you okay?" Jack looked at her intently.

"Yes," she lied, "I feel fine. Let me get dressed and we'll go."

Jack gathered his pants and pulled them on. He was confused by her behavior. He thought he'd given her what she wanted, had even been careful with her. He helped with her shift, adjusting it over her shoulders. She hadn't looked at him since they'd finished, but as she braced her arms under his hands and he lifted her to her feet, he saw that she looked tired.

"We've done too much."

"No, Jack. Now go get those drinks and the car. I'll be out in a minute." She kissed him lightly on the cheek and walked unsteadily away.

Martha wasn't sure that she should leave the house, was quite sure she probably shouldn't, but she had to get away from the smell of linen, the perfume of vanilla soap in the bathroom, the house itself.

She didn't shower because she liked the way she felt just then, slightly used, relaxed. Her skin still had dew on it, and her face was flushed. She slipped the shift off in the bathroom and kicked it so that it slid across the tile and clumped in the corner. She regarded herself in the mirror, turned sideways, and ran her hand from the top of her breast, over the mound of her belly and down her thigh. Her hand going over the curves reminded her of when she was young, when her body was tight and had not grown slack with age. For the moment, she thought her skin was stretched to its very limit, which pleased her. She splashed water on her face, under her arms, wiped the excess away with a washcloth. Her mood lightened.

She put on a clean pair of panties, fastened her bra, and with each article of clothing stopped to face the mirror again.

Martha changed into one of her husband's button-down cotton shirts and pants that were flowery and pink with a generous elastic waist. She slipped on shoes, but her feet were swollen, so she resorted to rubber sandals she'd picked out of a bin at the dime store.

She heard Jack in the kitchen: the opening of cabinets, the refrigerator, the smack of ice trays against the counter and the cubes cascading into the cooler. She wanted it to be a good day, and they were going to relax into their old habits of driving off to just about anywhere, as long as there wasn't a destination, just the requirement to see new things. It was how they started as a couple, and she had felt she'd found a kindred spirit, a man who viewed life as a thing not to be squandered or lessened by convention. But since they'd moved so far away from other people, and away from the city where on weekends they felt the need to get out of, they had become conventional, and now had resorted to keeping secrets from each other. The baby would solidify that. Martha understood the danger of it.

They took Highway 24 through Maywood then split off at Piper and drove towards Canaan Lake stopping to buy sandwiches at a small store. On the way, Martha rested her head on her door's metal curve and let the air blow through her hair. She had not felt a strong wind like that, nor a sense of freedom that she remembered, but the swing music on the morning radio – Ella Fitzgerald, Tommy Dorsey, Glenn Miller – seemed perfect for her mood.

When they reached the lake, the blue, wind-ruffled water that went slack inside the small bays, reminded Martha of home where her parents had lived. Despite what she had told Linda, leaving home was scary at times. There was a constant struggle between terror and relief, but then there were days such as this one, when the weather cooperated, the sun beat down and the sky cleared. Today was like that, she thought, as Jack helped her over to the wooden picnic table.

"Do you think the city will someday stretch out this far?" Martha asked. She was still in that space where things seemed to float.

"I'm sure it will." Jack went back to the Ford for the bag of sandwiches and small cooler from the back seat. "I think that someday people will cover this whole country, top to bottom, and there won't be places like this."

She hesitated and then said, "I wonder if that couple with the child just picked up and moved. I don't think I could live so close to such a thing as that and be reminded all the time."

Jack opened napkins over the tabletop that was etched with names and dates, plus signs, hearts. Someone had whittled a crude unfinished picture of a bear's head.

He opened the sandwich wrappers; chicken salad spilled out between slices of egg bread. The lettuce had wilted in the car's heat. He picked up half of sandwich and handed it to Martha, "Here, you should eat."

She took the sandwich and held its sponginess in her hands. "Jack, did you ever see the girl's parents again?"

"Is it important?" He said peevishly.

Martha set her sandwich down. "It's a shame, really."

"Oh?" Jack slammed the metal top off the root beer against the edge of the table. The cap flew up and he caught it on the way down. He considered his wife. "A shame? For them or me? It was an accident. The police took a report –."

"It just occurred to me." Martha said quickly then took a bite of her sandwich.

He took a slug of root beer. "It seems sort of a strange thing to ask."

Martha quickly said, "I didn't mean anything by it. I was just curious."

Jack worked the bottle around in his hand and squeezed it hard, "Would it have made a difference if I did?"

"I don't know. I think it would have helped, don't you?"

"I have enough guilt about it. That would have just added to it." He stood up from the picnic table and moved off a little.

Martha thought to drop the subject, but she couldn't. "What was the little girl like?" She watched him closely to see if she'd gone too far. She'd know by the way he held his head that he was on the edge. He turned to her and came back.

"Jesus," he said, "I wasn't drinking. That's what you really want to know. You want to know if I was really drunk."

"No."

"Bullshit." Jack put his sandwich back in the butcher paper and squashed it.

Martha was sorry she brought the whole thing up now. She wasn't sure of what to say to him.

"If there's one thing I've never done, Martha, is lie to you."

"It was wrong of me to ask." She reached out for his hand, but he turned sideways on the bench and looked out over the lake.

Time stretched on. Martha ate her sandwich and Jack coddled the bottle of root beer.

"She was four," he said, starting slowly. "She had on this little blue dress. It was a Saturday, and she had chased something into the street, an animal or something, that's the thing I can't remember. But she had dark, dark hair, fine and shiny and cut short, and these tiny little shoes." Jack shaped the shoes with his hands. "One had come off and I went into the middle of the street and picked it up and gave it to her mother." He was clear-eyed, seeing her all over again, and he stared off as if frozen. "I got real drunk after that and stayed that way for days. It took a long time to come off that one." He sighed and then got back up and left Martha at the table and walked to the lake's edge.

He seemed wounded and that is what attracted her to him. His shape moved in and out of the shafts of light angling down from the trees. She remembered the rush of their courtship where he'd only spoken in half sentences that trailed off as if she were supposed to catch them.

He resented having to pull that part of his life out again, and as he stood at the lake's edge, he almost wished he were back at the time just after he'd arrived in Kansas. Everything seemed new to him: the city, his job, and the apartment he lived in in the West Bottoms. Since then, he'd had a penchant for new things, and when the dealership gave him a new car for making employee of the year, he knew he'd made the right decision moving to Kansas and escaping everything he'd known.

Jack didn't think about his own family anymore. He had heard from a brother who tracked him down. His mom had died of a stroke, and his brother thought he should know. He didn't care much for the news of the others. He'd always existed outside their circle. Being the middle child of five gets you lost as if you were filed away among papers to be retrieved every now and again when needed. At fifteen, he found the taste for beer to his liking and it was a struggle ever since. Once he hit that little girl, the shame of it made him never want to see his family again because the hurt of it was so plain on his face. They would have thought that something like a drunken accident was inevitable and they wouldn't have believed him either.

The wind picked up the water across the lake and he heard the box elders sighing above him. He looked back and saw Martha coming down through the grass. She came up next to him. "Doesn't having this baby make you think of all the things you want to do right in the world?"

Jack hadn't thought about it that way, but maybe it did. "I believe so," he said, "I want to see about inviting my family up for a few days when the baby comes."

"I'd like that." Martha said, "I'd like to finally meet them."

"Then I'll call them the day he's born."

Martha laughed. "He?" and then she squeezed his middle. "It's not so frightening now, is it?"

"No, I don't expect it is." He smiled.

"Will you be alright with just Linda while I'm gone next week?"

"Of course."

Martha leaned into him because the day, he suspected, had ultimately been too much for her. He'd let her sleep in the car on the way home, but the water, its blue, now darkening from the gathering clouds, captivated him.

He helped her down into the high grass at the lake's edge. When he sat next to her, they disappeared and were enveloped by green on one side and deep blue on the other.

Airstreaming

Snow

Linda dressed for bed – a plain white t-shirt over loose cotton shorts (her father's) – and picked up a new Redbook she'd sent away for, carefully filling out one of the little cards in the last month's issue that Mrs. Miller had given her.

When the phone rang she waited for her mother to answer. On the fourth ring, not hearing any movement from her mother's room, Linda jumped out of bed and ran into the living room snatching the receiver out of its cradle at the fifth ring.

She didn't hear anything for a moment.

"Hello?" she said, as she looked at the clock. It was nearly 11pm.

There was still nothing except the faintest sound of moaning, and then a sharp cry. Linda dropped the receiver and ran into her mother's room. The television was on; blue light flickered over her sheets. Linda woke her up.

"You have to drive me out to the Pearsons' house. Hurry."

Her mother didn't move and said groggily, "Who?"

"To work," Linda shouted, already searching in her mother's handbag for the car keys. "You have to drive me to work!" Her mother still hadn't moved so she went over and yanked the covers down, and pulled her mother up out of bed. "C'mon Mom, Martha's in trouble."

Registering slowly, her mother slid into her slippers, took her coat from her daughter. "Who was that on the phone?"

"That was her."

"I didn't hear the phone."

"You never do." Linda pushed her mother out of the bedroom and through the house. Outside, the air was frost-stung. Their breaths escaped in lamp lit clouds. She didn't lock the front door, but rather guided her mother down the walk to the car. She put the keys in her mother's hand. "We have to hurry."

Once inside the car, Clare put her hands on the icy steering wheel and muttered, "I'm surprised that a woman that skinny can carry more than a bean in her belly."

The engine caught and the Mercury rumbled to life. Clare put the car in reverse and skipped it a little before easing it out of the driveway. She twisted her entire body around to see out the back instead of using her mirrors. "Where's her husband?"

"He's out of town."

The lights of houses grew farther apart. Stars emerged like spectral small-town points on maps. Linda gave her mother directions the entire way as though her mother had never driven her out there. Finally, Clare told her to hush, sit back and stop blocking her view. Linda had been so close to the front window that fog covered the inside. Her mother switched the defroster on high. Warm air hummed loudly from the vents.

"Well, she had the good sense to call you." Clare spun the steering wheel and the car turned hard into the driveway. The wheels slipped on the gravel which pinged their wells; each metallic hit made Linda jump and before her mother brought the car to a stop, she was out and throwing her weight against the kitchen door which gave way to darkness.

Inside, the house was slightly warmer. Linda switched lights on as she went, calling after Martha. She went down the picture-lined hallway towards her bedroom afraid of what she might find. She worried that they were too late. A small light angled from the slightly opened door and a sense of déjà vu worked through her. She had done this before with her father, had seen the same diffuse quality of light, and heard the same silence.

Going into the room, Linda saw Martha on the floor at the foot of her bed, the sheets pulled over her body, eyes closed. Martha lifted her head and a long wail came from her as a cold breeze sliced through an open window ruffling the bed sheets trailing down. Linda knelt next to her. She lifted the bloodied part of the sheet and saw the exposed crown of a baby's head slightly pushed from its womb. Martha's eyes were on her now as if pleading. Her face was winter white, child-like, her mouth open but emitting no sound.

From the doorway Clare stopped. This was the worst of it, she thought, the very deep of it. Seeing that Martha was alive, she bent to touch her cold skin. "Close the window," she said. She leaned back against her legs. She pulled a blanket from the bed and covered Martha, tucking it in around her.

Linda started to cry.

"Stop your crying, find a phone and call for help." Linda's mother steadied herself and felt for the baby's head. "Get some water heated. Do they have more towels?"

Martha screamed as another contraction wracked her body. The baby hardly moved as Clare pushed in around its head to release it and bring its head past the nose so it could breath but it didn't budge.

Linda got to the phone, dialed, listened and gave directions. Coming back from the bathroom, Clare took the towels that Linda held out and placed them around Martha's hips. Linda disappeared again, but light now streamed from the hallway

Clare heard clanging in the kitchen as she focused on Martha's breathing.

Linda reappeared, "I put water on the stove."

"Good. Now help me lay her down and then lift her legs. Can you do that?"

Linda kneeled next to Martha. "Yes." They turned her away from the bed and then laid her down slowly. Each of them took one leg and bent it up.

Clare said, "Now I need you to hold them apart. Ready?"

Each movement brought more cries from Martha who's eyes were wide, but not seeing; her breaths were short, hard rasps.

Clare pressed her fingers again around the baby's crown. What should have been wet was dry. "Warm water, Linda, please."

"It's still heating."

"Go run the tap then. Hurry."

Martha's breathing quickened.

Clare pulled the rest of the sheet away, split it in two and bunched half of it under Martha's pelvis. Linda handed her a soaked washcloth. "Here. Lift" she shouted to Martha to get her full attention, "and push as hard as you can." She took the other half and dabbed the baby's head, and handed the washcloth back to Linda.

"Wetter."

Martha screamed.

"Hurry!" Clare shouted.

Linda fumbled with the washcloth, disappeared again and then handed it back to her mother dripping wet. Her mother squeezed the water out over Martha's vagina, the inside of her legs and over her pubic hair and wiped the blood away.

Martha's head swung back in a cry, her hips lifted and the baby's nose and lips emerged. Again, Clare pressed and pried Martha open and the baby slipped farther out, but now she noticed the bluish color of its skin, the lack of movement.

"Martha. Push!"

The woman's body heaved. Her hands slapped the floor and her hips violently jerked up into the air before she let out a long sigh and then went silent.

The baby slipped into Clare's hands: its cord wrapped around its tiny neck, the body still as pond water, skin rubbery and blood stained as Clare gently unwound the cord. "I need a knife," she said to Linda who only stared. "A knife, Linda!" she shouted.

Linda left and reappeared with a large bladed kitchen knife.

"I need you to cut it," her mother said, adjusting the baby so that it balanced in her palm. With her other hand she pulled the cord taut.

"I can't," Linda could barely breathe.

"Do it!"

Linda's hand trembled as she lifted the knife over the baby.

"Quickly now!" Her daughter positioned the blade just above its penis against the cord and watched it fall away dripping fluid from its end.

Linda rocked back and forth, crying, holding the knife until it fell from her fingers.

Martha had passed out.

After Clare checked the baby for life and found none, there was nothing left to be done but wrap them both in blankets. She took the baby into the other room and sat in a chair holding its stillness. She listened to the furnace sputtering to life, and stared straight out the window into night's blackness. She began humming nothing in particular, but it seemed to momentarily draw that night's images from her head. The furnace metal popped as it heated, and over its muffled metallic sound she heard her daughter weeping and whispering between her labored breaths.

After covering Martha with blankets, Linda came into the room.

"You should call her husband. Do you know where his number is?

"Yes."

"Go do it now, then."

"The ambulance should be here soon." Linda said flatly.

"Good." Clare said absently and, for the life of her, couldn't understand why she was still rocking the baby, so she stopped and just held it.

Blood had seeped into the carpet. She had called Jack and told him what happened. She tried to tell him as matter of fact as possible, but before she finished he'd hung up and she assumed he was already out the door from wherever he was and on his way.

Linda didn't want to move Martha, but she lifted her legs slightly and slipped a new sheet under them and then pulled it under her hips. Martha's sleeping face wrinkled in pain. Linda thought that there was still some chance to save her. She assumed the baby must be dead, suffocated; so she went to work to keep Martha alive until someone came.

She placed her finger on Martha's forehead and moved a lock of hair into a graceful arc. The house warmed, her mother brought towels with the stove water, and the two set about cleaning up.

At last, the ambulance came and Linda greeted it outside. Freezing rain streamed through the air, circled around them and disappeared. Linda saw its icy crystals glitter in the ambulance headlights. The men ran in to attend to Martha. Her mother had stayed inside and she heard her explaining what had happened. She stayed a moment longer for the simple fact of air, and she sucked it in despite the ice, which lightly stung her throat.

When she reentered the house one man pronounced the baby dead, noted the time, wrapped it in blue cloth and placed it in a box. The other cleared away straps and supplies from a stretcher.

In the gray mist, Linda noticed a shovel sticking straight out of the earth in the garden. Though few people would know what happened here, how a woman lost a baby and almost her life. She thought of the telephone, its heaviness, how the receiver dangled off the edge of the bed, the transmission of pain over wires and miles. She wanted to talk to Jack again.

When she went back into the house, she found her mother at the kitchen sink, her hands resting on the edge of the counter, shoulders bunched up against her thick neck, shaking slightly. Water spilled from the faucet, and as Linda came nearer she saw that it had risen almost to the sink's rim.

"I wanted to soak the towels," her mother said, her voice scratchy and low.

"There's a bigger basin off the porch." Linda pushed the faucet handle down, turning the water off. "The snow is coming faster."

The two medics came through the kitchen with Martha strapped into their stretcher and carried her outside and into the open doors of the ambulance. One of them came back in.

"We'll take her into Kansas City. She'll make the trip okay," he said. "Better to get her to a larger hospital right away."

Clare turned around and stared at him.

"Is there something wrong?" he asked.

Linda walked to him and took his arm and led him outside. They looked at each other a moment. "Where will she be?"

"The KU Medical Center." The driver gunned the ambulance a little and a great cloud of steam came from the tailpipe. "You know where it is, don't you?"

Linda had no idea. "Her husband will know."

The medic pulled a sheet of paper from inside his jacket. "This has all the numbers." He handed it to her. "Your Mom's okay? I can give her something."

Linda nodded. "The snow will make it hard for you."

"We're used to it," he said, and backed away.

For the first time Linda noticed his face, how white it was, free of any markings, how blank and open it seemed. "Hurry," she said.

The young medic opened the back of the ambulance and slipped inside and firmly closed the door.

She watched its red taillights trail away. She looked back to the house and saw her mother peering out the kitchen window; the harsh overhead light blasted her forehead but darkened her eyes. She couldn't tell if her mother was seeing anything or was just remembering now.

The night wore on. She took one of Martha's sweaters, shouldered it on and walked around the house.

Linda pulled the indoor clothesline across the back porch and hung each of the towels and clipped their centers with clothespins. She inspected them as she went to make sure there was no trace of blood left. Her arms ached from scrubbing out the stains. When she was finished she went outside for a moment to let the steam and perspiration dry on her face. Across the wide expanse of land the day had awakened on the fine line of the horizon.

Airstreaming

Cleaning

Jack spent his days working at the dealership while Martha was in the hospital. He didn't know what else to do despite Carl, his closest friend there, telling him to stay home, take care of himself.

He collected condolences from his co-workers, giving only a mutter back until they finally kept their distances. Stopping to see Martha at the hospital on his way home, he brought her pictures of the house and the landscape's promise of spring: crocus. He sat for an hour or so waiting for seven o'clock to arrive to be ushered out by the volunteer night nurse who swept the rooms for visitors before leaving herself.

On his way home, he ate dinner at Casey's, a small all-night diner and ordered the pot roast most every night. He had no taste for variety now, no sense of the need for something new, only the expectation of the next day, and the next. The world had lost its color, just as the snow had blanketed the ground in whites and grays.

The temptation to have a drink with dinner was overwhelming, but he couldn't get up the courage to order one. Sitting at the counter with all its accoutrements: salt shakers, ketchup and Tabasco bottles, menus, creamers and sugar cubes, they looked as forlorn as he felt under the harsh light.

He kept Linda on to look after the house. During the first few days, she worked to rid the bedroom of the stains and smell. She dusted the carpet with baking soda and let it sit until just before she left when she took a vacuum to it. She did it three days running watching the milky clouds rise up in ribbons in the light across the room.

The mattress had been spared, but the sheets and blanket weren't. He had driven with Linda into town to Spencer's on a day off and bought new sheets. He noticed that by the time Linda was through with the bedroom there was very little evidence save for a faint stain in the bathroom grout that would not be removed. Some things are permanent, he decided; some things need to be left as a reminder. He wouldn't tell Martha about the stain, as faint as it was, she'd let her remark on it if she found it.

There was so much to do in the first few days that when they were over, and the house had returned to stillness, he sat in the kitchen at the banquette and stared out across the low, snow-covered hills, folded and refolded a cloth napkin, thinking how the light had flattened, how the sky was not so different from the land.

"Maybe we should look for another job. I can see the writing on the wall. She'll come home and there'll be nothing for you to do." Linda's mother had moved the TV back into the living room having woken up one too many times with the test pattern's squeal blaring at four in the morning. She thought she should make herself simply get up off the couch, switch the T.V. off and go to bed, but on several nights she was found stretched out, her slippers dangling from her toes, head caught in the wedge of pillows, and the station's Indian head target wavering from the diminished signal.

"Martha will be home soon." Linda whirled a pinwheel that had held candy, a gift from Martha that Jack had brought to the house. It had been stuck in a bouquet of white Easter Lilies. Light sparked from its silver metallic leaves.

"You didn't mention it." Her mother pulled herself up and planted her feet on the ground between the sofa and coffee table. "You didn't say a word."

"She hasn't come home yet – a couple days from now really." Linda waved the pinwheel quickly to see how fast it turned. It made a sound like a bee.

"I would have liked to have known that after all we did."

"I should have told you, but you'd have started in like you already have about finding a new job."

Clare looked at her, annoyed with the whirligig. "You've had ample opportunity to say something, anything, sitting there spinning that thing. Can you stop for just a bit?" Linda grabbed the head of the pinwheel hard, bending the foil leaves for good, ruining its perfection.

"I didn't mean for you to break it." Clare leaned into the coffee table, picked up a glass of water and took a drink. "Honestly, Linda, I think you need a change. I'll start asking around again for another situation."

"No."

"Your mind will go to jelly out there with nothing to do all day but wait until the next bad thing happens."

"I can't imagine anything worse," Linda said.

"Well, I can," her mother said, and took the empty glass into the kitchen, flipping the light on as she went. White incandescence spilled into the room erasing the television blue. Linda stared blankly at the TV; over its chatter her mother's muffled voice called out. "You should try and keep up with your friends at school. You don't even call anyone anymore." Clare ran the tap filling the glass then shut it off. "How about that Parker girl, the one with the pretty hair. You used to spend time with her."

"At school, I did."

"You can still call her once in awhile. You have your weekends." There was a crunch of ice being gathered out of its freezer tray and then the clink as they hit the glass.

"Have you heard the phone ring from people looking for me?" Linda asked.

"You have to make an effort, hon," Clare said, coming out of the kitchen, switching off the light, and returning the blue to the living room.

Linda dropped the pinwheel to the ground, tired of its uselessness, its promise of cheer. "What would I talk to them about? What could we possibly have to say to each other now? That I scrub floors and dishes, make beds and wash clothes, clean the stains out of other people's bed sheets?" Linda fingered the sofa's worn cloth.

"You don't have to be fresh. I was only trying to think of ways to get you out of the house. I'm no example, I know. I just sit here all night watching any old program that comes on." Clare spread herself out on the sofa, pulled a pillow under her head. "It's awfully quiet now with the Miller's gone. Barbara must be enjoying all that nice weather in Arizona." Clare glanced at her daughter to see some reaction, but none came. "Have you heard from her?"

Linda got up off the couch. "Where are you going? Big Valley is coming on."

"Martha needs me," Linda said, and looked down at her mother. "So does Jack. And I'm going to stay no matter what." She left the room, the bent pinwheel lying face down by the chair, as Clare settled in for her program, and another Saturday night where she'll fall asleep before Barbara Stanwyck stands on the porch, legs apart, with hands on hips to call her boys home.

Rain fell in the morning. Linda huddled under the covers for an hour after she was fully awake. There wasn't any sound save for drops hitting the windowpane muffled by heavy curtains that darkened her room. Once in awhile, she heard the slush of rain under car wheels carrying the neighbors to their Sunday services throughout the neighborhood.

Linda missed the sound of her father playing hymns for the Baptists, though they weren't Baptists themselves. In fact, she never knew what religion they were. It was always something her father refused to discuss. But while he played, her mother and her sat in back where each note ricocheted against the curved ceiling and landed just behind them. He'd match the strength of the congregation's voices by turning single notes into chords during the powerful Yonder Stands the Mountain or play delicately during gift-giving as the round, gold platters were passed down each set of pews. She never understood why her mother always put a couple of dollars in them.

A wash of shame swept over Linda after the church had cleared as one of the deacons came from behind the alter with an envelope holding money collected that morning and handed it to her mother.

She turned, the bed too soft in the center, curving her back wrong. Grey light leaked around the curtain's edges.

A Late Winter

Jack's visits to the hospital should have been something she looked forward to, but all Martha felt was that she'd let him down even though his hand, when he touched her, was warm and inviting, and though another woman wouldn't have wanted to be touched, she wanted to be. She wanted his hands all over her, inside her, filling the empty cavity.

Shortly after he left each night, the nurse came with medication to dull her mind, which she welcomed with an open palm and gratefully swallowed the pills.

The three weeks included her recovery from the birth, and then surgery to repair her uterus, which was torn and infected, and was painful when she tried to sit up in the first two weeks. In the days after her arrival, having lost so much blood, she was weak and slipped in and out of consciousness remembering only the shapes of faces and hands coming toward her and disappearing.

She understood what had happened even so. In the last moments at the house she felt it leaving her body as a stone pushed from an eroding cliff, dislodged by something greater than itself.

At some point she screamed at the doctor and nurses in the room to not touch her. She pushed their hands and tools away, brought the blanket over her face and wept for two days until she was dried out: her tear ducts, the milk that was just filling her breasts before the miscarriage, the fluids protecting her baby - gone. When she was as arid as a desert she stopped, was clear-eyed, assessed her surroundings and refused to speak to anyone except her husband, and only then in barely audible tones. For the remainder of her stay she kept silent, accepting what came to her in the way of food, small gifts, the long nights.

In the third week, the weather changed. Having been bitterly cold, the air, though still freezing, carried moisture. Her lungs loosened; she breathed easier. When she fully awoke, she went to the window and saw heavy snow falling in the largest flakes she'd ever seen. They were big and flat and glistened like sliced sugar cubes.

Back at the hospital bed she gathered the heavy blanket, slid her feet into her slippers and stole to the open doorway to see if there was anyone in the hall. The corridor was as bright as the night was black. The contrast not lost on the large windows at the end that only reflected the corridor back on itself in its darkness. She knew of a door that opened onto a sort of patio where people went to smoke while visiting.

Martha snuck down the hallway, past the empty nurse's station, past the lounge, the two elevators silently lifting and descending. She picked up her slippers so as not to scuff, held her breath, and tightened her grip on the blanket at her shoulders.

When she was at the door, she turned the handle as quietly as she could and slipped outside. She did not know, and did not stop to check, that the door locked from the inside. Instead, she turned away and let her breath out in a cloud of steam. She looked out over the tops of the city's buildings, their mechanical workings, pipes and ducts, saw the snow blanketing them, perhaps working the motors and vents harder, or breaking them down. The cloud cover was dense and low. She loved that the night was shrouded in gray.

Martha tightened the blanket around her and slid down against the wall to the cold concrete under the eave. She put her open hand out to catch the snowfall. Flakes hit it and melted instantly, running down the creases of her cupped palm, pooling the water at its center. She sucked it into her mouth and drank.

For the first time she felt remorse for leaving her mother the way she did, stealing off. She understood the abandonment, and why her mother refused to contact her, even after she'd made the effort to let her know where she was, that she was fine, happy.

Martha remembered the photograph of them, the one that sat by itself on a table in her parent's dining room, her mother's thin fingers on her shoulder, eyes gazing just past the lens' focus. It was her mother's favorite.

"You are so beautiful," she said, picking it up one day, "So how I imagined you'd be before you were born."

She knew her mother loved her, but it was a lost love, made sudden by her leaving. She must have grieved. Now grief was present and made her believe that loss was permanent, irreplaceable. In this case, there was no picture to prove that there was something, was a life.

As cold overtook Martha, fragments containing the dark car ride with her father for hours to her Aunt's home, who lived alone just outside Minneapolis, and being sequestered as much as possible from the neighbors waiting for her and Morgan's child to come to term, the drive to hospital and afterwards, when there was nothing but white and the baby gone, came to her. Fragments from the train ride: the stolen eighteen dollars and fifty-eight cents she took from the petty cash box at the nurses' station, paying for the nine-dollar ticket on the Twin Star Rocket in the early morning holding half the money to eat with, being nervous and scared at the same time as she watched down the aisle between seats until the train pulled away from the depot. The four hours with her face pressed against the window watching the flat land, the endless trees and lakes passing into low rolling hills. Then the train arriving in the underground of a great building, steam billowing up, vapor light giving it shape, and the rush of people meeting each other on the platforms. Her coming up from the tracks to a great hall filled with impossible light streaking across the floors and a clock, the clock that said five-fifteen. Or is that time just the time she'd heard through a wall of pain when her baby was born like a stuck needle on a scratched record in her mind. Fragments of the odd jobs she worked for years, living on the street the first few months near the West Bottoms, that when the flood dissipated in 1951, it left the empty fences and mud and the few stockyards that survived, which held endless fascination for her. The days she spent walking along the now forgotten tracks, looking at the tired men who were broke and living out their daily existence. There was the rented room, and the waitress who slipped her food that lived across the hall. She'd been invisible until one day when Jack followed her, had to know her name, and her just barely hanging on. And both of them lifting each other up, slowly, him from alcohol, her from everything, but it was a well of strength she'd had when she was young, but was now depleted.

Every now and again, the hairs of the blanket's fabric caught a flake and soon it was as if she were wearing sequins the way the beaded water caught the hospital light. She cried for her loss, the snow like a curtain, and the whirring motors making her sobbing soundless. She huddled there and didn't try to go back inside. Instead, she stayed, haunches up, back against the hospital wall, eventually falling asleep, deep, the gray ebbing into black.

A half hour later, on her break, the night nurse came outside to smoke a last cigarette before her shift change. She opened the door and placed the empty pack between the door latch and its catch. She lit up and threw the flickering match toward Martha, now almost blue, unconscious. It flamed out against the wet blanket and then the night nurse screamed seeing the woman there.

When he got the call, it was as if he were already out the door and on the highway before he realized that he was, indeed, on his way. He'd left the house in such a hurry he reminded himself to call Linda, tell her that he forgot to lock the house, that it was his fault. But then there'd be her questions about Martha, and though he had tried to keep her apprised of her condition, he could not decide if he should mention what had happened.

Jack arrived in time to see Martha's body lifted onto a gurney, his gait so heavy and lumbering, defeated. Martha looked as if she wasn't going to make it. When they wheeled her down to the bathroom, which had the only tub in the ward, and had been filled with warm water, they stripped her of her clothes and slid her in to bring her body temperature up.

It was several moments before she woke, thinking that she was still outside, that the snow had completed covering her and the surroundings, but the sound of several voices, orderlies and nurses, ringing off white tile, echoing, changed that perception. She turned to look sideways: a wan smile curved her lips.

Then she felt her extremities tingling, a burning sensation at the tips of her toes and fingers, lashing down her legs and arms. Her energy was spent and she could do no more than lie in the water, accept the ministrations of Nancy, the night nurse, who said, upon seeing her patient's eyes flutter and open, "Martha, honey, you sure gave me a fright."

Jack stood behind her, closed the door to the rest of the ward, and looked down at his wife, limp in the water. It was dawning outside; the windows were turning a pale blue. The smell of disinfectant sharpened as the steam expanded its fumes. His eyes watered easily because they had deepened and grown heavy these past weeks.

He couldn't sleep at home alone. Every sound was sharp and present as if the cause of it were directly under the bed. He traced every car by its definable engine down around the bend until finally it was blocked by the low hills. Because his eyes were so tired, they'd grown sensitive to light; he hung blankets over the thin curtains to keep out the moon's shine.

The nurse tapped his leg, motioning for him to come close. Her arm had tired cradling Martha's head so that it remained just above the waterline.

"Can you take over a moment?" she asked, slipping her sore arm out of the tub and shaking off the water.

"Of course." Jack knelt beside her and pulled up his shirtsleeve.

"Run the hot water every few minutes to keep the temperature warm." Nancy toweled her arm. "I'll be back in a few minutes."

When the door closed, Jack adjusted his arm under Martha's head; her brown hair swirled about and settled over his forearm. She opened her eyes intermittently and turned slightly toward him. He didn't know if she wanted to say something. He was still reeling from the sight of her: at her enlarged breasts and nipples magnified by the water, her flaccid, white skin, and the still swollen abdomen.

He took his other hand and wiped the perspiration from her forehead. She moved her lips as if wanting to say something. He leaned in.

"I didn't mean to..." came in breaths punctuated by silent gaps.

"I'm here now," he said, "I'm here now."

Seeing her like this made him believe he had to do something - anything extraordinary.

The nurse came back with a thermometer, towels, and Martha's robe from her room. She knelt next to Jack and slipped the thermometer into Martha's mouth, checked her watch and tested the water's warmth. In the time that it took for the mercury to work in the glass tube, Nancy recounted to Jack how she'd found his wife, and that it was lucky to have needed a smoke, and how her bad habit had finally done some good.

Later, when they returned Martha to her bed, Jack crawled in next to her when she fell asleep again and whispered in her ear about the places they'd see. "We'll go northwest to start: through the Black Hills, the open ranges of South Dakota, Mt. Rushmore, on into the flats of eastern Colorado and then the sharp rise of the Rockies extending up into Canada. We'll go to Yellowstone, see the geysers, buffalo. You've always wanted to see them. We'll just go, you and me."

This was going to be the extraordinary thing.

Linda thought that Jack was at wits end. She'd arrived two mornings after Martha had gone to hospital to find him in the den, slumped like a weight, swallowed by the chair's worn fabric, the lamp lit, drapes closed.

She had gone into the den and stood over him, waiting for him to feel her presence. She did not dare to reach down and touch him, to startle him in any way, but when his eyes opened and saw her there, he blinked to see if she'd go away, let him sleep just a little more.

"It's past time for you to be going to work."

He pulled himself up in the chair, and saw light leaking around the drapery's edges. "Can you call work?"

"No, Jack, I can't." Linda was surprised at herself, the hard tone she took with him. "And why are you in here and not the bedroom?"

Jack said, "because I can't sleep without Martha there."

Linda softened and took his hand to try and lift him from the chair.

What little effort he made to rise up was erased when he sank back down. Linda went to the drapes and swept them open. Light struck the room like lightning. She went to where the records were kept and pulled out any old record, this one happening to be Glenn Miller, took the vinyl disc from its sleeve and put it on the record changer, switched on the receiver, and dropped the needle down in the middle of a song. Horns blared like a voice going from octave to octave, note to note.

"You've made your point." Jack said over the music.

She made him take her to the market to buy food, coffee, and ice cream. He loved ice cream. When he'd finally leave for work, she made sure to make the bed, put his clothes away, clean the bathroom and make sandwiches that she'd leave wrapped in cellophane on a plate in the refrigerator. When she left in the evenings, she'd leave several lights on, turn the furnace up, and leave a note detailing the things that needed attention, even if they didn't so that he didn't come home to a dark house, that it felt warm, that there were things for him to consider.

Linda was pleased, that in the days before Martha was to come home, that Jack combed his hair, shaved, and pretended to be a man that wasn't on the verge of losing everything. One more day lollygagging around in that chair, Linda thought, and he might have.

Linda arrived early the following Saturday, the morning Martha was being released from the hospital. It was her day off, but she wanted to make sure the house was clean, Jack and Martha's bed sheets changed. She was surprised that it was all done. There were even flowers on the kitchen table, on the dresser in the bedroom, and fresh towels. The carpets had been vacuumed, floors swept. After seeing all of this, she had to look in the refrigerator and, sure enough, it had been stocked fully with all the things Martha liked.

Jack was out back, standing and smoking a cigar. Overnight snow had dusted the crusty remnants of a storm a few days before. The skeleton trees, Black Walnut, Hackberry's and White Oaks were etched against the snow, dried prairie grass clumped at their bases. He watched geese come up the valley's center for their feeding and a short rest in the pond, which was created as a reservoir for the houses being built, one by one. Now was the time for change, he thought.

Linda was in the kitchen with the water running. The last corner of sun, going over the hill, sparked off the window frame.

When they came in through the kitchen from the car, Martha was dressed in a new, blue terry cloth robe over Jack's pajama bottoms. Jack handed her a bag containing her medications, told Linda to put them away.

"She'll sleep for several hours," he said, as he passed holding Martha's arm to steady her. Linda watched for the old signs of Martha's happiness, but she was withdrawn, weak, but she managed a smile at Linda, who reached out to touch Martha and welcome her home.

The first thing Martha noticed was the light stain, scrubbed rough in the grout of her bathroom. She didn't say anything as Jack worked the room, pulling the drapes, "No, leave them open," and turning down the bed, "No, I'd like to just see the house. Let me wander." When he left the room, she sat on the bed's edge and followed him with her eyes down the hall. She touched the new blanket's cotton fabric. She ran her finger along the stitching. It was here, she thought, right here.

Standing, Martha decided to spend as little time in the room as possible, to make herself busy. The room made her dizzy with emptiness, as the hospital room had, the people with their bright faces, perpetually smiling, working around her as they chattered about nothing. She hadn't wanted to talk – not to anyone.

Several days went by as Martha regained her strength.

She was good in the morning if she'd slept well, but by early afternoon she barely kept herself upright, needing to retreat to her bed to sleep. There would be an hour or two in the late afternoon when the pills effect had worn off, before the next two, when she was most lucid, present.

"Jack's usually home by now." Martha said between sips of water. They were the first words from her since noon. They felt thick, like cotton. She took another sip. "Usually he calls if he's going to be late." There, a little better, she thought and looked out the window.

"No word, yet." Linda said, hands flat on the counter.

"Did a ghost come up behind you?" Martha smiled.

"What?

"You shivered. Means there's a ghost sneaking around."

"Oh no. It's just that the counter's cold." She thought for a moment of the absurdity of the old cliché, especially now that there was a ghost in the house. Perhaps Martha was coming to terms, but each small step in the last week had been met by a shuddering back-step. The step out of the darkness and then the door shutting closed again.

Airstreaming

Silver

A week passed. Each day Martha gained strength. She'd lost weight in the hospital and the shots she'd received bruised her loose-skinned arms. Every morning, Linda fixed her a large breakfast of eggs, bacon, fruit and muffins that Martha picked at in the beginning, but by the end of the week, ate all of it. Lunches, too, were feasts, and the dinners consisted of their leftovers and more if Jack picked up food at the market on his way home.

The following Saturday, he left early in the morning. He felt Martha would be okay for the couple of hours before Linda arrived. He put on coffee, sliced some bread, put the butter out to soften. He didn't shower or shave to prolong his leaving, nor did he put the clothes away from the night before, which lay at the bottom of the bed over the wingback chair. He put on fresh clothes. He transferred his wallet and keys from pocket to pocket. He splashed water over his thick hair and combed it back so that his temples showed their angles, revealing a thinning crown.

He started the Ford and sat there a long time as people do when they are about to make a big decision or think on trouble. It was still frosty in the mornings, still that Midwestern wet, but the sky was clear and the damp air turned from hazy silver to pale blue. Jack pressed the gas a bit when the car slightly sputtered. In the rearview, he saw smoke rise from the tailpipe. Slipping the car into gear now seemed momentous, like those large ships in newsreels, having been christened, are pulled back into the water with ceremony, a kick of foamy water, a lurch into the unknown.

He'd passed the lot with the silver bulleted trailers twice everyday to and from work, never noticing all of the gleaming trailers lined up along the highway's edge like silver fish at a market. But one day he did look over because there was a storm coming on, and beyond the lot the sky was black in the direction of Olathe.

He'd worried that Martha might be home alone, but tonight it didn't stop him from pulling over, drawn to the reflections coming off the oblong trailers. A lonely strand of colored flags beat hard in the wind. A tall, reedy man sidled up to him, his fine hair flying around his head, clipboard in hand, pants buckled tight around the loose ends of a starched white shirt, and nametag announcing "Hank" hung crooked from the shirt pocket.

"That's top of the line sir, Airstream Sovereign Double. Over thirty feet of luxury, built in everything, double bed for you and the wife, plenty of space for storage, full kitchen and bathroom." The man flipped some pages on his clipboard. "Extra space and bed for the kiddies. It's even got a bathtub for the missus and shower for you. Hank here, what's your name?"

"Jack"

"Would you like to step inside for a peek, Jack?" Hank searched a ring of keys and opened the door, which looked like something off a rocket.

"I think it's a little big for what we need." Jack stepped to the open door anyway as Hank held it open.

Having worked in the car business, he knew that once you hooked the customer into sitting on new leather, feeling the velvety enameled steel, or admiring the clean lines of any excellent car, a good salesperson could easily lock you in, and have you driving off the lot in a matter of hours wondering what had gotten into you. So Jack held his breath as he went inside. What he found was a new sort of home, a feeling so deep that, when he looked down the narrow hall into the rest of the cabin, he felt a well of emotion come over him and sat on the upholstered couch. Here he found the means of escape from memory – for he and Martha.

Stepping off the steel step, the salesman said, "I could give you a few minutes alone…to discover this beauty."

It was cool inside the cabin. Jack's eyes roamed the submarine-like hull. It's interior an elegant sturdiness - gleaming wood, stainless steel fixtures, no nonsense appointments – a Midwestern appeal to everything including color and pattern. From a service manager's point of view he had an appreciation for how everything was put together: no wasted space, easy to maintain, easy to fix. He marveled at its simplicity.

He stood up and walked slowly down the corridor noting how the interior skin, riveted and screwed to the hull's bones, was seamless across the ceiling, how the cabinets were snug against the next thing – a window, the kitchen wash basin, Formica countertops, closets. The windows were rounded at the corners, screened from the inside, louvered, the sky perfectly reflected in them. From the kitchen area, he entered the master bedroom that contained a full-sized bed, a dressing area with closets that led to the bathroom. He poked his head inside and found a full-sized tub and shower.

The salesman, called up from the open door, "Plenty of water storage capacity – 40 gallons! Propane for hot water and the stove at 10 gallons a pop! A snap to keep filled. I'll show you the two tanks in a sec."

Jack paid no mind. He was hooked. He'd work out the details and sign the papers. He didn't need coercion – only time to plan. He'd have to go down a size or two; the Ford wouldn't pull a 30 ft. trailer; 24 or 26 feet would be more appropriate. He knew the towing capacities; he'd make some structural changes to his car at the shop, add the hitch, beef up the suspension, put it in for service and slip his guys some overtime pay.

Having signed papers on a new 26 foot Overlander, promising to pick it up in a week's time so he could modify the Ford, Jack left the dealership slightly dazed. He pulled back onto the highway and headed home. The sun sparked through the front window as the storm headed north: white clouds stacked towards heaven, the air washed and the fields shimmered from fallen rain.

Afternoon came and there was no sign of Jack. Martha was a bit worried despite Linda hovering around her like a bee, picking up plates, used glasses, trying to lighten the work. It was too much, really, and she had a thought they might not need Linda now that everything was diminished. Her strength was returning, after all. She watched Linda stealthily slip a dirty dish into the sink, wipe a counter, straighten the dishtowel, and set out her pills with a glass of juice.

"Sit down, Linda."

"It's alright."

"No, sit." Martha motioned to the banquette. "There. You're making me nervous."

They regarded each other. Linda didn't know what to say so she fiddled with the saltshaker. So this is it, she thought: my last day. Martha didn't need her anymore. Maybe she'll go back to school, catch up. She'd miss the house, the quiet, the rolling hills and green from spring through summer and Martha, despite her ups and downs. And Jack, also, the careful precision of him, not the intelligent kind, the work kind, his attention to detail much like her own father's piano playing – not fussy, but controlled and measured.

The two looked at each other, smiled.

Martha said, "I've put you through a lot."

"No big deal."

"Too much for a girl your age."

"Not so much," Linda pushed the shaker away with a finger. "You and Jack should be getting along fine now, I imagine." She wanted to be the first to open the door. "You're getting better every day."

"Is that how it looks?" Martha brightened a bit.

"Sure." Linda wanted to say it with more conviction, but it came out flat. Martha nodded her head as if she understood. And the inflection in that little word told her she wasn't ready to let Linda go, though she and Jack had talked about it. She reached across the table to touch Linda's hand, but a silver light filled the room for a second and vanished, then another and then a bounce of bright light. It was as if the sky had cleared a moment letting the sun spark the ground, or an explosion of light, but it was already sunny out. The women shot to the window to look.

Coming down the driveway was Jack in the Ford pulling a long, gleaming silver cylinder. The women pressed their faces against the glass.

Martha, wide-eyed said, "Would you look at that?" Her hand caught the heat when the light bounced into the glass. "My it shines, doesn't it?"

The gravel dust kicked up in puffs, crunches and pings. Rocks shot from under the wheels. Jack slowed the Ford to a crawl and inched forward until the trailer rested level. Clouds of dust rolled toward the house. The women's faces were at the window: shocked disbelief, and smiles.

Linda stood back from the window to let Jack and Martha have their moment to see each other through the window. She was stunned; this brought change. Whether it was good change she'd have to wait and see, but it was extraordinary this silver carriage, all door and windows and shined metal. It reflected all sorts of colors as it came down the drive: grass green, sky blue, flowers red, yellow, orange and violet. All the colors reflected perfectly, but chief was silver: a new coin, early mornings, water from a fountain.

They went outside to see the thing fully, Jack standing there admiring its impressive size thinking about the work to be done to make it home for trips he'd daydreamed about while Martha recovered.

He watched Martha,

"This is extraordinary, Jack, this contraption."

She ran her fingers along the trailer's metal, "It's cold, here, under the belly of it and then warm as I move over the top. And it's so smooth until the rivets."

Jack didn't say anything. He wanted his wife to take her time discovering it as he did at the lot.

"I don't know what to say." Martha sat on the sofa, which Jack had pulled out to demonstrate the bed and then replaced it in moments. Her fingers opened flat on the rough fabric. She took in the trailer, its angular shapes and features: the refrigerator and stove, the sink and floor to ceiling closet made from varnished wood. She wasn't relaxed enough to lean back so she sat ramrod straight supported by her hands.

"Kind of wild, I know," Jack said. "A bit of a snap decision, but we have the money – not an issue – and we talked about those trips we wanted to make."

Linda peered in from the outside. "Are you hungry, Jack?"

"Powerful hungry. Something this big takes a lot out of you," he laughed, still nervous about Martha's reaction.

"I am just stunned." Martha said. "Just beside myself."

"I know we didn't discuss this, but I didn't want to be dissuaded because I think this is the thing you need," Jack corrected himself, "we need."

"I'm not sure I'm ready to go anywhere." Martha didn't look at her husband when she said this, but rather out the window over the sink.

"We don't have to leave tomorrow. I want to do some adjustments, and then there's the car to work on a bit." He sat next to her and placed his hand over hers. "And you can think of things to make this more homey, more to your liking."

Martha was quiet awhile. She worked out slowly in her head the idea of departure or the willful act of staying and decided she might like the former. "Can we replace those curtains for starters?"

Jack relaxed and laughed, "Just say the word."

Martha leaned forward and turned to the door, "Linda, come on in and take a look."

Linda, hesitated at first. "Are you sure it's okay? Linda poked her head farther in, "I can see it later."

"Come on in," Jack bellowed.

Linda grabbed the door's inside and swung herself up avoiding the metal step altogether. The trailer lurched a bit and Jack took hold of Martha and put his hands on her shoulders. Martha flinched a little and then settled back into Jack's chest.

"Sorry, I wasn't sure about that step," Linda said as she took a look around; "What do you think? Jack asked.

"It's beautiful! All this space! It's like that bubble, Glinda the good witch get's to float around in – all shiny and new!"

Martha laughed. Jack was pleased.

From the pullout Travel Lounge Martha and Jack watched as Linda fiddled with the controls on the stove, opened the pantry door, and peered in the refrigerator. She moved down the corridor and stopped at the double bed with a window above it. She tested the firmness of the mattress.

Jack said, "They call that Airfoam... comfortable isn't it?"

"Yes!" Linda stood and opened the door to the bathroom "I can't believe there's a shower here," and then, "and a tub!" She started laughing and then going from cabinet to cabinet, opening and closing them, peering out each window at scenes she knew by heart now framed in silver. Martha and Jack laughed with her. "This is so amazing," she said, "Oh, I wish I could disappear with this, find some forest to hide out in." Linda stopped, looked at Jack and Martha, who were startled with the last, but then Linda kept on as she came forward, towards Martha and Jack. "I'd fill it with all my favorite food, all my stuff: lots and lots of Hershey bars and strawberries in the fridge. I'd put pillows everywhere and blankets and fit a phonograph in here so I could play my 45s really loud because there would be no one around. I'd sleep 'til noon every day and read my magazines and walk along the river. I could eat whenever I wanted, whatever I want." Linda stopped and leaned against the counter.

Martha and Jack looked at each other. Linda's sudden mood shift surprised them. After all this time, for a fleeting moment, she came out of herself. Martha noted how beautiful Linda was when she laughed, how her whole shape changed and radiated strength. It reminded her of herself not so long ago, and when she was young.

"Maybe someday, when you learn to drive and are ready, you can take it out for a weekend or two." Jack said.

Linda looked as if she didn't really believe that, but Jack noticed that she didn't dismiss it either.

They chattered on about what they'd do – fix all the curtains, stock it with supplies, outfit the bathroom with bath beads, luxury towels and special soaps. Both of the women went from each closet and talked about where they would store things. Jack sat back and enjoyed watching them. For the first time in a long time he felt confident around them. It was so good to hear laughter and how his wife prattled on like she did when she was excited. He hadn't heard that since the morning before he'd left her to go on his business trip. It was good for both Jack and Martha to see her come out of her sadness. When Linda left for the day, Martha said to Jack, "what a joyful girl she can be!"

The sun gave way to clouds; the weather still unpredictable in early spring. Weather skirted along the flat land: dust-ups, funnels fueled by wind, torrents of rain and sometimes hail. Weather predictions were useless and primitive.

Jack saw Martha stiffen a bit against the stove as if she had just remembered something. Her back, once smooth and pliant against him looked hard. He couldn't tell what she was thinking, but she went for the door and left the trailer. He saw Linda look at him as he got up from the couch to go after his wife. Outside, the wind kicked up, Martha's dress flapped against her legs. She walked close to the trailer letting her hand run along it.

"It's so smooth," she said, "warm to my touch."

Jack followed behind. "Yes. It feels good, doesn't it?"

"It feels like skin."

"I hadn't thought of it quite like that." Jack went up beside his wife.

Martha took his hand and guided it to the steel. "See?" She put his hand on top of his. "So smooth."

"Yes, it is." Jack said. He saw that his wife was still beautiful, her auburn hair tucked behind the ear on his side, a few freckles over her eye, her nose blunted slightly at the tip, her long arm and fingers over his hand as she moved it across the cooling metal.

"This is what he felt like." Martha said, "Just like this. When he came out of me, this was exactly it: smooth and warm, but losing his heat." She turned to him. "I wanted you to feel that somehow."

Jack cried and began moving his hand involuntarily – as if some unknown force was guiding him. For a long time his hand gently moved over the steel as if polishing it.

Martha released his other hand and stepped away from the Airstream as the sun broke through the clouds and struck the silver hull and then disappeared.

Airstreaming

Peace Piece

Linda heard her mother's car horn and then again, but longer, more insistent. She heard it, but couldn't see the car now that the Ford and trailer blocked the view of the road. She was sitting at the banquette, magazine in front of her, but stared off into space while Jack and Martha were in the den. For the last half hour Linda had leaned in hard to listen, but she hadn't been able to hear anything. She finally gathered her things and left the house. As she walked up the road, she turned and looked at the Airstream against the house and hills beyond and wondered how it might affect her.

She pulled the car door open and slid quietly into her seat.

"Honestly, Linda, couldn't you have remembered I have to go out tonight?" Her mother started the car and revved the engine.

"They had a hard day."

"And then you take your sweet time coming from the house. It's maddening." The car lurched forward from being thrown into gear.

"I'm sorry," Linda said.

"I'd be wanting to get away from that crazy woman as fast as I could."

Linda twisted her fingers, "She's not crazy."

"Did she not just try to kill herself out on that rooftop?"

"No."

"It sure sounded like she did. All that fuss about her – and you always cleaning up afterwards."

"I guess it's all in how you want to look at it." Linda said, her heart beat fast and her arms beaded up from the heat heading back into town and her rising anger.

After some quiet, her mother said, "Maybe we should look for another situation." Clare looked over at her daughter who was gazing out her side window. "You know, the young women at work – the newest secretaries who are barely out of high school – they're making more money than I did at that age.".

Linda didn't say anything. She was thinking on the twenty in her pocket, the extra one she kept. So far she'd stashed nearly four hundred dollars. There was nothing she spent money on except for records here and there: Billie Holliday, Chet Baker (not because she loved the trumpet so much, but for his pictures on the covers, which were often of his head cocked to one side, hair in a short pompadour and slicked back, full lips, skin as smooth as wet soap), and everything by Bill Evans.

Her father had played *Everybody Digs Bill Evans* until he'd had to replace the record twice after the vinyl wore and the pops and hiss made listening to the stark piano on *Peace Piece* and *Some Other Time* unbearable. Tonight she'd listen to him, her new copy clear enough to hear those final notes ringing out and then the long fade into silence.

Later that night, a Saturday, blue light filled her bedroom. The streetlamp's glow lit up the sheer curtains against which shadows slid across when cars turned the corner, headlights elongating branches and leaves.

She lay on her bed, the phonograph playing, and waited for each new car to come home and send its light across her curtains. She thought about Barbara and where she might be, her father sitting in a prison somewhere, lying on his mattress playing that moment he tossed his wife over the banister through his head, whether he was filled with remorse. She didn't understand the way of husbands and wives, their private thoughts, what they say to each other behind closed doors that bring them together or drive them apart. She wanted to know what secrets were told among people in love, or what was held back.

She wanted to see Barbara again. She was her last friend – or friend her age – all of the others had fallen away. She wondered what that meant to her. She had heard nothing of Barbara; she'd be in Arizona with relatives until she turned eighteen and could be on her own.

The Miller's house sold, but no one knew who bought it. It remained empty through winter and spring. The gardens that Mrs. Miller had obsessed over were now overgrown and leafy; the aggressive plants overtook the smaller, delicate ones.

On a weekend, a kid from across the street, had thrown a rock through one of the square panes at the side of the large front window. He chased down a raccoon that tipped over their family's garbage can that was set out on the sidewalk for pickup the next day and when he threw the rock, his arm's velocity, the raccoon's distance and his imprecise aim sent the stone far over the critter's head shattering glass as it went.

A few days later a truck arrived and a man stepped out and efficiently boarded up the window within ten minutes. Several people came out of their homes to watch including the Adderley's and Mrs. Cuthbert who sat on her porch most days anyway. The open window might have been a portal for which the house gave up its secrets, but no one could muster up the courage to approach it.

Linda heard her mother in the bathroom getting ready to go out; the clink of glass vials, the medicine chest opening and closing, water being turned on and off.

Her mother hummed. Saturday's meant Smith's – a bar that served fried food with steaks as big as a house. Surf and Turf to them meant steak and fish sticks, but it was the one extravagance her mother allowed – heavy on the tartar sauce - which she also used on the steak to make it juicy.

Smith's décor was a bit too nautical for Clare's taste, and the Midwest, quite frankly she thought: dusty wooden sailboats behind the bar, posters of ocean maps with filigreed compasses stretched across the walls. The table lamps were fluted; their bases wide as if made for oil, but instead votive candles were replaced and lit each night. Smith sometimes wore a sailors cap and captained the bar to which he'd attached half a helm. When it got busy, he'd yell at one of the help – most of the time it was Stuart who really didn't work there, but sat at the corner of the bar reading racing forums escaping his stay-at-home father. One heard "Take the helm, Stuart!" several times during the evening so Smith could deliver plates of food to his customers.

Smith never got over his naval days after the war.

It was the theatre of it all that attracted Clare. She'd sit at a booth with the nighttime paper, cutting away at her steak, looking up now and again to see who had entered and whether they sat at a table or the bar. Smith tapped her table every so often as he swooshed by after delivering or taking up plates and she'd look up in time to see the tail ends of his apron ties switch back and forth at his rear.

These nights, these three short hours, she'd forget her lost husband, her job, and let her mind rush and create stories for each of Smith's patrons. The stories were all better than her own: she didn't allow darkness or death, or poverty, or loneliness – all had wonderful lives, even Stuart, who had not once noticed her, was mechanical about pouring the drinks, forgetting even the garnishes so that drinks came back wanting for olives, or those cocktail onions, cherries for Roy Rogers or Shirley Temples.

So Clare imagined him as Cary Grant, women wanting him from across the room, but keeping a respectful distance. He could be Earl Victor Rhyall: rich, debonair, aloof in The Grass is Greener, or John Robie in To Catch a Thief – mysterious but fun.

The reality was that his father's mind was deteriorating and he'd come to live with Stuart. She'd heard that he wandered from home often, so Stuart had a bracelet made with his phone number and address on it. And Stuart's sister came and relieved him Saturday nights bringing with her their father's young grandchildren, born late to her, but in time for him to understand who they were when he was lucid.

After dinner, Clare left her table and moved up to the bar. She waited until Stuart returned to his corner and his forums because Smith always gave her the first drink free. But it was only for that reason; secretly she longed for Stuart, was attracted to him like all broken things.

He had coarse strawberry blonde hair, cut short at the temples with strands at his forehead leading to more over his crown. He was far different from what her husband had been. Stuart made his body seem smaller than it was the way he always leaned or stooped or squatted on that chair. Once in a while he'd have to stretch out his back and then Clare could see how tall he was. Whenever Smith needed a new bottle of something from a high shelf, Stuart was the one to get it. And every time he looked up, it was as if he was looking out from under a baseball cap, but he never wore any kind of hat.

She watched him absently stroke his earlobe, cross his legs, his forearm muscles flex and repose wiping down the bar, the way he held his cigarette at the tips of his fingers while the others clung to the newspaper. His blue jeans were always clean, and were always the same. She predicted that he wore the same ones every Saturday, but he did change up his shirt and tonight he wore a white shirt with blue pinstripes with opalescent white snap buttons, the kind that were rounded and soft to touch.

There were no racetracks nearby, but he'd make Smith turn to 780 to listen in on race reports from east to west. She was not sure if he gambled, but saw his slight smiles or disappointments when races were called.

Clare worked the gin and tonic for as long as she could.

Smith leaned against the back of the bar. "Can I get you another, Clare?" He came forward and swooped her glass up anticipating a yes. He flipped it a couple of times in his hand.

"You break many glasses doing that?"

"Not anymore," Smith said, filling the glass half-full with gin, squeezing a lime. "Good drink for the start of summer."

"I like them in winter, too, you know." Clare scooted back in the swivel stool. "Has Stuart won anything today?"

"Not so as I can tell," Smith said, returning the glass full, slipping the napkin under.

His fingers moved efficiently, effortlessly, which Clare admired. She wondered if he were that good with buttons and laughed to herself. "Elaine home tonight?"

"She's at the movies with the girls." The girls meaning two women who lived together across the way from Smith and Elaine: it was a relationship that no one talked about. One a retired schoolteacher, the other widowed early and never remarried. They were together as long as anyone could remember and Elaine, fifteen years their junior, included them in all their family parties and twice-monthly outings to the movies. Many times they came by after for a drink and to discuss the film before the girls took their car and left Elaine to catch a ride with Smith.

In the months since her husband's death, and when Clare decided it was time to leave the house and get out she'd seen the four of them at To Catch a Thief, several rows in front, Smith's arm draped possessively over his wife's shoulders and the women ramrod straight in their chairs. Though the chair backs blocked her view, Clare thought the women, once the dark took over, put the popcorn bag between their opposing knees as a sort of connection like she and her husband had.

Her gin and tonic had become watery, the ice melted. Clare studied the swirling opaque liquids at the bottom of the glass. The gin soaked onion slipped along the bottom. She plucked it out and placed it between her lips tasting its sweetness and sharp tang. The steak and potatoes absorbed the first drink; the second determined how the night would go.

Stuart was there with a fresh one minus adornments. Clare didn't mind so much, two onions were enough in an evening.

"There you go, Clare."

"You're an observant man," she said, holding up the empty for him to take. She dropped the glass in his palm, its cold sweat trickled down his lines of skin, pooling under the glass' bottom.

"I see everything," he chuckled, "I sit in the same spot because it's the best one."

"The newspapers are just a ruse then?"

"No, I read them too. Four hours is a long time to fill on Saturday nights." He closed his fist around the glass and turned to deposit it in the sink. "How was your steak this evening?"

Clare was glad he noticed what she had for dinner. "It's such a relief not to have to cook, it made the steak better than it probably was."

He laughed, "I'll let Smith know." And then he winked at Clare, who laughed with him.

The hundred neon beer signs shot color all across the counters and into the liquor bottles. Electric transformer buzz was the white noise in the bar lowing under people's voices, under their pulses, the clinks of glasses, the hiccups, the light love slaps on thighs, the scratch of denim under fingernails.

"How's your daughter?" Stuart asked. Clare felt he was trying to keep the conversation going.

"Complicated," Clare said, "and getting more so everyday."

"The air is thick with complication at her age."

"She got too much of her father, I think, and not enough of me." Clare sipped now; her last drink of the evening was to be savored. "She holds onto things, like this job she has. Just like her father who played piano even on out of tune instruments, or with dead keys, or when there were just two people left listening. It was over compensation or something." The third drink was just about loosening her up.

Stuart tapped two fingers on the bar like playing piano. "I remember he could play."

"Linda is probably sitting at home listening to his old records."

"A young girl like that should be out having fun."

"I'm part of the blame for that," Clare admitted, "part of it all in her mind, I'm sure."

"I miss him playing at the hall. About the only thing I looked forward to on those nights - your daughter leading him up there, finding his place; Sort of like Ray Charles, who I saw once in town when he breezed through. I could tell he'd be tough to work for. Guys like that with all that talent has to have something going on, but your husband was nice as summer."

Clare quickened them out of the past. "I'm coming out of the mourning period. I think people are starting to allow me a certain freedom."

"Freedom?"

"I can talk to men now. Like I'm talking to you. I can be alone at the bar." She laughed nervously.

"I never thought you cared about what other people think." Stuart smiled, "When my wife left me years ago I could feel the air in church charge up like a heat storm, which is why I quit going for awhile."

"It doesn't matter whether I care or not," Clare said, "it's just the cost of living here, and I can't afford to move."

"Moving is the easy part, don't you think? Clare leaned in close to him and caught his eye so he couldn't look away. So tell me Stuart," she said, "Tell me how you get through these years when you are hated by the only thing you have left?"

Stuart place one palm on the back of her hand, "That's a bit much, no?"

"The thing she's learned from the job I made her take was how to take care of herself." Clare looked at the ridges and freckles, the bent strawberry-blonde hair on Stuart's hand, how the knuckles had tiny work scars among the folds of skin, the veins blue and meandering and swollen, mapping the muscles. It was the first time someone had touched her tenderly, even if it had been absent-mindedly, even if the way he left it there was only for comfort.

"Is it such a bad thing?" Stuart asked. "I suspect your husband's death would have compelled her to. She had somewhat taken over the job of caring for him all those years while you worked. I suspect she didn't have much more to learn."

Clare wondered if they'd talked about this. How did he know what Linda was like before? Coming to Smith's was something she did after her husband had died. She hadn't said two words to him the first ten times she was there so wrapped up in her grief and what to do next. Then she remembered Smith's wife, Elaine, at the office and them talking through lunches. She discovered she had to be careful with her: she was one of those people who were slippery good at extracting information, putting little nuggets of it together to formulate the whole. Clare imagined Elaine up at night making Smith a conspirator, and then Smith, from his neon-lit pulpit, beer glass rings reflecting into his customer's eyes, disseminating information with as much discretion as a dog in heat.

Which meant that his first mate, Stuart, knew everything.

"It's not like she did everything," Clare said, her voice a little strident, "Without me he would have squandered it all away."

Stuart, a little chastised, said, "I don't mean to suggest..."

"No, you did. That is the belief around here," Clare narrowed her focus on Stuart who removed his hand. "Even at work. And I don't mean to get preachy here, I don't mean to lay the whole women's suffrage thing at your feet, but people don't take into account circumstance. Sixteen years ago I was one of those women expecting to have married, stay home with the babies, all that nonsense. But things were different for us."

"You don't have to explain it to me, Clare, really, there's no judgment here, none at all."

"Are you sure, Stuart? Can you sit there and tell me, with your experience of how it is with men and women..." Feeling that Stuart was hurt and that she'd been too caustic, and seeing him back away from his side of the bar, Clare abruptly softened and lowered her voice, "the thing we have in common is that both our spouses left us. I'm willing to meet you on that one." Clare took a large sip; let the cool run down her throat, healing the heat that had risen up in her.

"I don't suppose you want another drink," he said, pausing a moment to see where the Captain was, "before Smith comes back." It seemed to Clare that he wanted to end the conversation suddenly. He'd paid deference to her for the first time, but for Clare to have brought up his wife's leaving was a thing she was suddenly shameful for.

Clare just shook her head.

"I'll go back to my reading then," he said, turning, and then headed to his corner stool.

Clare watched him go, sorry for the anger that had no place rising up like it did. It was all disappointment and the fatigue that goes with it. She felt defeated in almost everything – she missed the routines of her husband, her daughter's deference to him, work didn't offer the pleasures of escape it once did. When her husband died there were those few weeks of sympathy from her friends at work, and then the gradual exclusion from conversations, events, weekend dinners. Not so much because she wasn't asked - she was asked several times to fill the odd seat - but it was because there was nothing she could relate to. The standard lines of family were broken. While she was never as involved in Linda's activities as her father, she was always keenly aware of them.

Now Linda didn't talk to her at all. At home she was sullen and angry. She didn't engage in anything other than working for that crazy woman. Linda came home and either left the house for hours on end or she holed up in her room, squirreling away hours of silence that Clare thought she used against her as punishment.

Smith came back to the bar. He stopped near Stuart, his back to Clare, but she watched him as he wiped down a bottle of cognac, and leaned into him. "You say a proper farewell to Clare," he said, "you go over there again."

"I'm fine where I am," Stuart said.

"I'm tired of seeing you waste your time away in this corner, tired of seeing the both of you port to starboard in this bar." Smith put the filigreed bottle up and wiped clear down to where Clare was a gulp away from the end of her night.

"How are you doing there?" Smith asked.

Clare wasn't doing well at all. Smith wasn't one of those bartenders who offered advice, but in a blunt way dispensed with his thoughts no matter the fallout.

"Looks like you and Stuart are inching towards each other." Stuart put the bottle up and then turned back around. "That's a good thing, no?"

Clare just looked at him and smiled, giving away nothing.

"Tonight's on me if you go tell Stuart good night," he said.

Clare bought time by downing the last of her gin. Ten dollars without tip was something and she felt bad with the way she'd knocked Stuart down a notch or two.

"Just give me the bill," she said, resigned to the night ahead, the ride home, the moon-washed houses, the car's headlights forging ahead like in those Hitchcock movies – all dread and high violins, the thump, thump – but her movie was without any expectation of what lay ahead, only Linda, that piano music emanating from her bedroom reminding her of her husband every night until the thwack of the needle against the center made her steal into Linda's room and snap the record player's arm back in its cradle. Only then could she see the remnants of innocence on her daughter's sleeping face and remember how much she loved her.

"Here you go," Smith said, slipping the bill to her, which was a couple of drinks light.

Clare did look up to find Stuart, his eyes low, but on her. She nodded and smiled. She thought she saw him shift a little forward on his stool, but she could have been wrong. She set a ten down on the bar and thanked Smith for so many kindnesses over the last many months and left.

Boxes

Over the gray unexpectedly cold weekend Martha lined boxes along the walls. She'd rescued them before being smashed by the box boys at the grocery store in town - all were various sizes to hold different things that would eventually find a home in the Airstream. She divided the items up between paper goods, cleaning supplies, kitchenware, bathroom towels, sheets – some of which she was able to glean from items they already had. She'd made a pact that anything she hadn't used in the house in over a year would find a place in the trailer or was off to Goodwill. Otherwise, she went to second hand stores and picked out discarded plates and silverware, a toaster, pots and pans, knives needing sharpening. It was her way to create order.

Jack abandoned his spring routine to customize the trailer; he installed new curtains (white with yellow daisies and green vines trailing down) that Martha had sewn, a matching shower curtain for the tub, a soap holder above the sink. He paused often to just sit on the couch at the back staring down the short hallway still dazed by his purchase. He built additional racks for clothes and linen, became familiar with how the tanks worked for water and propane, how the electric fed off the batteries and how to keep them charged.

Saturday, Martha went out to the trailer with plates of food, sodas and an old tablecloth she found. Jack snapped the table in place and they sat together, like two people sharing a booth at a diner, but sitting on one side so they could touch. This seemed new to both of them, or foreign, or as if returning from a long trip. There was no negotiation between them as they returned to the time before any talk of a baby, the casual, almost silent exchanges between them. Smiles were genuine, laughter unforced.

The trailer's cabin was warm from the heat of the light Jack worked with; the louvered windows were shut tight and Martha had pulled the door closed behind her when she came in. Jack's forearms glistened from sweat and Martha moved her arm against one as they ate their grilled cheese and chips.

Jack didn't want to spoil the mood by saying anything so he ate hungrily, downed the soda, the bubbles coming back in a belch. They both laughed. Maybe they needed a new project. Maybe they needed something they could talk about again that made them focus outside themselves. Jack's thirst had been powerful until Martha showed signs of strength again, and the trailer consumed his thoughts. That ache for the familiar; a glass cupped in his hand, or twined at the tips of his fingers. He'd passed more than a few bars in the last months, the flickering neon, the anonymity of their front doors, darkness inside even on the brightest days.

He planned a couple of weeks to get the trailer ready, get it stocked, which he'd left most of it to Martha to do. The mechanical work he took care of, making the space under the couch at the front of the cabin the place he stored the tools, electrical supplies, tire patches, flashlight, flares – all things he picked up from work at a discount and some from overstock.

"This is quite comfortable sitting here," Martha said, "I could see us living in this quite nicely for a couple of weeks."

"We'll go as much as we can, depending on work."

"I need a plan," Martha said, "I need a date." She'd been thinking in the morning that she had to have something specific to work toward. She'd stared at the calendar, days infinite now needing to be filled, days against whatever weather came across the rolling hills.

"I put in for some time," Jack kept this unspecific to make sure of Martha's progress. "They've been generous with me for some time now." He didn't get any reaction from Martha so he knew he'd need to find a date. "How about a test spin over a long weekend?"

"Good idea."

"Test out the systems, how it trailers."

Martha heard about a place down toward Emporia. "Two weeks from now?"

"I'll ask Carl."

Martha left the trailer and walked to the house, then turned to look at the Airstream. Her husband had spent nights polishing it, had put such force into his circular motions that it gleamed in the light just now. Colors blended over its hull until the silver white at the top. She had continued to trail her fingers across it, but Jack had been possessed by it since he first pulled up in front of the house. He'd photographed it at every angle; Martha was placed against it for scale because he wanted to record its beauty and put them in a notebook. He'd gone over every rivet to see that it was sound. The coating he'd polished until his fingers and wrist were so sore they hurt, but even still he polished from the moment he got home until Martha coaxed him in.

Jack wasn't quite sure what got into him. His thoughts turned to penance; to a willful act of making things so clean they'd reflect back goodness and light. Two things he wanted returned to him.

The cream paste he used left a waxy residue, flaking as it dried. Jack's circular movements could be seen in the paste. He tore towels in two and buffed out the residue leaving a shine. Most people would have done this once and called it good, but Jack was on his third coat when Linda had come up behind him a few evenings into it.

"I don't think you can get it any more clean," she said, startling him out of his work.

"Hmm? What did you say?" Jack stopped, but didn't look back at her.

"It's just that you've been at this for several days. Polishing…"

"I don't think I'm done yet."

"Aren't there other things to do?" Linda went to touch the hull.

"Don't." Jack put his hand between hers and the trailer.

"Okay." Linda stepped back "I'm leaving for the day."

"That's fine." Jack folded the rag over itself.

"Go inside for supper, Martha's waiting on you." Linda walked up to the road and waited on her Mother. She looked back at where the trailer sat and watched Jack almost in silhouette now against the silver. She worried more now about him than Martha who seemed to have come out of herself in the past couple of weeks. She was intent on her projects in the same way as before – haphazard, randomly going from one thing to the next like a bee alighting on flowers. Her projects seemed to fill her up with purpose again, whereas Jack had become compulsive, addicted to a thing he would never believe was finished.

It wasn't long before Linda's mother swung onto the roadside curb and scooped her up.

Jack kept on until there was simply no light.

The next Saturday, Carl came to weld metal pockets onto the side of the hull where the main door and windows were. Jack had bought an awning and had measured the space between where the pockets for the rods needed to be. Carl tested his welding torch, lowered his faceplate and clicked the starter a few times before the fire leapt from the end of the torch. Jack marveled at his amateur ability to weld and how it kept him busy on weekends. He was surprised Carl hadn't turned it it into a business rather than working for someone else, but his wife wanted stability and encouraged Carl to keep it as secondary income while the babies were young, which kept him at the dealership.

Jack held the sprocket in place with thick gloves over his hands. The solder melted between the hull and the metal plate as Carl fused them with fire. They worked in silence until the second metal plate was in place. Carl stepped out of the Airstream's shadow and lifted his faceplate.

"I think it'll hold alright, don't you think?

"Rock solid, Carl. Nice work."

"It's a good rig you've got here, Jack. I was suspecting it was something to behold the way you talk at the shop, but not this nice." Carl turned the torch off and set the nozzle across the top of the propane tank. Jack had gone on about his trailer for some weeks now. It had supplanted the subject of the new baby almost overnight. It was as if Jack had made up his mind to not talk about what happened. Carl said, "the Airstream has an almost translucent quality about it, not metal at all anymore, but a reflection that sort of makes me uncomfortable because I can practically see myself in it."

"That's the idea," said Jack. Coming up beside Carl to stare at the trailer.

When Martha lost the baby, Carl had come out to the house the minute he heard to tell Jack how crushed and ashamed he was to have ever said the things he did to him at the party. He tried to make it up to him by covering all his shifts for the days he needed.

Martha came out from the house with some water and glasses. "You two are working hard in this heat."

"It's not so bad," Carl said, as Martha held out a glass to him. The ice clinked. Jack watched Carl hesitate and look her over. Martha was frail, he thought, her arms thin and very white, the skin hanging loose under her arm. Her eyes were sunk deep in their sockets and her cheekbones were high from when she carried the baby.

Carl took the glass, then said pointing to the Airstream with it, "Are you ready to take this out for a spin?"

"I've been ready a week now. Just waiting on Jack to make up his mind that he's done everything he needs to do to it." She smiled at Carl and gave another glass to Jack. "He's worked so hard night after night fixing it up." She moved up next to Jack.

"It's about ready to go," Jack said, joining the conversation. He was still fixated on the roller pin for the awning in his other hand. "I expect a few more nights ought to do it."

Martha laughed. "It's ready to go now. Just put that awning in and we're off!"

"It's good to see you smile, Martha," Carl said. The air heated between them. Martha glanced at Jack. Carl finished his water.

Martha looked away and said, "That's nice of you to say, Carl." Then she turned back to him and put her hand out to retrieve the glass. "I'll bring more out in awhile."

Martha went back in the house and Jack, furious, turned to his friend. "Carl, you missed your calling. You should be some fucking psychologist or something. You've got more leading questions than a detective, always trying to figure people out. Us anyways. You've seen Martha maybe six times in your life and you say something like, "Good to see you smile again..." For fuck's sake, just let it be."

"I meant nothing by it, Jack, nothing at all."

"The hell you did. I remember the night at the party. You and I spend a lot of time together and I tell you things, but not everything."

"I can't forgive myself for what I said. I've played that over so many times."

Jack gripped the roller pin harder. "Well, you were right, Carl, but you didn't have to say it. Sometimes it's good to just not..." Jack's voice trailed off and he sat down in one of the lawn chairs set up in front of the Airstream where he and Martha sat in the evening together as if practicing for the real deal. Two black clouds hung in the air off a tree across from the two of them. Carl stood where he was. "I never saw it... him, Carl. They whisked it away, put it in a tiny little box and we put him in the ground. In some ways it feels to me like it didn't even happen."

Carl made a feeble gesture and attempted to talk.

Then the cloud broke apart above the two men; blackbirds in a flighty clump scattered and reformed across the field and then blackened an entire tree.

"The night I brought this trailer home Martha remarked how when she touched it, it felt like the baby did when he came out and all I've wanted was to feel that."

Carl said, "So you wait awhile and you try again."

Jack stifled a small laugh, which seemed inappropriate and said, "No." The doctor had been rather emphatic that it was now an impossibility that Martha would conceive again. It was a cruel turn and the laugh was really about him, his own failure. He stood up suddenly, "Can you cover me one last time next Friday?"

"Sure I can."

"We're taking this out." Jack pointed to the Airstream and took the roller pin and slid it through the center of the rolled awning. "Help me hang this up and we'll see if it works."

The lowering sun made deep valleys of shadows in the sloping hills. The cicadas buzzed in the grasses. Cars rushed homeward on the road before last light. It seemed more and more cars used the road in front of their house as the city stretched out of town. Carl left before being invited for supper. He told Jack he needed to get back home to Susan and the kids. Jack watched Carl pack up his welding kit, take a look back at the house and then the Airstream.

"It's a beautiful trailer, Jack," Carl said, shutting his car door, "I'm sure you and Martha will have a lot of fine times."

Jack went back to polishing the silver hull. The colors from the sky reflected back like a warm-hued rainbow. One of Jack's fingers slipped off the rag as it bunched in his palm. He suddenly stopped polishing. His breath caught in his chest. The hull's skin felt right now as the air cooled it. He dropped the rag into his other hand and pressed all of his fingers into the smooth silver and wept.

Martha was in the lighted kitchen, her cardboard boxes almost filled with the supplies they'd need for their trips. She had catalogued their contents on a piece of paper so that she'd have a list for replenishment. While she worked, she hadn't realized that it was getting dark outside and that Jack hadn't come in yet. Of course, supper wasn't even started. Perhaps she'd collect the glasses and bring them in. She went outside and her eyes adjusted to the gloaming as she approached the trailer. She saw Jack silhouetted against the darkening blue sky, kneeling on the ground, one hand on the trailer. She stopped for a moment and thought to back her way to the house, but she stood and watched him, his shoulders heaving. She knew then that they were in for the long haul of marriage, that things would right themselves over time. She went to him and put her hands on his shoulders to calm him, kissed his neck and put her face in his hair. There were no words; only a box in the ground that contained their past lives and boxes in the kitchen that contained their lives going forward.

Jazz

While her mother was at Smith's, Linda wandered the house as music filled it. She had stacked several records atop each other on the Garrard turntable so they'd drop, one after another. Saturday's was her night, too, since her mother was gone for hours. There was no work, nothing to do, but listen to the hi-fi that her father had spent precious money on to have the best. The sound came out clear as if snow and only instruments filling the air could quiet the world.

From outside, her figure's shadow floated across the sheer drapes undulating sheaves. Tonight she was more restless. She felt Martha and Jack were changing and getting ready to uproot their lives. Her mother's anger had receded, replaced by the drone of work and melancholy that lifted itself only on Saturday mornings when she had something to look forward to.

Linda had no desire now to return to school; she had been forgotten. Her time was simply her own when she wasn't working. Her mother seemed done with raising her; expectations were dashed. The two lived together out of necessity and their conflicts were meaningless, scaled down to irritations.

As the music played, Linda moved over the wood floor in her socks, flattening her toes and then arching them to pivot and swing. If there was one thing she loved, it was music. Her father came back to her in it, the pull of him in the syncopated rhythms of the snare, the staccato trumpet or the piano in an arpeggio holding it all together. He had taught her to listen to the details; discordant notes that led into elegant notes, a slap of a hand against the bass as an A flat pulled and stretched.

During the past few summers, they stood in the doorway at The Blue Room, one of the last remaining clubs at 18th and Vine. Her father had recounted the history of the district to her and how, when he was in college, they came down to listen to the likes of Sonny Stitt, Dexter Gordon and Miles Davis and how he'd run into Bill Evans and how his girlfriend at the time described him smoking alone after a set in the alley, leaning against the back of the club, the air smelling of tobacco and how delicate Mr. Evans had held the cigarette in his fingers. Black was only a concept, her father said, and joked about being truly color blind. Every time they went he asked to be led around to the back of the clubs where all his senses, save for his eyesight, heightened. On some nights when the air was heavy, the mix of music coming from the various clubs was like an orchestra tuning up. But on other nights, you'd only hear a piano, or a trumpet riffing for long stretches of time. He could sense people gathering around him, smell their aftershave and perfume, heated and close. They would all listen as long as it would take the player to find their way to the end of the song.

Linda remembered the nights standing outside The Blue Room, the area now a mix of cleaners, bars and shops save for this one vestibule of music where her father would stand still, hold her hand and listen.

With her mother gone tonight, she could leave without questions, and she was missing her daddy. She'd get to The Blue Room, take the bus she and her daddy always took down off Proctor Road and across town. She went into her room and put on warmer clothes, a jacket, scarf, and hat. The days were warmer, but the nights were still cold. She took money from her stash of twenties and rolled them up into her sock. It was half past eight and most likely would take an hour by bus into downtown. She walked the few blocks to the station. The buses ran further apart on the weekends, but she seemed to time it right and after five minutes the low rumble could be heard down the street and she saw the amber lights atop the bus coming toward her. She had not been on a bus since before her dad passed and had forgotten the acrid smells of them, the worn leather seats and cold metal handrails. She sat two thirds in among people who barely acknowledged her. They kept staring straight ahead or gazed out the windows like prisoners longing for escape.

The bus meandered through the city, through tree-covered slopes with large brick Tudors, various small neighborhoods alternating between houses like hers and mansions with elongated driveways edged by perfectly maintained lawns. Then through north Terrace Park into Independence Plaza where a number of folks got off and on. She stared out at the huge fountain, water spouting at its center in a circle. Now up Prospect Avenue along low brick buildings as the city grew darker, more worn; the building's facades were boarded up by plywood or hideously covered with aluminum siding. The bus passed East Truman Road and pulled up to the 18th and Vine district and Linda got off. She walked the half block to

18th and turned right, remembering the way from the summer before. Even in the past year, the district had deteriorated further.

There were people lying about in the park, some in clumps. Car drove by, with rolled down windows, music blaring. Women stood in small groups on corners and a few dogs flitted from overloaded trashcans, and rooted through their contents spilled on the ground. She thought that this might not have been such a good idea and she almost crossed the street to take another bus home, but she had to go and stand in The Blue Room's vestibule tonight, just to remember what her and her daddy witnessed and listened to. She remembered being wide-eyed and fascinated how the ruins of the district fit so well with the music. She rounded the corner and spied the neon sign with its cursive The and Blue block letters stretched vertically to an edge of lit piano keys under the word Room. The club seemed to be the last lighted building on the street and its own façade was in disrepair.

Much of what had been a bustling, lively district was now bleak and weathered. Down the street, women stood away from the curb only coming out of the shadows when a car passed by. A few men stood together talking, smoking rolled cigarettes. One of the men looked at Linda. She caught his eye, but looked away. Cars pulled up to the corner and people climbed out and went quickly in the club. She was close now and slowed. There were a mix of white and black men and women on the curb outside the club. Smoke curled up into the lamplight, men whispered into the ears of their women who stood close to them.

As she moved up to the front door, she could hear a trio of trumpet, piano and drums playing. The music was fast and the trumpet swirled furiously around the piano lines, which were, in their own way, sharp and dissonant. Linda recognized it as Be Bop, a jazz style her father had defined for her over the years. She was glad to be here she decided and moved up closer to the door where the music was loudest; every time the door opened a blast of music burst into the street. There were others gathered outside just listening, heads intent at the doors opening. Some of the men were young, stocking caps pulled down to the tops of their ears, worn jackets, and the pockets warming their hands.

Linda wanted so much to go in, but there was the doorman, not tall, round-faced and blocking the entrance with his girth covered in a beautiful coat, its shiny fabric reflecting blue neon.

Instead, she stood for a moment at the building's corner against the cold brick. People continued to filter in, but none were leaving. Saturday nights they were in for the long jams that went until dawn, the inhabitants at an entirely different cycle from the rest of the world. Linda's time constraint was centered on the last bus back home, which allowed her a few hours, but her curfew only allowed a couple though she knew her mother would never hear her come home.

The doorman noticed her after awhile and nodded his head at her. She recognized him from the summer before and now she had been discovered as she bided her time listening, watching for signs of his impatience with her.

An hour passed and she'd grown cold, but hadn't noticed fully because of the music and what it brought to her. Some of the other listeners had left because of the cold, but the others stood steadfast. The doorman finally walked over to her, smiled, but kept his distance.

"Miss," he said, his voice deep and resonating a clear, rich tone. "Miss, how long you planning to stand there?"

"I don't know." Linda said.

"Are you waiting on something?"

"No, just listening." Linda looked at the doorman.

"Just listening?" The doormen laughed a little. "A young thing like you just listening?"

"Yes."

"Well, I'll be." He came up closer. "No one your age just stands out here listening." Ain't it a little late for you to be out?" He was more patrician than threatening.

Just then a deep red Cadillac pulled up to the curb. A man, dressed in a dark pinstriped suit under a black overcoat, maneuvered his way out stopping to pull a horn case from the rear seat. He walked slowly toward the front door – painfully working his legs. The doorman made a move to head back to his station, but the man just waved at him and entered the club.

"You know who that was?"

"Jimmy Forrest." Linda looked at him and waited a beat before she smiled.

"Wow. You are here to listen." The doorman was bemused and a bit surprised and examined her a bit.

He made Linda a bit uncomfortable. "I used to have to describe all of the musicians for my dad."

"You used to describe them…?

"My dad was blind." Linda offered. The music went suddenly silent. The doorman didn't respond for a moment. He turned his head toward the door as some people exited to take a break from the heat and smoky interior.

"I remember you two," the doorman said, "You used to hang out back though, not up here in front. It's been awhile since I seen you two. How come you're here alone?"

"He died." Linda said as a statement of fact.

"That a terrible thing, miss." He looked back at the door. "Come stand by me. I need to be there for the breaks." Linda followed him. "How long he been gone?" The doorman motioned to a spot just behind him for her to stand.

"Almost a year."

"Lot's can happen in a year, no?" He held out his gloved hand, "I'm Barkis. And Barkis is willing to get to know you. Good to have you here."

"Linda." She took his hand and smiled. "Barkis is a different name than any I've heard."

"See David Copperfield. I'm not anything like Barkis, but my mama loved that movie and so I'm stuck with it!" He said lightly. "I'm Barkis, The Blue Room doorman. I know everybody." Then he laughed and winked, "and I know their business." He studied Linda a bit. "You miss your pop. You're really not supposed to be here, but here you are. You're a bit of a sass... a bit of tough, but you've got something soulful going on. I can read people and you, my young Linda, are a heavy book already."

"I remember you, too, from before. My dad and I used to spy you from down the block and enter into the alley. We could never afford to go in. Daddy wanted to so bad, but we'd sit out back, sometimes meeting the players on their breaks."

Barkis said, "That would have been the place to be."

"We saw everyone," Linda said, "Even Count Basie who came to the club a bit ago."

"Everyone comes here now since we're one of the last places left. It breaks my heart to see what's happened here, but time makes a mess of things."

A group of four who'd been standing outside turned to go back in the club. Barkis nodded at them as they passed. "Evening Mr. Marcius, Miss Lenore. I seen you brought some out-of-towners tonight. Always good."

"Good evening, Barkis," Mr. Marcius hesitated for a moment. "They're in from St. Louis this weekend."

Barkis extended his hand to the visiting gentleman while acknowledging the woman with him. "I trust your train ride was a smooth one." The woman nodded and Barkis let go of the man's hand in deference to him. "Welcome to The Blue Room. It's going to be a swinging night. I know you'll want to stay late so if you need anything just let me know." Barkis pulled the door open and Linda stepped up from behind him to look inside. The foursome noticed and Barkis moved slightly in front of her. "Enjoy the music." The club-goers disappeared into the blue-bricked walls dotted with black and white portraits unfolding the club's history.

"Patience, Miss Linda," he said, turning to her.

"I've always wanted to see inside," she said, stepping out from behind him again.

"You don't need to see jazz, Miss Linda," Barkis said smiling, "you need to feel it just like your daddy did."

For three weeks every Saturday Linda stood behind Barkis at The Blue Room door. She watched the patrons come and go, most of them dressed to the nines for the evening; men in fine woolen or silk suits, women with tight dresses in bright colors covered by long, fur coats, their heads topped with beautiful hats. Linda could tell what they were like from their hats; some wore complicated, frivolous ones with beads and ribbons surrounding the crown and brims that swooped around their heads like spinning tops. Some wore simple, tight hats that fit snug over their hair; these were usually of one color with a ribbon offset or a simple brocaded flower to one side. The striking thing to Linda was that they were all different and she never saw the same hat twice. She was simply in awe of the more outlandish hats, ones that added a foot to the woman wearing it or so detailed with wide feathers they'd have to turn just so to make it through the door. Sometimes, Linda burst out laughing once the woman in question was safely inside and Barkis would look at her, a complicit smile escaping his otherwise professional demeanor.

"The women call them 'crowns'," he said, "they are a sight some of them, but it is a tradition that goes way back and you will not see a woman without one on a Sunday church meeting or out on a shopping promenade."

Linda loved Barkis' formal speech. She hadn't heard someone speak with such formality since her days waiting for her father to finish playing the organ in church. People treated Barkis with true affection, a clap on the shoulder, or an inquiry after his wife and children. Some leaned in to ask for a special favor, often tipping him before they went into the club. He'd disappear for a few moments inside, have Linda step around to the side of the club facing 18th street and reappear having performed the task efficiently. He'd motion for Linda to come stand behind him again and whisper to her, "Anniversary" or "Birthday." From the stage Linda heard the bandleader call out a song and she'd know that Barkis had slipped a piece of paper to him.

At home, Linda practiced Barkis' elegance in the mirror; his slight bend of the head forward as if taking something in confidence, the wrap of his hand over the back of the arm, how he swept his eyes across the patrons and then closed them as if offering privacy or the slight step backward and sweep of his whole arm gathering all of the arriving guests and guiding them into the club.

One Saturday night she arrived to a crowd of people in line around the block. There was no marquee on the building, but word had spread about that night's show. There was a buzz through the line as Linda walked by, but she couldn't hear specifics. Barkis was busy shifting people gently away from the door and directing them around the corner. He was offering condolences to the regulars as he was stepping aside to let invited guests in. He spotted Linda.

"A special night," he said nodding at an incoming guest. "Horace Silver's Quintet. Do me the favor of helping me keep the line against the building."

Linda nodded and moved down the line, embarrassed slightly, holding her arms out to make the people clear the sidewalk. She used all of Barkis' moves she'd practiced and people, first surprised by her, responded to her elegance and direction and willingly kept in line for nearly an hour until the band was finished setting up, doors opened and the stream of people were allowed to enter. She followed the last of the people in line, who'd brought her into their conversation about the coming night, one of the men bopping to a song of Silver's in his head.

Before rock n roll hit, Horace Silver could have filled a room ten times the size of The Blue Room, but jazz had fallen on hard times just as 18th and Vine had. Gone was the Hey Hey Club, The Gem Theater, the dance halls off the Paseo near 12th Street; countless clubs and businesses were vacant lots, strewn with debris and rotting wood. Gone too were the musicians who either passed on or moved to New York and New Orleans for consistent work. The people who stood in line were the true fans left for the occasional greats coming into Kansas City every so often unlike before, when a night like this was a regular occurrence, and people went from club to club all night long when rumors filtered through the crowds of who was playing where.

And so the people tonight, standing outside the only club left, were giddy, and Barkis poured on the charm and was all smiles, and before he knew what he was doing he'd ushered Linda in right through the door, stood her in back and let his elegant fingers put a beautiful hat on her that had been left behind one night by a drunken patron.

Horace took the stage, older now, but still upright at the piano, attention on the audience and then on the quintet, a slight nod, blue light shone across every black surface, his skin, the light in his eyes and all he said was, "Ladies and Gentleman, we're going to work through *Serenade to a Soul Sister* from top to bottom." The first staccato notes of *Psychedelic Sally* rang out from his fingers and the horns. Linda could not believe her luck, could picture her father next to her and she could now not only see the music, but feel it.

The hours passed too quickly and now it was two in the morning before Linda noticed. In her slight panic she looked around for a clock and when she found it, she panicked more because bus service had stopped an hour ago. She had no way of getting home and she was fifteen miles at least across town. The music was still going, Horace Silver had long gone past the new music and was reinventing songs from the past, the crowd was as intent as from the first note, drinks flowing, more rowdy, and talkback had escalated. There was a back and forth between the audience and band and some of the couples had retreated to the corners and some had gotten up to dance. There was more gospel to this music, more melody.

Linda looked for Barkis who remained outside nearly the entire time. He had not forgotten about Linda, but rather had let her get lost in the music.

The owner came up to Barkis, "What's this girl doing here this late at night?"

Barkis said, "She's come to find her father," which, to Linda, seemed somewhat true. "She'll be no trouble sir," he added, and shielded her from the big man.

"Just this once," the owner said, and disappeared back into the club.

Linda burst outside, "I've missed my bus!" Panicked, she looked up and down the street to figure a way home.

"I will take you home," Barkis said. "If you'll let me,"

Linda regarded him for a moment. She had never accepted a ride before by anyone other than her mother, let alone a black man. "You'd do that?"

"Of course. If you'll wait just ten minutes and inside the club while I walk to get my car from my apartment, I'd be happy to."

"I can walk with you."

Barkis cut her off, "Absolutely not. Go back inside." Barkis took the hat off her head and ushered her inside. He put it back in the small nook for lost things among the gloves and cigarette cases. Linda had forgotten it was on and now she felt conspicuous and apart from the crowd. She stood now just by the door as Barkis went for his car. Horace Silver finished up his set with *The Preacher*, but slowed down now, funereal, his playing lovely, the notes in combination with chords and color. The room's mood changed; what was once a celebratory evening finished on a melancholy note, and Linda wished Barkis could have heard it.

People streamed out, some in tears, quietly, slightly off-kilter from their cocktails, but snapped into a sort of reverential silence; some of them glanced at Linda, but most didn't notice her. Barkis arrived and asked after the crowd's mood and then he took Linda's arm and guided her to his old Studebaker quickly just around the corner from the club and opened the door for her.

As they traveled across town the silence was punctuated by Linda's directions home to Barkis. Finally, Linda said, "Thank you for tonight."

"I'm pleased you were able to see the show. Thank you for your help earlier."

"Oh, I didn't do much, really."

"Did you enjoy it?

"Very much. It's the best night I've ever had. I will always remember it."

"Then I'm pleased," Barkis said, "I can't guarantee you more nights inside the club."

"I didn't expect so. Tonight was enough." She might have gone a few more times, but she was worried her mother would finally catch her. Linda motioned for Barkis to turn right. They were now in neighborhoods so different from their own. Stone pillars held large glowing globes, trees hid houses from view, but there were lit windows that showed how large the houses were. Barkis shifted in his seat. "You live near here?" he asked.

Linda laughed, "Oh no, but not far. You'll see how fast the neighborhood changes."

Over the last bridge they went and now the trees were not dense; the houses bunched together like square monopoly pieces. The driveways shortened and there was a small group of shabby stores clumped at the corner where they turned: a convenience store, hair parlor and a Laundromat with a large Maytag sign lit up in blue. Utility poles lined the night sky.

"Reminds me of home," Barkis said, "Not too different from where we left. A little more trees, less cement." He chuckled and asked, "Will your mama be upset you being out so late?"

"She probably won't notice." Linda saw their street and pointed it out to Barkis. "Take a right there. I'm just up the block a bit." Linda pointed to their tiny house. There were no lights on and she was glad of it. "Just there," she said.

The car rolled to a stop as Linda turned to Barkis. "I can't thank you enough for tonight."

"Think nothing of it. You come back again. You study up on what you heard tonight."

"I have it right here." Linda pointed to her head.

"Then you need to put it here." Barkis placed his hand over his heart. "Now get on inside before trouble arrives."

Linda smiled at him, her eyes sparkling, tears welling up from memory. "I don't believe in God or heaven or anything like that, but I do believe my dad is happy."

"I'm glad for it. Now off you go." Barkis looked in the rearview mirror. Linda searched up and down the street for anyone coming. Then she slipped from the car, closed the door as quietly as she could and walked up to her home.

She looked back to see Barkis watching her, and when she opened the door, he put the car in gear and disappeared into the night.

Airstreaming

Trouble

In the dark, Linda's mother waited with a glass of water. She had returned to the couch from the front window and took a sip. Clare saw the car, the black man at the wheel and Linda hesitating to get out. She'd been home from Smith's for three hours and gone to bed, TV rolled into her bedroom on its casters now that Linda had stopped watching it. In the past three weeks, Linda only listened to her music, the records stacked three high, and the only reprieve Clare had from the noise was the twenty seconds it took for the next record to drop.

When she woke a couple of hours into the Indian head test pattern, she'd gotten up for water, gone to the bathroom between their rooms and didn't hear anything, no music or see a light on under her door. There was usually one or the other at all times. Linda fell asleep with lights on and music going and Clare had gone into her room several nights to turn both off.

When she opened the bedroom door and discovered Linda gone, there was a slight panic dulled by sleep and Smith's extra drink. Clare turned the light on and looked around the bedroom. Linda's room was as it always was, spare except for the records stacked leaning against the wall.

She went into the living room and then the kitchen to run water for the glass in her hand. She took a sip and quenched the dryness left from the alcohol. The water ran a long time as she drank and held the glass at her lips. She thought of freedom.

She turned the water off and left the kitchen. She stood for a while at the picture window staring out into the street. It was the kind of dark outside left by clear skies and no moon. She'd woken warm and the coolness of the house and window felt good. Clare was at the window for a long time and then she sat on the couch and was about to doze off when car lights scraped along the houses across the street. She went to the window and kept herself behind the drape. It seemed like several minutes until the old Ford's door opened and Linda started up the steps.

She put herself back on the couch, sipped from the glass of water and waited until the front door opened.

And she waited until Linda closed the door and turn to go quietly into her room.

"Who's the colored man?" Her voice was gray and quiet.

Linda, startled, stopped in her tracks.

"I won't ask again."

Linda stood and looked at her mother for a moment on the couch. Window light lit one side of Clare's face and sparked the crystal water glass. Linda thought to answer her, but thought better of it and continued to her room.

"It is after two in the morning and you are being driven home by a black man who let's you out of the car on our street."

Linda disappeared into her room. Clare waited for a moment to hear the door close then she got up and took her water glass to the kitchen. She set it down on the counter and waited two beats and then headed toward Linda's room and swung her door open.

"You come waltzing in here and you don't say a word to me. Not a single word," she hissed, "Not a single, solitary word."

Linda was at her closet removing her cardigan sweater. She could feel the heat rise in her neck and shoulders.

"You come home with some colored man and you don't have one thing to say. The neighbors will probably be all gossiping tomorrow about it the way they do. Have you nothing to say to me?"

Linda turned around and slipped off the sweater's last sleeve. "No."

"Did he touch you?"

Linda stared at her mother, dumbfounded now as she started to laugh. "I can't believe you."

Clare face twisted up, her lips pressed together hard, "Your father would not have allowed this, not for one second."

Linda stopped laughing and burned her eyes into her mother. "He's not here." Her back was against the closet door. Clare moved in close to her daughter and loomed large over her.

"Where were you? I want to know where you were."

"I don't ask you where you're going every Saturday night." Linda said.

"That's none of your business and you know perfectly well where I go."

"This is the first time you ever cared."

"This is the first time you ever came home after two in the morning."

"How would you know? You come home most times smelling so bad from whatever you're drinking. You don't think I notice? I go in most Saturday nights and turn the TV off. You don't think I know what you've been doing all night?"

The ceiling light disappeared behind her mother's head; the dark shadow of her face grew even closer.

"Did that man touch you? I won't ask again."

"What if he had? What if I wanted him to?" Linda was in dangerous territory and she knew it and steeled herself for what was coming. Clare coiled her arm back and brought her hand full force at Linda's face.

Linda ducked and her mother's hand hit the closet door hard, which gave way and shut completely. Clare howled and spun around to follow Linda across the room near her bed, her hand throbbing, but her anger so elevated she only saw frames of images: the bed lamp, a sock on the floor, her frightened daughter's face. She saw the stack of records on the turntable and peeled them off the spindle. She raised them high over her head and slammed them to the floor. Vinyl shattered in fragments. Linda screamed.

"You tell me what he did to you." Clare went to the stack of records and started pulling them from their sleeves, one by one, and smashed them to the floor. The sound was deafening, splintering the air like breaking glass. Clare, now out of herself, every hurt from the past year roiling inside her, her lost connection to her own family spinning around her, storming her very home.

Linda reached up to stop her mother, slipped on the vinyl, and fell into a sitting position on the floor.

Black vinyl flew around her. Shock overtook her as the last things she loved broke at her feet.

Later, sitting rigid on the edge of her bed in the blue TV light, Clare stared at nothing. Her mind was clear of everything; a cigarette burned down to her fingertips, the slippers that were on her feet were now on the floor. Her room was silent; the house was a cavern. Eventually, Clare fell back against the bed and went to sleep. The cigarette had long since slipped from her fingers to the wooden floor and went out, its ashes strewn around the tip. The rage toward her being left alone, to losing the thing she fought for – her husband – that had gathered up for so long in her was released, which soiled the house and left it stained.

Linda, still dazed in her room, her records in shattered black shards around her eventually stopped crying. She saw among the pieces some records that did not break. Slowly, she picked them out, read their centers and found the matching sleeves and gently slid them back in. She took the small stack and put them in a knapsack, got up off the floor and pulled clothes from her drawers and put them in a suitcase. She found her cardigan and put it back on.

Linda looked at herself in the mirror, rubbed out the streaks that ran down the sides of her face and smoothed her hair with her fingers. The rims of her eyes were red and tired and her arms felt heavy. She peeled a couple of pictures off her mirror: one of her father and her sitting on the front steps of the house, her arms and legs akimbo and her father laughing, head held high in the sunlight. The other of her and Barbara, much younger, in dresses standing at the front of her parent's car awkwardly smiling. She put them in the pocket of her sweater.

Linda went to the very back of her closet and reached under a stack of clothes for the sock she'd put all the money she'd saved from her job. There was almost four hundred dollars. She placed the sock in the nylon pouch inside her suitcase, closed both its latches, gathered up the knapsack and left her room.

She would not be back, she thought. She would never be back.

Linda started the long trek to Olathe on foot, knowing the way by heart. Halfway there, the sun crested over the flat earth and grasses and lightened the sky to a pale blue. It was Sunday morning. There were few cars, and none of them had wondered enough about a girl walking down the side of the road to stop. Linda had thought of Barkis, who would surely have given her a ride, kindness coming from him fluently.

Linda rested frequently, shouldered her knapsack off and sat on top of her suitcase. She had been up for nearly twenty-four hours and was bone-tired, but she was still wide-awake.

Hours stretched on as the day warmed. Linda was very thirsty and passed a house and saw a hose lying on the ground attached to a spigot. She stowed her knapsack and suitcase behind a thicket of climbing white roses at the head of the drive. She looked in the windows for movement and saw none. The light was still flat enough to see through them, but she also saw her reflection. Her hair hung down close around her face, slightly matted now from sweat and running her hands through to keep it back. Her eyes had a hard time focusing and she constantly blinked. Her shoulders rounded down in pain from carrying so much weight for so long. A blackbird skittered behind her and broke her stare and she crouched down under the window.

Linda turned the water on and drank. The cool wet ran over her lips and face. She removed her sweater and ran the water down her arms. Her shirtsleeves got wet at the shoulders, which also felt good. The icy water dripped off her fingers and light refracted in tiny smooth globes at their tips. She put her tongue out and flicked each drop into her mouth. Water cascaded out of the hose onto the ground before she realized it was still going. Reaching down, Linda turned the handle and hoped the house's inhabitants hadn't heard the water running through the pipes.

She gathered the suitcase and swung the knapsack on. Many more miles were left to go. She'd been walking for six hours having left at three in the morning. She figured three miles an hour or less with stops, which equaled eighteen. Six more to go. A game in her head named the songs on the records left in her knapsack from memory, their order and which side they were on. She said the album names out loud, then each song until she remembered them right.

Clare woke up late in the morning. The westward light through the curtains sent streaks and shadows over the wall. Disoriented, she slowly opened her eyes to the dish-like ceiling light, its faux gold rim shining. The room was warm. Her skin had a slight film of perspiration. She wiped her hand across her mouth, her eyes and felt her chest just below the neckline.

After a while, she sat up. Her nightdress hung loose about her. It was as if she were waking from drunkenness, or out of a drug-induced stupor like when she bore Linda. She startled herself awake thinking of her daughter and pulled herself from the bed, the air giving a chill to her body, to the wetness, as she moved quickly down the hallway. She opened the door to Linda's room, saw the chaos of the early morning before; black shards circled an open space in the brown carpet where Linda had last steeled herself against her mother.

"Linda?" she called going from her bedroom to the living room and into the kitchen. "Linda?" Her voice rang out, hollow and shrill, into nothing Out into the front yard she went, standing under the elm, eyes scanning the street up and down, the neighboring houses empty because they were all churchgoers and Sunday mornings beckoned them into their cathedrals.

The high sun dappled the sidewalks through the trees; broken black walnut shells peppering the neglected lawn hurt her bare feet. Clare went down the narrow side between the old Miller place and her house to the backyard. Vines had grown up over the fencing. She swatted them away and tore through until she emerged out of the thicket and into the backyard finding it empty save for the two wooden chairs, now mossy green, that her husband had entertained neighbors and friends in. It struck her, that sight, how empty the chairs looked, forgotten. She couldn't remember the last time she'd been in the backyard. Winter had come and gone, then spring and summer. She hadn't thought to water the plants, but the summer storms and rains had kept them alive.

The backyard once bustled with activity, been the center of their lives once it was warm enough to stay outside. Most neighbors screened in their back porches, but her husband always wondered what the point of that was. Mosquitoes and flies were part of the deal of summer, he said, so were bees and wasps. They were just doing their work, he'd go on, and if you let them do their work, they wouldn't bother you.

In the hottest afternoon hours they sat outside listening to the cicadas sing, high pitched, otherworldly. They heard train whistles blow as millions of bushels of wheat were moved through the train yards miles away.

Clare went to the chairs and sat in one. There was an occasional dog bark, but mostly it was quiet. She didn't need any more evidence that Linda had gone. She wondered how'd she got so mean. Did it start before her husband died, the way she was jealous of how close her daughter and he had been, the world she was excluded from? Or was his death just the trigger for thinking that she'd settled – a blind man, her own mother had asked, how on earth would she manage that? Clare stopped talking to her then – a teacher – she would have thought her own mother would have believed that Clare knew what she was doing – that she married because she was in love and damn the practical matters. Clare used to imagine her mother being better than she was, but she wasn't. And now she was no better than her. She should be out looking for Linda – calling the police, the people she knew, canvassing the neighbors, driving down streets, but she knew where Linda was going and she would drive out there soon enough to retrieve her, but now quiet – and in the quiet, she remembered thinking of freedom last night at the sink, that if she had it she might start her life over again – after all, thirty-eight was not so old.

She leaned her head back, felt the full sun on her face and thought of their lives before the trouble began, how perfect it seemed from this distance.

The sun had traveled across the sky, reached its zenith and started its western decent. Linda walked twenty-four miles, her feet ached and a blister burned her heel and her shoulders were nearly cut from the knapsack's straps. Her face and arms were sunburned, her lips dry, and the cardigan she wore for warmth was hanging down over her knees, tied at her waist. She looked down at the house she knew so well, saw Jack shoveling, the sun like a beacon off the silver trailer and the driveway's slope to a thing like refuge.

Martha, washing zucchinis, tomatoes and carrots, looked up from her business for a moment to see if she couldn't see Jack standing like he did at the head of his garden admiring his work. Instead, she caught the sight of someone at the top of the drive silhouetted against the white sky. It took her just a moment to know by her shape that it was Linda. She wasn't expected on a Sunday afternoon and Martha sensed something wrong. She dropped the vegetables in the sink and ran out the kitchen door, up the drive and called out for Jack to come help.

When she reached Linda, who stood like a statue looking past her, knapsack on her back, hand still holding the suitcase off the ground, Martha put her hand to Linda's face and brought her focus to her own.

Reaching out for the suitcase, Martha said quietly, "Here let me have that."

Jack ran up the hill and circled around the two of them, ended up behind Linda and removed the knapsack. Linda didn't say a word as Jack and Martha took her things. To Martha, Linda looked dazed, dehydrated. In a flash, she crumpled like she'd been shot. Jack flung the knapsack over a shoulder and slipped his hand under one of Linda's arms just in time. Martha had her by the other arm and Linda fell against her. She and Jack stole a glance at each other and worked to right Linda against the two of them.

The three stood on the highway for some time as Linda worked through her cries and Martha held her while Jack put his hand on her head and rounded them both against him.

After they led Linda to the house, fed her and gave her water – and after Linda fell asleep on the sofa in the den, Martha and Jack walked outside and sat in the Airstream. They talked of their plans, the idea of going away.

"We're almost there, honey." Jack said.

"I know." Martha twisted a towel in her fingers, the one she carried from the kitchen. "I have everything ready to go, everything put away. I want to go just as much as you. But now, Linda..."

Jack nodded, "I want to know why she walked all the way out here. I want to know how a mother could let her daughter walk all the way out here by herself."

"She hasn't called. Maybe she doesn't know."

"She knows." He had not liked Clare the instant he saw her, had even hesitated to consider Linda then to come to work for them because of her. She didn't exude warmth, nor any compassion, just all business.

"We really don't know Clare all that well."

Linda didn't speak of her mother much. Jack thought of Clare as someone stuck in a situation, very lost in the damage left behind by her late husband. He put his hands over Martha's to stop her fingers from twining the towel she held in knots.

He said, "Why don't we wait until we find out what's happened. We'll let her sleep; let her sleep all day tomorrow if she has to. I think she'll come 'round and we'll figure out what to do." He stood up and went over to the bench and pulled it into a sofa and moved the pillows around. "Come here," Jack said, sitting on the upholstered cushion. He reached down and pulled a blanket out of the drawer underneath him. "Come here," he held his arm out, two fingers giving her direction.

Martha left the towel on the table and moved over to Jack and crawled up into him, his smell and dirty clothes. "We'll help her," she said and looked into him.

Jack floated the blanket over the two of them and tucked the edges under. "Yes," he said.

Streaming

Martha woke in the early dark. The trailer's batteries emptied, and the small lights went out. Jack lightly snored; his leg dangled over the cushion and Martha worked to extricate herself from him as lightly as she could. Jack shifted and Martha spread the blanket over him and stepped out of the Airstream into the night air, shivered and noticed the quiet. Stars were still bright; the constellations obscured by the Milky Way's translucent mass. She stood back from the trailer - its ghostly silver hull reflected a deep blue.

Inside, the house was still warm from the day. She hadn't opened the windows for the cool air like she usually did. She turned the kitchen light on and walked into the living room illuminated slightly from the bending light. Linda was deeply asleep.

The phone was quiet all night. She wondered if Clare thought to think her daughter might be here. Martha couldn't think of where else Linda might have gone. Back in the kitchen, Martha picked up the phone and carried it just outside the door, its cord uncoiling catching in the doorjamb. She dialed.

"Hello?" a flat, sleepy voice answered.

"This is Martha."

"Who?"

"Martha Pearson." Martha, annoyed, touched her bottom lip to the receiver and held it there until there was recognition.

"Oh yes. How's my daughter?"

"You know she's here?"

"She didn't have another place to go did she?" Clare's voice came stronger now.

"I wouldn't know, but yes, she showed up yesterday." Martha couldn't help let the next slip, "You should be ashamed of yourself."

Silence. And then Clare's deep breath and controlled anger. "Has she told you why she left?"

"I fed her and gave her water and she went to sleep straight away." Martha, who was leaning against the house, slid slowly down the wall so that her knees were at the same level as her chin. "She has blisters on her feet and she's sun-burnt."

"That's a choice she made to leave that way."

"She must have had a very good reason." Martha said with a finality that surprised her, but damn her politeness as she added, "It seems I woke you."

Martha sat at the banquette for the remaining hour before daylight running over her conversation with Clare. How could a mother be so unloving? How would she know what to do with Linda? Clare would surely come collect her when she woke and take Linda back. But what did Linda need?

Morning revealed the Airstream. She went to it, found Jack as she'd left him, removed the blanket, began unbuttoning his shirt and jeans, and took his smell deep into her. Jack woke and put his hands on her waist and guided her in his hazy waking. Martha lost herself coming back to Jack and when they finished, she lay across him like some attachment – moss to a tree – feeding off his strength.

"Welcome home," he said.

"Yes." Martha held him inside her as long as she could. "I'm sorry for not being ready for this until now."

"No need," he said, and kissed her, "anything is possible now," Jack was thinking that it was true, that the air had changed, gears had locked into place instead of spinning out of control. Sparks returned to the plugs, diodes lit up behind headlamps and the night-darkened road revealed the lines by which to navigate the future.

As they dressed, they talked about Linda, what to do. Martha told him of her conversation with Clare. They decided to wait and find out what happened with Linda, to see what she would reveal.

They left the trailer and Martha made breakfast while Jack showered. Linda came into the kitchen.

"I didn't expect you up so early." Martha said, breaking eggs into a bowl. She motioned Linda over to the banquette, "Here, sit."

"I'm sorry I just showed up like that."

"Sorry isn't a word we use around here anymore." Martha set a glass of orange juice in front of Linda. "Drink this." Linda emptied the glass. Martha poured her more. "Jack and I want you to stay as long as you need to. We talked about it earlier." Martha put her hand on Linda's head and moved it down smoothing her hair and then cupped her chin. She returned to the eggs.

Linda regarded the offer. Her body ached and she lapsed into silence. She watched Martha work and began to think of ways to not go back home. Maybe she'd leave again. She could take the four hundred dollars and buy a ticket anywhere. She noticed the kitchen was clear of the boxes and assumed the two of them were ready to go. She'd feel bad if she kept them from their trip even if it was a test run for the new trailer and that they were only going to be gone a few days.

"Your boxes are gone."

"Finally, can you believe it?" Martha laughed.

"You're about to leave."

"Well, yes." Martha put down the fork she was whipping the eggs with. "We won't if you need to stay. We can go whenever we want."

"I can go to another place." Linda lowered her eyes from the lie.

Jack wandered in, hair wet, the top of his trousers unbuttoned. He was vaguely aware of things around him because he was in good spirits for the first time in a long time and that drew him into himself. He was startled to find Linda in the kitchen.

"This is a surprise," he said. He moved close behind Martha, gave her a kiss on her neck - theatrical and possessive. "The resilience of the young."

Martha laughed, "You're not that old." She reached back and squeezed his side and brought him tighter against her back. Then she pushed him away and pointed to the banquette, "go sit."

She split the eggs over toast across three plates and took them to the table. She put the coffee percolator in the center with three cups and slid in next to Jack leaving plenty of room for Linda. She didn't want to crowd her. Linda had only followed Martha with her eyes the entire time she made breakfast. Martha felt entirely new in this. Motherly. A sensation she liked. Their eyes met several times and when Jack came into the kitchen, she was embarrassed at his show of affection. But then Linda smiled and dropped her eyes giving them privacy, but when she lifted them again, Martha saw a trace of tears.

Jack made short work of breakfast and noticed that Linda didn't touch her food. "You should eat."

"I know."

"Take your time, sweetheart." Martha shot a look at Jack, reached over to Linda and stroked her forearm. "You just eat in your own sweet time."

"I want to," Linda moved her fork along the plate's edge. "I'm not that hungry."

Linda's arrival circled the two of them around her. Like bringing home a stray. Wonder, Fear. Joy. Emotions and actions that had been missing for several months was a problem to be solved. Martha worked around the edges of Linda's need for quiet until she could wait no longer. So the next thing she said she presented carefully: "I spoke to your Mother earlier while you were asleep. I had to let her know you were here and being taken care of."

"Did she ever call here looking for me?"

"Not that I know of, she might have, Jack and I fell asleep in the trailer overnight."

"Did she care?" This came sharp.

Martha, who didn't have the capacity to lie, said, "I don't expect she did or she didn't indicate she was coming to pick you up."

Linda exhaled slowly like letting go. "She will when she needs something."

Jack asked, "Do you want her to?"

"No."

Martha felt the need to investigate.

"Linda..."

"I hate her." Linda swept her eyes over both of them. "I won't go back. I'll disappear where she won't find me."

"What happened, dear?" Martha gingerly asked, now needing something in her fingers to roll up and keep her hands busy.

Needing to talk like she'd been closed up for days, Linda's voice like a stick breaking, words spilling forward from a great chasm said, "She broke all my records. Smashed them all on the ground. She screamed at me because I came home late. And she goes out all the time and I make my own money and she takes it and I don't go to school and there's nothing left because she sold the piano and took all his clothes away and I can't crawl in their closet anymore where his clothes used to be or sit on the piano bench and just put my fingers on the keys. I only have these records I carried. I want to play them and I want to listen to them like we used to listen to them and when my mom was gone I played them over and over until she got home and told me to turn down the music even though I put the dial only at two. And the Millers are gone and my daddy's gone and I want to tell him so much but I can't. I wanted to tell him about you and your baby."

Martha caught her breath. Jack closed his palm over her hand.

"I am far away from everyone and now you will be gone and winter is coming and snow and I will be stuck." All this realization made Linda sit up straight where she sat and she got a faraway look in her eyes while the two across from her reeled from the wave of words. "I'm stuck," she said again. "I'm stuck so hard."

Silence overtook the three. Steam rose from the percolator leaving behind coffee's earthy smell. Outside, noise and clatter could be beating the air, but they wouldn't have noticed.

Martha formed plans for leaving. The mention of snow wrenched forward the loss of her parents, the one memory she had being carried from the house after she lost the baby. Finality. Snow had an ending quality, the touch and taste of it on her at the hospital's roof. The thing she dreaded coming: its relentless white silence.

Then Linda ate. And Jack and Martha watched her clear the plate.

Change so mercurial in her, Linda did the only thing she knew how to do. She stood up, took all of the plates, the egg-coated bowl from the counter, the frying pan still warm off the stove and put them in the sink. The forks and knives clattered, the glass rang like bells. She turned the water on and felt the cold disappear.

"I can still do this." She said over the running water, over the clank of dishes, "Can't I? I can stay and do this?"

Later, the steam from the bathroom escaping, Linda inside cleaning off the road, the dust, the remnants of her squatting behind trees and bushes along the way, Linda leaned against the wall under the cascading water. Standing at the place where a life ended. She was intent on plans. Going away plans.

Linda felt different in the house. She was not working, not going about her chores, not thinking forward to the day's end. The shower felt good on her body. She surveyed the shower's bottles and soaps. Head and Shoulders for Jack. Milk Plus 6 for Martha. She washed her hair with it and ran her finger in the blue Noxzema bottle and rubbed the cream over her face. She wondered if she looked as beautiful as Grace Kelly, white covering her. She washed her face clean, turned the water off, stepped out of the tub and tucked the towel left on the sink around her. It all felt new. She wasn't cleaning after others.

Martha left clothes for her on the vanity counter. Linda picked up the pile, brought it to her face to smell. She had left everything – from underwear to socks, a red shirt with a light plaid pattern and blue jeans that were a little snug, but fit at the length. Linda stood at the mirror for the first time in a long time and stared at the red shirt, how it made her seem tall and thin. The cut was tight at the waist giving her shape. She was reminded that the boys at school shot looks at her and then retreated to their whispering groups. She missed school, it's clamor, and the way the days could have been about anything. Maybe now, here at Jack and Martha's, it could be that way again.

Brushing her thin hair gave it some life and she tucked strands of it behind one ear. Opening the drawer where she knew Martha kept her perfumes and lipsticks, she examined the colors by pulling off the lids and putting the red or pink tips up against her lips. She did not dare to use them, but she wanted to imagine some kind of otherness like she'd felt leaving for the dance so long ago.

After she'd put Linda's clothes in the washer, Martha found Jack in the front clearing away the debris he and Carl had left. "Hitch the Airstream to the Ford."

"What?"

"Let's take the trailer out. We'll stop at that lake we used to go to. We'll pick up some fixings for sandwiches."

"But I have to go into work. It's Monday."

"You're sick, you couldn't possibly work today," she said, lightly. Now she begins to lie, she thought, "I'll call Carl."

"What if he calls later to check up on me or there's some sort of problem."

"Oh, Jack, I would have said something like that not too long ago." She went over and worked her arm around his waist. "Hitch up the trailer." Then she placed the palm of her hand on his cheek, the stubble flicking her lightly and her lips on it again for the second time that morning, "Please. Let's go streaming."

"Where on earth did you hear that?"

"From you," she said, "While you worked." The dream quality of a word like 'streaming' that Martha had misheard Jack muttering over and over as he polished.

"Airstreaming," he said, when he was outside one evening, clouds buffeted by strong winds strafing the sky, tornado season afoot, their translucent reflections streaming over the mirrored surface.

"Yes," Jack said, "Let's go streaming."

Independence

Clare woke after one in the afternoon, the room stuffy, light hazy but sparking dust motes hanging in the air. It was a slow waking. She opened her eyes, wiped across them to help her vision clear. The phone call to Martha came back to her and the night before, the confrontation with Linda. She pulled the blanket down and uncovered herself to her knees hoping the air would cool her, but it only served to expose her and make her uncomfortable.

She put her finger to her temple where it throbbed for relief. Last night's drinks were still on her tongue despite the water she drank. Finally, she swung her feet to the floor and sat on the edge of the bed. The phone call with Martha came back to her; the woman's obvious judgment of her in her voice scratched at Clare. She looked at the clock, put her hands on her knees for support and stood. A sharp pain stitched her lower back, but she ignored it and went into the bathroom between their rooms and turned the shower on. The water came through cold and she turned it slightly warmer so that the water was just cooler than the air. She slid her nightdress off, stepped into the shower and stood under it for several minutes lost in thought letting her body cool until she fully woke.

She tried her voice, which came out hoarse and low. She said her husband's name and then Linda's and cried.

She warmed the water enough so that when she got out, the air would cool her. In the last remaining moments, she washed her hair, soaped her face and scrubbed the night off. Stepping over the lip of the tub she felt new – the long year scrubbed away, battles with her daughter were wounds closing, her husband's death a palpable, but receding hurt. She was once loved, she could be loved again despite the pain she'd inflicted. She'd act like a mother again to Linda.

Driving out to Olathe, Clare could not get comfortable in her seat. She rolled down the window, she turned music on, she put her hand out the window to wave air against her face and feel it in her hair. She stopped at the A&W for a cheeseburger, root beer freeze and fries and watched families order, eat and go: little girls hanging on to their mother's dresses, a father palming his boy's head like a basketball making him look up at the menu and make choices, them sitting together, eating, reaching across to wipe mouths, share fries, look at each other with that easy way of knowing what each were thinking.

She remembered all that, the years when Linda was young, but it had always been some sort of competition for her daughter that her husband dismissed. It was clear the two shared a connection. When Linda entered her teens, she was hopelessly lost to her daddy and Clare was left to go to work and come home, circle around them needing a sign to be included, just a little, to feel connected to them. She dreaded the moment she and her husband left the bed in the morning, the confines of their small room where they talked, stroked each other's backs, made love, burrowed into each other like animals in winter. She was glad of his blindness, for his hands were his eyes, and he would move them across her as if constantly finding her. She was glad when the years turned and Linda no longer needed the safety of their bed and they returned to their private nights and mornings. When he died there was no one to explain this to. And her anger engulfed the space she held for love.

Coming upon Jack and Martha's house she had a sense of contrition, that she'd explain herself and make amends to Linda. At the top of the drive she sensed something different. The trailer was gone, and their car. Drapes were pulled across windows. She came to a stop, got out and walked down the drive knowing that a knock on the door would be futile. But she knocked, waited and knocked again. All the thoughts of contrition and humility were now replaced by fear and a rising anger again that they would take Linda away without calling, without some sort of note left.

She walked around the entire house and peered in the windows she could. Looking through one of them she saw Linda's empty knapsack draped over an armchair. Clare continued around the house looking for some sort of entry into why Linda was gone and where the couple had taken her.

The trailer bounced the back of the car up and down when they went over rough road. Jack kept looking in the rearview to make sure that it was still there.

"I think Carl and I are going to have to make some sort of sway bar or something to keep the trailer from bouncing and shifting back and forth." Jack said to no one in particular.

"Maybe he can come out on the weekend." Martha said. "I'll fix supper."

Linda sat behind Martha and watched the land sweep past the window. They'd left any sort of town and were out in the low rolling hills. Martha was all giddy and light remarking on the day's adventure and holding her husband's hand on the seat between them. Jack's arm rested on the doors lip and his finger held the wheel.

Linda rolled her window down. Air swirled around the car's interior, swirled her hair around her like sugar in cotton candy makers.

"Oh, that feels good on the neck." Martha said, "Can you imagine doing this everyday of your life, Linda? Just moving from place to place, your home attached to you? All you have to do is pull over and set up house!"

Linda didn't respond.

"Well, I can. I can do this the rest of my life. "

Linda watched the back of Martha's head, how she'd flick a finger back and scratch just behind her ear often enough to be some sort of tic. She had not seen this before. She did it more when she talked so as Martha rattled on about living on the road, Linda counted the times she scratched.

"Can you imagine the things you'd see and the people you'd meet?"

One... two...

"Not a care in the world..."

Three...

"How about food and money?" Jack said, his voice of reason rearing up like a sentry.

"We'll do odd jobs. Work for a bit and then move on."

Four and five... Linda used her hand to count.

"That's a fine idea," Jack said, snapping to the wishful thinking like he was catching on to a plan. "We'd work fields and take some of the harvest for food."

"Exactly." Martha laughed. "Now you're talking."

Linda began opening the fingers on her closed hand.

"The three of us could make a go of it across all those small highways. We'll stay off the interstates like bandits." Martha turned in her seat. "Wouldn't that be an interesting life, Linda? Wouldn't that just be, oh, I don't know, the world just opening up to us?"

Linda snapped her fists shut, smiled at Martha and said, "I suppose it would."

Martha slid closer to Jack and he worked his arm around her shoulders stopping her tic. Linda studied the two of them. They launched her into memories of her own father and mother, but the roles reversed, her mother driving and father up close to her. It was too much like the past and because Linda was overly tired, deep feelings welled up in her so she shut her eyes to the coming tears and rested her head against the door.

When she woke, they had pulled to a stop at the entrance to Pomona Lake. From where they were they couldn't see it, but a sign directed them forward through tall oaks and poplar trees breaking the light.

Only the trailer's rattle was heard as the three of them waited for the view to come over the slight rise. And now, cresting the hill, the lake was shining blue, trees bright green and the late summer grass turning gold defined the horizon.

Jack pulled off and stopped the car. All three left it without a word and just stood looking at the view together. Jack satisfied, Martha serene and Linda remembering what beauty felt like.

The weekend campers and people had cleared away back to their cities. Just a couple of campers remained, one set up for the summer's duration, the other locked and cleared of any chairs or camping equipment. Jack backed into one of the stalls after going around the campground twice to find the best and deepest stall to hold the Airstream and the car.

"Well, I think that about works," he said, checking the side view mirror. "You girls happy with the spot?"

Martha leaned in and kissed Jack on the cheek. Linda got out of the car. She walked to the lake. Spartina grew from the marshes and there were a few ducks just outside the reeds bleating, upending themselves to feed. Blackbirds hung on the taller reeds and darted to and from overhanging branches to the water. Linda hunched down and scooped water in her palms watching the bending reflections of her eyes and sky. Water dripped through her fingers.

Jack came up behind Linda and sat on the gravel. Martha had stayed behind and gone into the trailer.

"You've had a go of it, eh Linda?"

Linda let out a "hmmm" and let the rest of the water go. She dried her hands on her thighs and sat back next to Jack.

"We didn't realize how much you were dealing with." Jack pushed on. "Martha and I want you to know that you can stay with us as long as you need. We'll have to let your mom know, of course, but the offer's there if you want to take it. You've been good to us in our time."

"You wouldn't mind if I stayed?" Linda let out a long sigh.

"Wouldn't mind at all. In fact, I think Martha would quite enjoy it."

"I don't have anything."

"We can work on that. We'll fix you up with some clothes and fix up the other room for you."

"All I have are my records."

Jack laughed, "I thumbed through them while you were sleeping. They look like good ones."

Linda smiled at him finally. "They are, but some of the best ones were broke."

"Maybe you go into work with me one day and spend some time walking the stores and go find yourself some of those records to replace. I'll give you some money."

Defensive again, Linda said, "I have money."

Jack considered that. "I know, but you have to start letting people take care of you again."

"I'm not so good with that."

"Well, give it a try. I'll make sure Martha doesn't smother you too much," Jack said and chuckled. They sat for a while and looked out over the lake and then Jack said, "Do you want to go back to school? You know it's starting up again real soon."

"I'm too far behind, a whole year. I'd feel like a dummy."

"No harm in going back, given what you've been through."

Linda let the school talk drop and fade. She looked over her shoulder to the trailer searching out Martha. "Is Martha okay?"

"She seems fine. Seems she's gotten through the worst of it. You helped a lot with that, you know. That's something…"

"I didn't do all that much."

"What is it you most want to do in the world?" Jack asked.

Linda looked out to the water and then to Jack, "You're going to laugh. Because it really doesn't amount to much."

"What?"

"I want to learn to drive." Linda surprised even herself. Maybe it was the freedom of it, watching Jack handle the Ford or having the opportunity to just up and go anywhere. Of course, there's the matter of owning a car, but the idea of it – just the ability, the thought to be able to leave at any time would be enough.

"Ok, done." Jack stood up, held out his hand to Linda and pulled her up. "After lunch you'll have your first lesson."

Martha had set out paper plates, napkins and cups on the table inside the Airstream. She'd been fixing sandwiches and watching Jack and Linda at the lake's edge from the louvered window. She'd opened it up to let the breeze through. She saw them talking, which was good. Jack could draw Linda out the way she couldn't.

Martha's comfort in such a small space as the Airstream surprised her given the hospital and her need to escape outside to the cold. But the work! The work itself was the pleasure. Fixing sandwiches for three. She took care in slicing the tomatoes, tearing lettuce, pulling the turkey apart, spreading mayonnaise and putting it together. When they came in, she'd have it all ready, drinks from the cooler, chips, cookies. It is not a small thing to do this, she thought, not small at all.

Jack took a moment to unhitch the trailer from the Ford and wind the wheel down to stabilize it. He'd forgotten to do it when they arrived to take the weight off the Ford, but it was all in the learning he figured. He'd work to learn the set-up for staying awhile in one place, setting the wheel blocks, unhooking the rear light electric cable, pulling the awning out and hooking up to the outside electrical line, but after lunch and after the first driving lesson for Linda.

When Jack entered, Linda and Martha were at the table, which Martha had pulled out and covered with a picnic cloth. There was an array of sandwiches and sodas in the center. So much of what Martha did now was with detail. Nothing was out of place, not a single thing; the silverware, pickles, chips, cookies did not go forgotten. Jack bent to kiss Martha lightly on the forehead, "Looks great, hon."

"I hope everything is good." Martha said, reaching behind and touching the back of her neck.

Again, Linda thought, but decided to concentrate less on that than on the lesson she and Jack talked about on the way up from the lake.

"Did Linda tell you what we're doing this afternoon?" Jack sat and took a sandwich from the collection. Martha shook her head.

"We're giving Linda driving lessons."

"Now that's a surprise." Martha said, delighted.

"It's time she learned, no?"

"High time."

Linda sat low in the Ford. They both laughed as Jack tilted the seat back forward and went to the trailer to retrieve a pillow for her to sit on. Now she could see over the dashboard fine. Jack slid in next to her and began describing knobs, what the letters on the instrument panel stood for as the red needle pointed to them when she pulled the handle down attached to the steering column. He described gears and gauges, acceleration and braking, speed and how the engine worked. He was patient, methodical and extraordinarily happy. Linda asked a few questions and he answered. All the while, Jack was thinking that he would have been doing this with his son sixteen years on, but here was Linda and he relished the idea of passing on what he knew to her; the things he'd learned about cars all these years.

Jack had put the Ford on a straight line down the middle of the camp road. He assumed there would be no one coming and for the next hour they circled around the camp, lurching at first and then, as Linda learned her foot's pressure, the car glided over the gravel. They stopped and started several times, kicking the engine over so Linda could feel it. The instrument panel fascinated Linda who asked what each dial and number, letter and gauge was for two or three times even after Jack had explained them until she understood. The Ford wagon, unencumbered by the trailer's weight, was all sun-sparked glistening chrome and steel as they drove under canopies of oak trees; their branches elongated over the protruding teal hood and shadowed the window.

Linda was mesmerized by the power beneath her. Her mother's Mercury was nothing like this car. It felt strong, like it could go for days without stopping – the touch of her foot against the pedal meant freedom, independence so that now, all she wanted was to hurry through the lessons and get her license. She could think of nothing else throughout the day when they circled back to the Airstream, and Martha, and the walk the three of them took along the lake's edge until they met the brackish marsh water and watched pintails and the land's ubiquitous blackbirds cartwheel through the tall reeds.

After the driving lesson, Martha came up behind Linda and placed her hand on her shoulder. She brought her in tight. "I understand Jack told you, you could stay as long as you want. I'd like that and I just wanted you to hear it from me. I know you all depend on what you earn from us. We'll figure that out. I hope you'll consider it."

Linda didn't quite know how to respond. If it meant learning to drive and being away from her mother until she could figure things out, then she was all for it. But it was more complicated, she knew. The fact of her mother as a force, her own tornado, destructive as she might seem would be a strong thing to put down.

Linda said, "I think you might have a fight ahead of you with my Mom."

"We'll try and reason with her." Martha said, thinking they had the trump card of Clare's bad behavior toward her daughter and, to her mind, sheer negligence. Letting a 16-year-old child walk all that way, or giving her cause to do so nearly caused her to call the police.

"Would you like to stay with us for the time-being?" Martha took her by the shoulders and turned Linda to her. She wanted a clear confirmation from Linda before she entered into the rocky terrain of Clare. It was clear to her that the next conversation with her would be difficult.

"I would." Linda said.

"That's all we need to hear," Martha said and pulled Linda in for a hug.

Linda was unsure of all of it. To her, Jack and Martha had been good, yes, but she'd never considered them before as more than people she worked for despite their troubles and her being available to them. But the events of the year changed all that. The time she'd spent she'd learned a lot about them, but how would she fit in? She hung back as Jack and Martha stepped closer to the lake's edge. Martha's weight returned to her so that her shifts and jeans filled out now and Jack had lost weight, trimming up from the diner food he'd grown accustomed to. Both had returned to the world where she was still unsure of it, battered by events, the chaos of death, anger and leaving. Maybe their offer had come just in time.

The three of them watched Canadian geese circle and come in to land against the reeds edge. There were five of them, shuffling the water off their feathers, gathering together after a day's flight. Their long, black necks with the etch of white at their cheeks, gleaming black beaks, rounded breasts reflected in the settled water making them seem larger. They moved closer together, watchful for a moment before languidly floating away from each other because they felt safe.

Linda moved up next to Jack and Martha, the sun's heat against them, its lowering a sign for them to head home.

Airstreaming

Wind

In the dark, Jack drove. Martha relaxed against the seat and Linda slept. It was an eventful day and Jack had learned much about how to trailer the Airstream: the pulling away, the braking and how it tugged slightly on the back of the Ford. It was easy to hitch it up and take it off. He practiced it a few more times while he was on the road and away from the safety of their home. The silver was dulled by gravel dust.

In only a few hours Jack could see the change in his wife. She looked out and up now, where before she kept her head down like she was counting to herself and trying to keep numbers in her head before they disappeared. She had tenaciously taken to the details of going away and he feared the intensity was too much. He feared her latching on to Linda – maybe they both were as some sort of life raft, but he'd work something out with Clare. His anger toward her did not abate and he hoped he could keep it together if she showed at the house. Martha had been practical a year ago, but he'd only seen fleeting moments of it since the baby. He was watching for signs of her lapsing into silences or melancholy. This day had been a gift, and he felt certain that the path ahead was right. During the drive, he watched Martha hold her hand out the window and open her fingers to let the wind flow through and then close them to make her hand into a kite. It reminded him of their drives just after they met.

Linda fell asleep on the way home, which gave them satisfaction that she was comfortable enough to do so. She stretched across the back seat, which was now dark from the receding horizon light.

"Thank you." Martha said, stretching her hand out to place it on his thigh.

"For what?"

"For what comes next."

"We'll see what happens. I just don't want to rile our hopes up and have Clare come down hard on us about Linda."

"I was thinking about us. Whether Linda stays is really more up to her than Clare or what we say."

"I suppose you're right," Jack said, his mind filtering her words, realizing she'd returned to her practical self. It was good to hear. "I think you like this," he said, sweeping his hand over the dashboard as if he were showing her the whole outside, "I think we could survive doing this, streaming, like it was just us and the road."

"I know I would," Martha pulled her hair back, touched her neck, "I know I would like being away. The house is all memory to me now."

"Yes."

"You could quit your job."

"I could. How about we think about it in the spring now that we're coming on fall?"

"We could go to California for the winter. Can you imagine a winter without snow?" Martha said, turning to Jack.

"Now that would be something."

"I don't think I've ever had a winter without snow." For a moment the two of them silently drifted, their minds conjuring warmth. Martha scooted across the bench seat into Jack. He lifted his arm and drew her in.

"Let's see what's in store for us the next few days," Jack said.

Thirty minutes from Olathe, the sky disappeared. Jack felt the sideways tug from strong winds at the rear of the Ford. Martha was upright in her seat. The languid day was replaced by concern. Linda was still asleep. Jack pressed on; he felt the need for them to get to the safety of their home as quickly as possible. They were at the tail end of tornado season and hundreds touched down across the Midwest each year.

He had a fascination for how the sky turned red and everything became silent: the insistent cicada whir stopped, the air smelled of steel and electricity and the deep pockets of lowering gray funneled and collapsed like darkened paper lanterns. Jack loved the work closing up the house, pulling all the loose tools into the garage and making everything ready. Sometimes, he'd stand outside until the last bearable minute that Martha could stand just so he could watch and then down into their cellar they'd go, waiting for danger to pass.

This storm didn't seem nearly as severe and he turned on the AM radio, which woke Linda. The static combated with the radio voice and now all three were intent on sorting out the weather news.

Jack tried to calm Martha and Linda a little, "These guys can't know what's going on. I swear they just read some report coming from some far off place from some station. I know they aren't right here, right now. I can't see anything more than a few gusts."

"Jack, the station's out of the city."

"I know, but we're miles from the city."

The wind whistled through the black rubber around the windows. The car's back swung abruptly and then shifted back into place. She'd never felt exposed to weather before. Always, at home, her father had seemed as confident as Jack. He could smell a storm miles away and waited for the quiet to settle in before taking her and her mother down to the basement, which had only happened a couple of times in her entire life.

The three of them had traveled enough now to see the lights of Olathe in the distance. The rolling hills of scrub, oaks and black walnut trees were curved horizon lines and the sky turned gunmetal gray with shades of purple. Lightning started flashing through the cloud ceiling like exploding light bulbs sending rumbles overhead.

Martha gripped her hands into one fist and everything in her tightened. Jack sensed her and drew her in again. Linda watched the sky unfolding: an overture to the impending storm.

"A few minutes and we'll be home." Jack said.

"Can I stay with you for the night?" Linda asked.

Both Jack and Martha looked back at her.

"Of course you can." Martha said. Had they taken too much for granted already? Did Linda really belong with them? Martha's mind twisted around so many questions suddenly that she forgot about the storm.

"You can stay as long as you want, Linda, you know that, don't you?" Jack chimed in because the thought of Martha being set off worried him.

"I guess I wasn't sure." Linda said.

Martha turned in her seat, "We will fix the den up for you. Make it yours. We'll call your mom, when we get home."

"I don't want to talk to her." Linda said, flatly.

Martha took a beat and reached over the seat and touched Linda's hand. "You don't have to, but we should tell her you're safe. All mothers want to know that despite what happens. I sent postcards and letters to my parents, but I never heard a word from them. But I always felt that they wanted to at least know I was alive." Martha held onto Linda's gaze a moment and turned back in her seat.

The sky continued its show and they all listened for the next sonorous booms and orchestral tympanis, and Jack wrestled the cars steering wheel to keep the Airstream and car on the road.

When he swung down the driveway, he saw Clare's car before anyone else did. The sky lit it up intermittently like a warning, so he slowed the car and trailer to a crawl to at least let Martha and Linda take in the idea of it before they pulled up next to her.

"Linda, your mother is here." Jack said.

Martha shot straight up in her seat. Linda leaned forward to look and make sure it was true, that it was their car. The pit of her stomach churned and she nearly felt sick. The air in the car heated.

Martha turned again to her and said, "You stay here with me."

Jack braked the car slightly behind Clare and turned the engine off. He peered through the front window to see if he could see Clare's shape in the darkness. "It will be ok. I'll go and see if she's in her car. I can't make anything out." A flash revealed Clare's outline above the seat amid a swirl of smoke. Jack was all determination now – anger coming to the surface, that sensation he got when he was ready for some sort of battle.

He stepped out of the car. A gust of wind caught the car door and pulled it open, but he held it fast and then shut it hard. The bombast outside of wind and drums sent him to Clare's car faster than he might have gone and his anger at this woman he barely knew caught him up as well. He rapped on her window and Clare looked up at him, pulled the cigarette from her mouth and extinguished it in the ashtray. What Jack saw was defeat, the woman's eyes tired and drawn, mouth slack. The anger left him just as quickly as it came. He stood there looking at the woman, the wind whipping around him and into her car. He didn't know what to say.

"Is Linda with you?" she asked.

"Yes."

"That's all I need to know."

"Don't you want to see her?"

"Of course. But I doubt she wants to see me."

"No, she doesn't." Jack felt the first drops from the sky opening up. Lightning burst from the clouds in long, jagged tendrils beyond the hills.

"How long have you been waiting?"

"Two packs worth," Clare said, holding out a near empty package of Pall Malls. "I should be going – the weather, you see." Clare turned the engine over which idled like low thunder.

"You can't drive in this rain. Nor should you be out in the lightning." Jack looked back to the car and imagined the two were waiting on him, expecting Clare's car to back out of the driveway, the moment in question to be easily resolved. "I need to get the other two inside. Can you wait here?"

"If I leave now, I can get home before the worst of it."

"It's starting now. Shut your engine down and just wait." His irritation was returning like a slight tremor.

Clare turned the engine off.

Jack went to the Ford and opened the door, looked in, two expectant faces looked back and said, "Why don't you two go in to the house and let me get Clare situated?"

"She's not leaving." Martha said as if as a statement of fact.

"It's too dangerous out to drive back to the city. Linda, if you want to go back into our room or the den and wait it out, that is fine with me, but I want you two inside now before it gets too bad."

"I'll put on some coffee," Martha offered up.

"That'd be fine. Now get going and I'll see to Clare."

Martha and Linda went into the house, Linda to the den who listened intently to the inarticulate sounds coming from the kitchen. Martha busied herself scooping grounds from the Folgers can, putting them into the percolator's metal cup, filling it with water. The new stress of Clare waiting there for them confused her. She couldn't see to how this woman thought about things. And just when Linda might be comfortable with the idea of settling in their home for a time. She wondered how Clare could face even her after their morning phone call let alone her driving her daughter to walk all the way out here like she did.

The water had already started boiling up into the percolator's see-through top before Clare came in followed by Jack. Martha leaned against the stove and steeled herself. She'd let Jack take the lead.

Jack motioned to the banquette and told Clare to sit. "Martha will have some coffee for you. I'll be back in a moment."

Clare sat at the banquette with her eyes down, not making any sort of contact with Martha until a cup appeared before her with coffee steaming up in her eyes so she had to look up. Martha stood a few feet away. Clare could see she was waiting for something from her..

"I owe you an apology for the phone call this morning." Clare had never believed in contrition until this very day: the prospect of losing absolutely everything a possibility.

"Jack and I were going to call the police. It's absolutely shameful what you've done to her." Martha was over her, coffee pot in her hand, steaming.

"You haven't any idea how hard it's been." Clare cupped her hand around the coffee and watched Martha warily.

"To see a young girl at the top of our driveway in the shape she was. Missing her whole year of school."

Clare shot back, "I believe she was a big help to you."

Martha took several moments to answer and went back to the counter and put the pot down. "Yes, of course..."

"And you know our situation."

"Yes," Martha said, deflated."

"I feel about as bad as any mother could," Clare said, "as sick and pained by what Linda has been made to do and troubled by the things she's seen. But I can't change circumstances."

"She doesn't want to go home." Martha said.

"I'm not here to make her go." Clare began to gather her things to leave. "I just wanted to make sure she was safe."

"How come you waited so long to come out here then? Any mother would have done anything she could..."

"I knew she was here."

Martha hesitated, "I think an apology would be appropriate to your daughter. Do you have any idea of what she did to get here?" Martha's voice rose slightly though she was trying to tame it.

Clare eyed her car keys on the table wanting to take them up just then and bolt out the door into the night and the devil may care with the storm. She wanted out. She'd apologize to Linda later, but now she just wanted to go. But outside, the storm was bearing down, water lashed the windows, wind pushed at the door slamming it shut on escaping. Every few minutes, blue light flashed against the cupboards and across the countertops and shortly thereafter, the house shook from its explosion. Though no tornado would come of this, the summer storm's violence tore trees apart and downed power lines sending sparks across streets. The storm proved to be a conversation starter for weeks to come.

Clare took a sip of coffee, "I didn't know she left until I woke in the morning. If I'd heard her, I would have stopped her."

"She would have left any way she could given her determination. You could see it in her eyes." Martha said. "She was terrified when she arrived and exhausted."

Clare was grappling at things she wished she knew about, Clare who was once imposing to Martha was now rumpled and insignificant. How does a year take hold of one's life and utterly destroy it? She knew the last, indeed. Maybe Jack left them together here in the kitchen's safety because he knew that both she and Martha were somehow equals and could talk about their losses.

"And I am sorry for it." Clare said. A statement. "The last fifteen years got tied up in ten minutes the other night - all of them. All of them came together. Like something you can't break. I couldn't stop it and I'm sorry. I know Linda will never forgive me for it, but I do want her home. She's all I have left."

"I don't think she's ready to go home."

"That may be true, but she's still mine."

"That may be in question as well. I don't think Jack will let her go with you tonight. I know I won't."

"Is that a threat?"

"No."

"You think you can just lay claim to Linda like that?"

"No, I'm not laying claim to Linda."

"She's not some replacement..." Clare wished she had stopped before her mouth opened.

Stunned, Martha said, "How dare you," and moved away from Clare farther into the kitchen behind the cupboards that separated it from the banquette.

Clare stood up and went to Martha and stopped just in front of her. She reached her hand out and touched her cheek. "I don't know how I've gotten so mean," she said, and for a moment the two women stared at each other, "I was here the night you lost your baby. I cleaned up after you with Linda. We wiped your bathroom's floor clean. We burned the soiled sheets. We saw you to the ambulance and spent the night cleaning. We worked until morning." Clare, who couldn't control her shaking, stepped in close to Martha and hugged her and then abruptly turned, took her car keys from the table and left the house into the dark night, the storm rising up, the air pocketed by an upturned boiling cauldron of light and cloud.

Jack heard the door slam and came down the hall to find Martha standing still in the kitchen. He went out the door and watched the red lights of Clare's Mercury turn onto the road and speed away, rain kicking up from the back tires. Rain soaked him. Rain came down hard on the house. Spectacular rain that floods and washes everything away and in the morning light, when the sun appears, everything is absolutely like new, but Jack knew that this rain was different and watched the lightning light up the Airstream's silver hull like a large blimp floating in black.

It took several minutes for Linda to emerge from the den. She'd heard the door slam and saw Jack run past.

She wasn't aware of what had gone on between her mother and Martha, but she knew it was her mother's fault. She trusted her own instinct on that. Linda came into the kitchen, the door wide open, and water cascading in off the roof over the clogged gutters onto the floor. She shut the door and went to Martha who was standing in the kitchen's center.

Linda took Martha's hands between hers and rubbed them together. She was somewhere Linda couldn't get to. "Martha," she said, "she's gone."

"I didn't know." Martha said, "I'd forgotten the whole thing, how it happened."

"How what happened?"

"And your mother…" She drew her face close to Linda. "Clare helped. You both cleared everything away."

"Yes." Linda said, at first not knowing what she meant and then remembering the night.

"I want to go away."

"Where do you want to go?" Linda, her voice low, controlled. "What are you thinking about?"

"We need to leave this house."

"We just got home. It's not safe outside."

Jack came in, water dripping off him leaving puddles. Linda, helpless, looked at him and shrugged her shoulders. He came to them and looked Martha right in the eyes. "Clare's gone. No need to worry."

She came back to Jack, "I'm not worried. I'm not anything. I just want to leave."

"We will, honey."

"When?"

"When everything is squared away."

Linda went to the kitchen window and looked out on the driveway and the rain coming down hard in the outside light shining from the doorway. She wasn't sure where she'd be from one day to the next, whether there would be a time she could settle, and be quiet again. Every part of her being wanted that. She wanted the family that existed before it was complicated by death and its new configuration. The wind drove the rain into the glass, but she was protected by it and she wondered whether her mother would make it back home through the storm.

Airstreaming

Refuge

Clare fought the planes of water sweeping the road. The tires, so old now the treads were barely visible, skated through the slick, but the car's heaviness, its thick steel, glass and iron kept it firmly on the road. She fought her own thoughts too and wondered if, when she crossed the brown, rising Kansas River, whether a sharp turn into it might be the thing to do. This thought scared her more than the storm. Her compulsive behavior made her leave without the one thing she stayed all day out in Olathe for: her daughter, who she only caught a glimpse of in the darkness behind Martha when they left their car and had gone into the house.

Her Pall Mall burned bright in the car's cabin held between her fingers clutching the steering wheel. The smoke's calming effect, not so much the inhaling, but its whirls and elegant streams, settled around her like a blanket. She had wanted just a moment with Linda – more if she'd let her. Forgiveness wasn't it, that would take longer, but she wanted to take Linda back to the time before her husband collapsed, to tell her that they could be there again, and that Linda could trust her to make it right. Now there was simply nothing.

Clare didn't want to go home. She passed the road she would have taken there and continued on to Smith's hoping his benevolence was in high gear that night, and that his bar's noise might drown out her thoughts. Its nautical theme might be more appropriate with all this water, she thought, lifting her spirits at the prospect of it. She was hungry as well, dry-mouthed from the day's smoking, and she felt weak. She'd ask for more kindness from him since the few dollars in her pocketbook could barely cover the cost of a meal and several drinks. She counted on the storm for this. Maybe Stuart was there as well.

There were few cars surrounding the white, dilapidated building, but the lighted neon blurs in each window were like beacons, and the roadside sign was brightly lit in the sheeting rain. Clare pulled the car up to a ragged stop, the lurch of miss-timed clutch and throttle down. She gathered the last of her cigarettes, pocketbook and keys, clutched them to her and ran to the front door.

Inside, Stuart with his racing forums and bourbon was sitting with his father upright next to him who was staring off into nothing. A young couple she'd never seen sat at a booth. Smith and Elaine were sitting together in their usual spot at a table just off center in the room. They all turned and looked at her when she entered; surprised that someone else was out in this kind of weather.

Smith, formal to the last, shouted, "Mrs. Wallich!" and leapt from his chair to get her inside, shut the door behind her and lead her to their table. He went to get a bar towel so she could dry her hair and shoulders.

Elaine, startled by Clare's appearance, inched her chair slightly away so as to avoid the shower of wet coming off her. "Clare, what on earth are you doing out on a night like this?"

Clare dumped all her belongings on the table and took a long while to answer Elaine. She didn't know how to answer her, whether the truth would be helpful, so she offered a half-story, "I've just come from Olathe."

"What were you doing in Olathe during all this?"

Elaine was going to press it and Clare was all shambles and dripping wet. "Going after Linda." So there it was and she'd have to explain it. But then Smith came up and handed her a towel. Clare lowered her head and put her hair in it, tamped the wet out then wiped her shoulders.

"You need something warm and medicinal. Be right back." Smith went off behind the bar.

While she was drying herself, Clare looked over to Stuart who watched her discreetly, his face hidden slightly by his father's shoulder, but she could see his eyes, the green flecks around his pupils reflecting light. Smith barked over to him, "Stuart, get up off that stool you're cemented to and help Mrs. Wallich with her coat."

Ever the captain, Clare thought.

Elaine stood up. "Smith, hon, I'm right here. I'll do it." Smith shook his head, poured a generous helping of whiskey in a deep brown mug and then coffee into it.

Stuart didn't move.

"It's on up about oh-eight hundred on a Monday night and we're usually closed this night." Smith said, bringing the mug over and setting it down in front of Clare. "Here you go. This'll treat the wet."

"What are you doing open?" Clare asked.

"Stuart needed a place to store his papa that was bigger than his house during this ruckus." He nodded his head toward the other couple and lowered his voice,

"Those two just wandered in from the road like you. Guess I should have locked the door, but I'd prefer to provide some sort of refuge than let people risk their lives out there." Smith sat down. He smiled and continued, "Elaine here doesn't like all the noise, but she likes me well."

Elaine chimed in, "That last part might be overstated," and laughed. It seemed to Clare they'd been there awhile and the drinks had poured generously between them. Elaine pressed, "Where is Linda?"

"In Olathe, with the people she takes care of."

"At this hour?"

Clare thought to shut her down, but her mood softened and regret came rising up. "I don't want to talk about it now, Elaine." Then she added, "I'm sorry, I really am."

"Drink up then." Smith offered.

Clare brought the mug to her lips and took a sip. The whisky felt thick on her tongue, delicious. The coffee, she knew, would keep her awake until late, but she didn't mind. Sleep wasn't coming soon or this night. She'd call in sick tomorrow or make some excuse up about the storm and damage it made.

Two mugs in, the conversation shifted from the weather. Smith, in his miraculous fashion, had pulled Stuart over to join them by guiding his father over and setting him up with a bowl of cashews and a pop. He shook the bowl so he could hear them and moved the man's hand in to touch the cool drink. Stuart had to follow him and Smith filled his glass again: vodka over rocks, olives with their bright, red centers circling the ice as he absently swirled the swizzle stick.

Clare noticed how similar Stuart and his father looked: their hands were weathered and strong, their noses blunt and wide, mounted over carved cheekbones that carried light and shadow like photos she'd seen in Life of railway workers, dock workers and farmers. They were both thin and wiry, but tall. Thus, the basketball talk, Clare surmised, thinking that Stuart probably had played in the past.

He and his father weren't that far apart in age, perhaps twenty-five years, but seemed as if there were decades more. Stuart's father shuffled along and their eyes were telling: Stuart's were busy and his father's glazed over from cataracts and dementia.

Elaine invited the young couple over who'd been traveling through from St. Louis, crossing the state making their way to new jobs in Wichita. The woman made her husband pull off when the storm dropped down. She hurried over when the invitation rang out through the bar and the man she was with ambled over wary of strangers.

"I'm Abby, and he's Paul." She had wild strawberry blonde hair she kept pulled back, freckles dotted her face, which was broad like a pan and eyes bluer than any of them had ever seen. "Thank you so much. I overheard you say you were usually closed so a double thank you to you, sir," She nodded to Smith and eyed the rest of the group and quickly sat down before the invitation might expire.

The young man was dark featured, pensive, each move a calculation. Clare pictured him the steadfast of the two, honest to a fault but rigid. They probably made a good match, eyeing how she was free with her hands on him and he never once flinched or turned her away. He was probably glad for the attention after a slow start in love. Clare smiled when the two of them caught her studying them. Then she looked over at Stuart who was also watching them and gripping his glass.

After a time, Smith heated up the fryer and cooked up a batch of chicken and French fries. He brought out the mayonnaise and mixed in ketchup for dipping sauce. Everyone was hungry. They talked about the new interstate, how houses kept cropping up until someday Olathe and Kansas City would be all one big metropolis. Stuart and Smith had a side conversation about basketball and the high school boys team. They all devoured the chicken and fries, mouths slick with grease, fingers slippery and wet.

After it was all gone and they had sat for a while, the conversation trailed out when Elaine said, "Honey, why don't you see if the rain has let up some?"

"I'm quite enjoying this impromptu gathering."

"But people are tired and might want to go home." Elaine was looking at Stuart's father who had remained silent the entire time, the cashews enough for him.

Smith went to the door and peered out. He came back to the table saying, "It's let up some, but I'm sure there's debris all over the road and it would be mighty treacherous to be out in the dark."

Taking that as a sign that they were in for the night, Elaine looked across the table, "Stuart, why don't we get your father to lie down in one of the long booths? I'm sure we've got a blanket around here somewhere. Hon, go see if you can find one." Elaine got up from her chair and went over to the old man and put her face right up to his.

"Mr. McClaine, why don't you come with me and we'll get you settled." She held out her hands and took his. Stuart put his hand under his father's arm and the two of them lifted him from his chair and led him over to a booth. Stuart pulled the table out so they could maneuver him in.

A deep feeling came to Clare. The entire evening, Linda's dark shape following Martha into the house had haunted her. But now, the surprise of something new caught her off-guard. Stuart tenderly laid his father down on the long, Naugahyde covered seat talking to him in low, soothing tones the entire time. He took his jacket off and placed it under his father's head as Smith arrived with a blanket that they both took the ends of and let it float down over Mr. McClaine's body. Stuart bent to kiss his father's forehead and placed a hand on his shoulder. He stayed there while Elaine and Smith returned to the table.

"I think he'll be just fine there." Elaine said, pulling in her chair. "Now where were we?"

Abby spoke first, arm entwined in Paul's. She was still ramrod straight in the chair as if the night, the long hours and beer hadn't taken their toll. The young couple's relationship was never quite defined and no rings signified marriage, but Clare had a sinking feeling that this trip was a test drive for Abby and Paul would quietly wander away from her soon.

"I think we should press on first light. We're supposed to be in Wichita by tomorrow and we need time to sleep."

"I think you'll get there in plenty of time." Smith said, still standing and taking the dinner plates from the table.

He stacked them all in the crook of his arm and took them to the back.

"Paul, why don't we go out to the car and see if we can't sleep a little before we get back on the road." Abby was already getting up and reached her hand out to Elaine. "You have all been so kind to us tonight. I don't think we should intrude further."

Paul said, "Thanks. Thanks for the food and beer," which he said to Smith as he came back to the table. "Let me give you some money." Paul reached for his wallet.

"On the house. It's been quite a night and you two have a long journey ahead of you."

"Thank you, sir. And thank you all for the company." The couple walked out of the bar. The four of them left watched them go: Stuart from where his father was drifting off to sleep and the remaining three at the table under the incandescent light surrounded by iron with rivets holding the light fixture together.

When Smith came back, he had brought a fresh pot of coffee, clean mugs and two-thirds of a bottle of Jack Daniels and put them on the table. Stuart rejoined them.

"I've never seen a man and a woman traveling together who aren't married." Elaine said and with a wry tone, continued, "The world is changing fast and I'm just trying to keep up."

"You should spend more time here," Smith said, laughing, "You'll see just about everything."

Clare reached out for the mugs and took two. She poured coffee in them and topped it with a little whiskey in both. She slid one over to Stuart, who wrapped his hand around it, slightly grazing Clare's fingers as he did.

"Here let me pour some for you two as well." Clare said, slightly embarrassed, a little nervous to be alone with Stuart, and wanting to make sure that Smith and Elaine would stay put.

But Elaine said, "I think I'll help Smith clean up in the back." She tapped Smith on the shoulder, got up from her chair and was halfway across the bar when she called back, "You coming, Smith?" And just like that, Smith was up and out of his chair as well, alternating his looks between Stuart and Clare until he turned away and followed his wife to the back.

Stuart chuckled, took a sip of coffee. "Clare, I..."

Clare cut him off, "I was mean to you last time we were here."

"No, I didn't get that."

"Well, I was, and I certainly do apologize for it."

"No need. I know what you're up against."

"You are good with your father." Clare looked at Stuart and smiled.

"He was always good to me and my sister."

"Maybe there are a few things I can learn from him."

"I believe it's too late." Stuart said looking up at Clare, eyes watering.

"You'll tell me some stories then?" Clare asked, and reached out and took Stuart's fingers away from his coffee mug and held onto them gently, but as if they were a lifeline.

"I've got lots of them." Stuart said, moving his fingers between hers and pulling her whole hand in.

After a time, Elaine and Smith rejoined Stuart and Clare at the table. Smith couldn't contain his smile – he'd seen that they'd be together so long ago it pleased him now to watch the slow way they were finding each other.

The four sat and talked, the hours drifting until the neon in the windows became less definitive from the gray light. From all the drink, the late night, and how she felt included among the other three, Clare unraveled the history of her last year, and finally the night with Linda and why she was in Olathe. There was no judgment from the others, only recognition in some parts, nodding heads and reassuring squeezes of her hand from Stuart. Oh, the way it all empties out and lays at the feet, Clare thought, the year of tumult and boredom, change and hurt.

Stuart asked Smith and Elaine to watch his father as he led Clare outside. The couple's car was still in the parking lot, the windows fogged from so much slow breathing. Clare imagined them inside, Abby wrapped around Paul like morning glory vines choking the strength of him, feeding off him. Maybe that's what Paul needed. Why did she think the worst thing of Abby when Stuart was here, leading her to her car, his arm tucked around her back?

Stuart said, "They are so young."

"Yes."

"We'll be quiet so they'll sleep." He moved in front of Clare, kissed her and took her into him.

Clare's fingers dug into him, not so much as passion because she was tired, but with a need for support. She wanted that, to not let go and be held up. When the embrace broke, she stole a look to the kid's car, "Do you think they have a chance?" Clare asked, and opened her car door.

"Everyone has a chance." Stuart said, guiding Clare into her car and then he paused, pulled the top of her sweater over her shoulder as she scooted into her seat, "Even us," he said, and closed the door.

When Clare got home it was very early, but she needed to sleep and she wouldn't be able to unless she called Jack and Martha. She poured a glass of water from the sink's faucet, lifted the receiver and leaned back for support against the counter. She did everything she could to stem the tide of hurt that found its way back. Letting it all out earlier at the bar had removed the anger. She went over in her mind what she would say several times until the dial tone began skipping causing her to press the button down and bring the fluid tone back. She dialed.

Jack answered.

"This is Clare," she said, her voice nearly a whisper, "Please keep Linda for as long as she needs." Her heart was breaking, but she kept on. "I will be here waiting, but please let me know how she's doing every few days. She doesn't need to know."

"I will."

Clare hung up the phone and slipped down the front of her counter until she was on the floor. Outside, the storm had moved on, but there were still cloud remnants and the debris left from all the rain and wind.

It was several minutes before she pulled herself up and made her way back to the bedroom where she removed her clothes, slipped on her nightdress, closed the curtains and her door so that the room darkened. She made up the sheets and carefully folded an edge down and slipped in under them and slept.

Airstreaming

Papers

Porches were now dotted with varying shapes and sizes of jack-o-lanterns, some carved with care, others by children whose skill at straight lines and curves were suspect. Leaves precariously dangled from branches waiting for a slight breeze forcing them to join the others carpeting the lawns and open spaces around Clare's house. The sunlight angled across Marion Street defining the houses, but the sky darkened by six and the incandescent lights warmed the windows up and down the street.

The Miller's house had construction workers carrying things inside and out. The neighborhood was buzzing about who would be moving in. Workers came to clean up the interior, replace the front window and plant flowers and shrubs in front. A stream of people came through during the course of two weeks. Mrs. Adderley sighted every one of them.

On an October morning, the air, crisp and with the sun warming her, Clare was caught by Mrs. Adderley to discuss the new owners, but Clare was in a hurry to rake the leaves, mow the lawn, and be ready for Stuart who was due by two in the afternoon to join her for the drive out to Olathe to take Linda's birthday present to her.

Clare was not so lonely at the house now that Stuart came by as much as he could. His sister, when she learned that he had started seeing someone, volunteered to take their father, or come sit with him in the evenings more often. Her kids now were off doing their own thing, she explained.

Clare went to his house as well, cooked the two men dinners, kept an eye on Mr. McClaine so Stuart could fix things around the house that were long overdue.

On the few Saturday's before, they'd gone to Smith's for dinner, held hands across the table, ordered their steaks and divulged their pasts. Stuart had been close to marrying once, but the girl, they were young, wanted out of Kansas and into a big city where she could be a part of fast moving change. He thought it'd be fine for a while, like being on vacation, seeing sights, but the real business of living and having a family seemed to him a thing you do in smaller towns. He'd dated after her, but then his mother died suddenly and left his father alone so his weekends were filled with hunting and fishing trips, days at the races and shopping for him. His sister helped when she could, but she had a family. Stuart and his father went to her house just as much as theirs. That went on for a good ten years, he said, and then his father started in on the dementia, and he became a full-time liability after which they sold his house, and his father moved in for good.

But he also said to Clare, that when "you came into the bar the first time, I saw someone worse off than me and I was instantly attracted to you." He'd chuckle and squeeze her hand and he'd repeat that line to anyone who'd listen.

Losing Linda for the second time was not as hard now because of Stuart. Clare's days and nights were full, but she kept Linda's door closed at home, kept it just how it was the night she left. Even the broken records were strewn across the floor to remind her of what she did so that behind that door, all the hurt could be contained.

Jack kept to his word and had called every third day to report on Linda. It was always late afternoon just after his day ended. Clare waited at work until the call or at home on the weekends, planning her schedule around it.

Linda had started at Olathe High School a couple of weeks into September, a week after the start of classes. A couple of weeks into October Clare took an afternoon off and drove to the school and saw the brick buildings nestled in among young and old trees. The sandstone buildings hadn't taken on the patina of age in the twelve years it had been there. Nor had the campus settled into the landscape like they do as their character takes on other buildings and play fields, and the children in their bright school colors. Clare walked around the campus to get a sense of what Linda's day might be like. Most of the children had gone home for the day. There were boys on the playfield in football gear. Whistles and shouts were mixed with voices singing coming from the auditorium. What sounded like a hymn drew her there.

She found an open door and stepped inside.

On stage were several children standing in a church that was suggested by a window, a few pews, and a cross hung down from the rafters. A false wall in back closed them in. A crescent moon was lit over the children. Their teacher stood at the lip of the stage, quietly directing a

girl and boy to come in through the congregation and
stand in front of another boy, a young preacher, Clare
surmised. She was tickled at how young they all were,
particularly the boy playing the preacher whose stature
did not indicate worldly knowledge. But their earnest
delivery of the hymn and their concentration delighted
her.

"May I help you?" A young voice asked, tapping Clare
lightly on her shoulder behind her.

Clare turned, "I'm just listening to them sing."

"This is a closed rehearsal. It's our last dress rehearsal
before the weekend," the young girl explained. She was
dressed in a costume that suggested an older woman in
the country, but she was somehow incomplete, her
straight, brown hair was parted down the middle and
long past her neckline.

"I'm sorry, I'll leave." Clare made a move out of the
row of seats.

"Stay until the end of the hymn. It's beautiful, isn't
it?"

"Yes, quite beautiful."

"I don't think I've ever seen you here. We had our
party with all the parents already, but I don't remember
you."

This upset Clare and she took stock of the girl. She
was too chatty. She felt like she was being found out and
tried to mask the annoyance in her voice. "I just
wandered in. I was looking at the school."

"Oh."

"My daughter just started here."

"What's her name?"

Clare hesitated and stared at the child. She didn't want to give Linda's name so she lied and said, "Susan."

"Oh? Susan what?" The girl asked, not really paying attention and watching the congregation begin to take their seats in the pews. "Oh, I have to go now. I'm in the next scene. I'm sorry."

Clare, relieved she didn't have to lie again, and followed the girl out of the theater. She changed the subject entirely on their way. "What's the name of the play?"

"Dark of the Moon," the girl said, "It's very progressive and we had to cut out the difficult scene."

"And that was?"

"We're really not supposed to talk about it, but Barbara, the main character is, um, compromised." The young girl pursed her lips and then put a finger to them mocking the forced censorship. "I don't know how Mr. Boyer got it through, but he did!"

It took a moment for Clare to understand her meaning, but then she did and said, "I see," She was startled by the girl's frankness and didn't want to reveal too much about why she was there. She was eager to end the conversation, "Good luck with your play," she said and began walking away.

"We hope to see you there!" The girl called after her.

Clare meandered through the courtyard and came to a low sandstone wall with a bronze plaque placed in its center honoring the school's founding father. She sat in the late fall sun and looked out across the small plazas and classrooms. If she couldn't actually see Linda, she wanted to at least know what she was experiencing. Jack and Martha had thought it best for her to return to school, and coaxed her back to this new high school where she wouldn't have a history and could start fresh. She entered as a senior, a year older than most of her peers and Jack said that she was doing as well as could be expected, that they were helping her catch up and bridge the gap from where she left off.

As she sat there in the sun, the kids from the play filed out of the auditorium in clumps, chatting tightly together, gossipy and excited. Clare smiled. The young girl with the long hair came out between two boys, her books tight to her chest, head back laughing, enjoying the attention. She looked over and saw Clare sitting on the sandstone wall and waved and continued on.

Clare was glad to be seen again, by this young girl, and by Stuart. It was a sensation she hadn't realized she missed all those years. To be looked at from afar, or up close in the eyes just after a kiss, or in the morning first thing before the realization that you didn't look your best, that what they saw was just you, sunk in. And to look at Stuart, too, and see what he might be feeling instead of a blank stare or fingers running over her face. Her need to be made up, to dress right, to make the world see her as something other faded away.

Maybe that was the source of her rising anger: that for years, no one saw her.

Now, with Mrs. Adderley nattering on with neighborhood gossip, Clare's hand on the rake, leaves gathered, Clare could only think of what lay ahead that day.

"Excuse me, Mrs. Adderley, but I must get this done before Stuart arrives."

"He's a smart looking one," she said, "When I see him come over, I can see he loves you."

"Is that right?" Clare said with a laugh. "It's a little early for that, don't you think?"

"Oh, I don't know. I think people know straight away, don't you? I knew when I met Harold, absolutely. And I waited for him."

"Well, I'll ask Stuart when he gets here. Put him on the spot!"

Mrs. Adderley picked up on the joke and said, "I'll do it for you."

"I'll leave it to you, then," Clair said and scooped a pile of leaves in the garbage.

"I do miss seeing Linda," the old woman said, "I miss her perched up there on the stoop at all hours. The neighborhood is changing so fast."

"I miss her, too," Clare said, "I'll give her your regards today."

"Will you see her?"

"Yes, it's her birthday." This was a half-truth. She hoped to, but didn't know for sure if she'd be there. Clare had to give some explanation as to where Linda had gone so the neighbors wouldn't think the worst. A week after Linda left, she'd gone and sat with Mrs. Adderley, knowing that she'd spread the news fast about Linda and Clare's work would be finished. She didn't tell her the whole truth, but that Martha needed full-time help all of a sudden and that Linda would stay on at their home until she got better.

"Oh, how wonderful." Mrs. Adderley was genuinely pleased, "You tell her 'Happy Birthday' from us, will you?"

"Of course." Clare said. And off Mrs. Adderley went; her arrivals and departures always abrupt so there was no way of stopping her one way or the other.

It left Clare to think about Linda, though, and her call the morning before, when she and Stuart were lazing in the house, the radio on, Mr. McClaine at his sister's and the two of them just getting up after a slow waking, making love, and then coffee on the couch. Linda, who hadn't called her mother yet, but who's voice had startled Clare when she picked up the receiver was nervous on the other end.

"Hello?"

"Linda?" Clare's voice caught in her chest. Her arms and legs suddenly broke out in bumps and her breathing quickened. "How are you, sweetheart? You're birthday is coming up."

"I know," she said, her voice distant, "I need you to sign papers for school. Jack and Martha aren't officially my guardians."

"They aren't, I'm your mother."

Linda hardly heard her. "And they wanted me to ask you. They didn't think it was right to do so. That it should be asked by me."

Clare hesitated a moment. She looked to Stuart who was lying on the couch, but he was lost in the morning papers. "Do you want me to?"

"It has to be done." Her voice was matter-of-fact. "If you'd like to come out and sign them, we were thinking around 3 o'clock tomorrow."

"Is there anything you'd like for your birthday?"

"No."

"How about some clothes for school?"

"I don't need anything. Just for you to sign the papers."

Clare could hear her breathing like a metronome, waiting. "Ok. Tomorrow then. Honey?" She waited to hear her say something, but nothing came so she added, "It's good to hear your voice."

Stuart popped his head up just then from the couch. "Are you coming back, Clare?" Clare quickly covered the mouthpiece and then heard a click on the other end and the phone go dead. "I'm sorry, are you still on the phone?" Stuart was now sitting up and looking at her as she lowered the receiver into her lap and cried. Stuart came to her and lifted her up.

In the afternoon, driving out to Olathe, Clare sat holding a small, flat box. After Linda's call, and after Stuart had left to spend time with his father, she'd gone into Linda's room and began cleaning. The black vinyl shards she collected and put them in the trash. She vacuumed their splinters, straightened Linda's bed and the clothes she left behind. The few remaining records, she put in a sack to take with her. On her dresser was a framed photograph that sat atop the piano. The family was invited to sit for a portrait outside of the Baptist church that her husband had played in. They were photographing the congregation's families and at the end, the pastor's wife came and asked if they would like a photograph of the three of them.

Linda was in the middle holding Clare's hand with her other on her father's shoulder. They were all smiling. It was Linda's favorite. Clare folded tissue around the frame, placed it in a small box, and tied a blue bow around it. When she left the room, she kept the door open.

In the car, scarcely a word was said on the way out. She had asked Stuart to drive. She didn't think she had the strength to drive home now that her regret wasn't fueled by anger.

She made Stuart pull the car over at the top of the driveway. He patted her leg and looked at her. She'd worn no make-up, had brushed her hair and wore a blue-patterned dress.

"You are a beautiful lady," Stuart said, reaching up to touch her cheek.

"I feel awful for having you stay here." Clare said, accepting his hand.

"It's the right thing to do. You go on. I'll have a smoke." Stuart picked a pack of cigarettes out of his pocket, smiled, "Good company, these things."

"I could use one."

"I'll have one ready for you when you get back. Now go on." Stuart trailed his hand from her face, across her shoulder and down her arm as she opened the door and stepped out.

She caught sun in her eyes reflecting off the Airstream as she made her way down the drive clutching her gift and carrying the bag of records. Maybe the records were not such a good idea, she thought, but clutched them all the same.

The kitchen door opened and Jack came out into the drive. Their phone calls had made things easier between them. Their conversations went from a sort of wariness and mistrust to longer, more detailed accounts of Linda's days. During one of the calls, she'd apologized to him for what she'd left Martha with. They had already "worked through it" he'd said, and Clare wondered what he meant by that, but didn't press.

Clare noted that there were papers in Jack's hand.

"So good of you to come out for this." Jack saw the bag in her hand, "Can I help you with that?"

"They're for Linda. Is she here?" Clare held the bag back from Jack.

"Yes, she's in the house."

"Can I see her?"

"Well, you see, that's the thing." Jack looked at Martha apologetically. Martha's jaw was set. "I tried to get her involved with this by having her call you and I was hopeful…"

Clare's hope cleared out of her. "I don't understand. I want to apologize."

"I know."

"We've come all this way."

"Is that Stuart up there by the car?" Jack squinted up into the white light and saw his silhouette leaning against the Mercury, watching the two of them negotiating in the driveway.

"Yes."

"Linda mentioned she thought she'd heard a man's voice on the phone yesterday. I didn't tell her about him when you told me over the phone. I thought you should do that." Jack reached for the bag. "Here let me have that, it looks heavy."

"They're the rest of her records." Clare said, handing it to him. "I wasn't sure whether to bring them."

"Can I go up and meet Stuart?"

"Why don't we wait on that," Clare resigned herself to the fact that she wouldn't see Linda. She felt that something was off by Jack changing the subject, "Why did it take so long for these papers needing to be signed?"

Jack hesitated and put the bag of records down on the ground and brought the papers up to show Clare. "They found out we weren't Linda's legal guardians from one of her teachers when she asked about her mother. Linda didn't know what to say to the woman and they called us to clarify. This paper just lets them know that you're her mother and are allowing this."

"She's been in school for a month." Clare was incredulous that no one from the school had bothered to try and contact her until now.

Jack took stock of her and let out a long sigh. "We just enrolled her like she was our daughter to make it easy on everyone given what had happened. I know it sounds awful, but you saw how things were, the turmoil created when you left suddenly. It was so hard to recover from that." And then he paused and lowered his voice. "It took me days to bring Martha around."

Clare didn't know what to say. She also wondered why Linda would go back to school after being gone a year. Were the two of them that persuasive that they were able to coax her back? She had a mind to just leave again, not sign the papers or demand that Linda come out so she could determine what was happening, why her sudden change. She had lost her way here, though, and she didn't feel like she could make demands or throw a tantrum. And Stuart was watching from the road.

Jack, who had also been faithfully sending Clare the money that Linda would have earned, was there in front of her now holding out the papers. She'd sign them, but then she'd do some investigation.

"I'm sorry to hear about Martha. Maybe someday soon she and I can talk," Clare took the papers and handed Jack the small gift she'd been holding. "Would you give this to Linda as well? It's a little something for her birthday."

"Of course," Jack said, pulling a pen from his shirt pocket. "Perhaps, by Thanksgiving we can all get together and things will be good."

Clare didn't respond. The holiday was over a month away, which seemed like a long time. She looked over the two sheets. They were on the school's letterhead and seemed in order. She noted the woman's name at the bottom so that she could remember it. She put them down on the Ford's hood and signed.

"I think she likes being back in school," Jack offered. "And I've taught her to drive. I'm not sure she wants to get her license yet, but it would be a good thing for her, no?"

"Who is going to pay the costs for that?" Clare asked abruptly, looking up at Jack, and then handing him the papers.

"As long as she stays in school..." Jack said.

"What if someday she decides to leave you two like she did me?"

"We'll cross that..."

"She may want to come back home soon." Clare caught her anger rising again and decided to leave before she said anything else. "Please make sure to give my present to Linda and tell her I love her." The last she said, quietly, but looked at Jack to make sure he would do so and accepted his nod. She turned and began walking up the driveway.

"We are doing our best," Jack said almost as an apology. Clare walked up the drive and met Stuart, who took her in his arms and guided her to the passenger seat. She didn't look back, nor did she acknowledge Jack's apology, which she'd found bothered her, because Linda was still her daughter, and though, Jack and Martha might be "doing their best," she'd been doing that all of Linda's life.

Rails

Linda took the papers to school. Jack dropped her off on his way to work every morning and she bussed home in the afternoons. Before she left the car, he handed her the gift from her mom, still wrapped in the blue bow. Yesterday, he'd put it in the car before going back in the house just after Clare left. He placed the bag of records just outside the den, which they'd turned into Linda's room. When Martha called for dinner, there was no mention of Clare's visit, nor the records left, but Jack and Martha heard the music from them throughout the evening and into the night.

In the school's drop-off circle, Jack pulled Clare's gift from the glove compartment, "Your mother wanted you to have this for your birthday," he said, "She also said she loves you. She seemed very sad."

Linda took the gift and put it in her knapsack with her books. "I'll open it later. Thanks," she said and opened her door.

"Good enough. Don't forget to give the papers to the registrar," Jack said.

"I will." Linda smiled and put the knapsack's strap over her head.

"We'll see you later and happy birthday!" Jack shouted after her, the door closing as Linda walked away.

School seemed like a foreign thing to her. The rules seemed not to apply. The bells marking the ends and beginnings of class that regimented the day didn't register with her anymore. Having been gone a year and having seen the things that the other children hadn't made her feel separate. Could they bring a child into the world? Had they saved a person's life? Did they know that the mysteries of other people's lives might one day be revealed as something ugly? Were there others around her that knew music wasn't just something from television, radio or 45s?

She drifted from class to class in a sort of rarified air that was like swimming in a crowded public pool, head underwater, a multitude of legs, swirling bubbles, creating motion, the sounds muffled and yet, feeling utterly alone because of the water's weight and motion.

When she dropped the papers off at the registrar's desk, it was more of a leaving than an appointment so that they got shuffled in with the daily reports and miscellaneous filings that were handled haphazardly by Mr. Holmquist late in the day.

It had been three weeks since she started. Her classes were all boisterous and the teachers alone in a sea of students Linda could get lost in. She spent the hours reading books from the library nestled behind her textbooks waiting for the day's end. Going back to school was a way to placate Jack and Martha, and Linda didn't really know what she would do all day at the house, alone with Martha, who had lapsed into periods of silence that she only came out of when Linda was deposited at the top of the drive. She knew Martha didn't do much during the day. On many of them, the kitchen remained full of breakfast dishes; cereal boxes and jelly jars were on the counter. Even their bed remained unmade with the bedroom drapes still drawn.

When she came home, Linda worked to clean the kitchen, and do the chores she'd done when she just worked there. It was a bit of a reversal and she didn't quite know what to do, but she'd keep it as much from Jack as possible, who had invested so much into bringing Martha back.

But it wasn't everyday. Some days she came home to find everything clean and Martha thinking about dinner, which allowed the two of them to work together. They'd go to the market in the extra cars Jack brought home to try out. Linda drove and Martha inspected all the different dashboard instruments, their radios and made adjustments to the seats.

Martha heard the bus brakes groan and stop. Linda would come in soon. She waited for her at the banquette; a couple of sweaters, her purse and the car keys were bunched together on the table. It was after two in the afternoon.

When Linda opened the door, Martha said, "Jack called and he's going to be late coming home and not to worry about dinner." As she stood up, Linda removed her knapsack and set it heavily on the floor. She took a look around and saw everything cleaned up, the counters spotless.

She gazed at Martha who was dressed in jeans and flannel top, un-tucked, but nice. She'd combed her hair, and clipped it in the back so that her face was clear and open.

"I want to take you somewhere," she said, "I've got a heavier sweater for you. Will you drive?"

Linda liked the prospect of driving. She missed the spectacle of neighbors from her street. There was no front stoop to sit on to watch their comings and goings. Driving was a way of seeing people in the nearby homes out working their yards or coming in from getting their mail at the main highway's edge. "Of course," she said.

The fall afternoon was clear and bright. The wind had cleared away the humidity, which softened everything: the trees, clouds, hills and low-slung houses seemed etched against their backgrounds. As they drove, Martha rolled her window down to let the cool air flow through the car sending her tied hair backwards over her seat.

"Roll down your window," Martha said, "Can you just feel how clean the air is?"

Linda rolled her window down. The wind blew past her neck causing a shiver. "Yes, it's nice."

Martha saw the shiver and draped one of the sweaters over Linda's shoulders. "I can't imagine anything better than this. The sunny days before the cold sets in are the best. Are you ok?"

"I've never driven this far before," Linda said, concerned that she didn't have a valid permit and that she had only driven to the supermarket and back a few times.

"You'll be fine. Where we're going is only a half hour's drive and I'll give you plenty of notice when to make turns and whatnot."

"Aren't you worried about the police?"

"Absolutely not," Martha chuckled and threw her head out and then to the side window to catch the wind,

"There are some things, Linda, I don't worry about and you're doing just fine."

The ride wasn't smooth at all. Linda's starts and stops were more abrupt than she wanted, but as they passed the fields and headed into Kansas City, the practice helped her to navigate the Mustang's power, which Jack had raved about the few nights he'd had the car.

"Will Jack be mad that we took the car?" Carl had followed him home with it the night it arrived. They had gone over it thoroughly in the garage. Jack had hung a silver cased light bulb with a long cord attached under the hood. They studied the engine like it was a work of art; running their fingers, when the engine cooled, over the different parts. Linda had sat and watched them marvel at its beauty and talk about gear ratios and rpm's and something about the new V-8 engine. She couldn't keep up, but the car was beautiful and bright red, which was as conspicuous as an elephant against the green rolling hills.

"I expect he might, but we don't have to tell him, do we?" Martha laughed again. She looked at Linda, who was intent on the road, her hands gripping the steering wheel. "It will be okay one way or another. I think he'll be glad that I just got out of the house," she added, "Don't worry anything about it."

Martha guided Linda through Olathe onto Interstate 35 past Overland Park, Merriam and into Shawnee Heights, and across the state line into the Missouri side of Kansas City. Every single car on the highway passed Linda who edged along timidly. Martha kept giving her words of encouragement while pointing out landmarks along the way that unnerved Linda because she felt compelled to look. Finally, Martha instructed her off the interstate and towards Penn Valley Drive, which was tree-lined on one side and opened flat on the other. It gave her a parallel view of the highway they were just on. She made another right onto Pershing Road and looming ahead was the mammoth gray Union Station.

"It's beautiful, isn't it?" Martha put her hands on the dashboard and her face as close to the front window as possible. "It's the most beautiful building in all of Kansas City."

On closer inspection, the building's façade was in need of repair and cleaning. The concrete blocks were streaked with mildew. The steps leading up to the gold-rimmed doors were pocked and their edges chipped. Neglect had taken its toll and worn down the buildings grandeur so that it felt to Linda like entering into a deep granite cavern. Inside, the large, open atrium dwarfed the women. Descending sunlight scraped the tile floor in an elongated pattern from the west end window. The light was dust-filled and streaked by the cross frames that supported the glass.

They had arrived between one of the remaining daily trains. Very few people were in the entrance hall. A single man stood at the one ticket window left open. Martha and Linda strolled over to the Lobster Pot restaurant. Two waiters were talking along the counter to a couple of patrons. Martha's mood darkened a little seeing the room so empty. Linda still wasn't sure why they were there.

"When I first arrived in Kansas City, this room was filled with people," Martha said, "Just utterly filled! You couldn't hear the person next to you from all the chatter and noise." They walked out of the restaurant and down into the great hall, a line of windows as large as the one in the entrance hall lit the floor the size of a football field, and ten sets of iron double doors along the east side were all closed. Martha continued, "And here, people flew by you on their way to somewhere. People streamed out of each of these doors that led to the tracks each train arrived or left on. It was quite a sight!"

A large clock hung from the ceiling modeled after a pocket watch suspended in time and space. The roman numerals on its face were dark against the yellow glow. It still ticked off the minutes after many decades. Martha took Linda by the hand and they jogged towards it and then Martha stopped them directly under it.

"Do you know how many people met each other here over the years?"

Linda shook her head.

"Once, I told Jack to meet me just like this, right under the clock. I told him I wanted to pretend that I was coming from somewhere or leaving to go off to some other great city. We met here and we kissed." Martha's eyes filled. "We bought round-trip tickets to St. Louis and went down to the platform and watched the trains come and go. When our train arrived, and it was time for us to get on, we looked at each other, laughed and watched it leave the station in a great cloud."

"Why didn't you go?

"Just knowing we could if we wanted to was enough, I guess." Martha looked over to a set of closed iron doors. "Now I wish we had."

Linda turned toward the long hall; the beautiful light and shadow across the great expanse changed her view of things. She stepped away slightly and into the hall and said, "I would have gone."

Martha came out of her reverie. She was stopped short by the possibility of her leaving.

It passed as quickly as it came when Linda asked to go down and see the train tracks and off they went, through the iron doors and down the stairs, Linda running her hand along the thick balustrades. They stopped at the base of the stairs and looked down the rails that came through lit tunnels from the outside on either end of the tracks.

To Linda, it was majestic: all of the tracks gleaming iron, the length of them leading out to all points across the country. She imagined them full of trains and streams of people getting on and off, families, lovers, soldiers, businessmen, the whole history of commerce and everything out there – away.

She wished her father could have come and listened to the echoes of what was. All those sounds would have given him vivid pictures in his mind and he'd describe for her what the train station had been to all these people. He'd have known how to do this unlike her teachers at the new school or anyone else. There on the worn tiles from so many footsteps, they'd have stood and taken in people's conversations and made up their stories. Her father would add a short little twist at the end to make it funny or strange: a couple with a new baby comes to visit the grandparents though they couldn't explain the blue tongue or a military man home on leave to meet his girl, but she's met this new girl and the three of them would be off on a night of adventure – the details of which he'd leave out. Or the four-year-old boy separated from his parents because he'd wandered off and now he's off to Alaska on another train where he'll grow up among the bears and come back one day with a bear show and spot his real mother and father in the audience one day, older now, and they'd reunite around the Thanksgiving table – all of them, bears and all, a new family, sitting upright delighting in turkey and cranberry sauce.

"You like this place," Martha said, bringing Linda back.

"I do." Linda had a small smile.

"What are you thinking about?"

"My dad used to make stories up about people all the time. This would have been a perfect place for him. I was wondering if my dad rode a train here when he came home from the war."

"He might have, but I'm sure he did ride the train at one point. Everyone in Kansas City must have or at least met somebody who did. Probably not so now, but if you're my age, I'm pretty sure they must have."

"Look how the walls are covered in soot."

"I'm sorry it all looks so shabby now." Martha said with regret.

"It's not so bad. Everything changes. The trains have given way to Jack's shiny new cars. How sad it must seem to see the change."

"At least we can still come visit." Martha said, looking at Linda in a new way, startled by her observation. They started walking to the stairs they'd come down. "We should get home before Jack does."

They came back up out of the iron doors and into the great hall. The sun struck their faces, which was now directly parallel with the large windows. The defining light burned the window's framework and patterns of sun and shadow across the marble wall.

Martha stopped and took a last look at the clock. She'd remember the time as five fifteen and then they passed through the atrium and out the doors into the remaining daylight and made their way home.

They talked nearly the entire way home. Glad for the conversation, Linda felt more comfortable driving now even in the waning light. Martha talked about her parents, the snow coming, the traveling she did to end up in Kansas. Linda spoke of how being back at school felt to her now and Martha encouraged her to keep at it, 'that it will get better, you'll see.'

When Linda pulled in at the top of the drive she saw the Ford wagon in front of the house, the garage door open and the house lights on. A little panic rose up in her. "Jack got home before us," she said.

Martha placed a hand on Linda's shoulder and said, "It will be just fine. I'll talk him down."

"But this car. We weren't supposed to drive it."

"What else were we going to drive?" Martha laughed.

They safely stowed the car back in the garage unharmed.

When they came out of it, Linda noticed that the Airstream shone particularly bright against the hill's black. The sun had lowered; the sky was clear and still in the last few moments before darkness set in. The trailer looked like it came from another world, its surface nearly translucent. Martha didn't see it and went into the house, but Linda walked up to its hull and saw her entire self nearly perfectly reflected back at her. Linda studied her reflection. It is only I, she thought: singular, tall, and alone now. She thought of the gift from her mother she'd unwrapped at lunchtime between classes: a picture of her mother and father, and she in the middle, standing stiffly in the churchyard. They were gone now. It was just she in the Airstream's blue shine.

"Come inside for dinner!" Martha called out.

When she came in the door, the kitchen was full of colored helium balloons and crepe paper ribbons. Linda looked around and then at Jack and Martha who stood together, full of hope, and smiled. Presents and a cake were on the kitchen table with a bucket of fried chicken, potato salad and coleslaw.

"I didn't know what your favorite color was, so I got all of them." Jack said.

"The trip to the train station was all a ruse so Jack could decorate." Martha laughed.

"How did you like driving the Mustang this afternoon?"

Overcome, Linda said, "It was fantastic," she brought her hands to her lips, smiled then added, "thanks for this…everything you've done…" She moved into their waiting arms and looked out the window to see the Airstream had lost its shine. She stood among the color and crepe, the presents and her new guardians. The trailer only reflected back the kitchen window's light and Linda wished she had a ticket to ride the rails from one end of the country to the other.

Airstreaming

The Returns

Jack and Carl went to lunch later than usual a couple of days after Linda had arrived, and after Jack had been able to bring Martha back from the disastrous confrontation with Clare. It was only a beer he had, but it was enough.

He'd ordered it and Carl didn't say a word, just sat and watched him sip it. It was the only time anyone had seen him drink anything alcoholic. He was just trying it on for size again, just to see if he could ease back into having a beer or two without crossing the line. God knows he'd been through it.

Carl said, concern in his voice, "I can't imagine what these past many months have been like for you. You deserve that beer."

And all through lunch, Carl lent an ear, much like he always did because Jack believed that Carl's life was great: the kids, the wife at home doing the work of kids, and Carl able to work at the dealership free of their worry. Carl didn't help matters when asked about how things were going. Always he said, "Fine, couldn't be better." Besides, he was more interested in what was going on with Jack because he'd told him he was a little envious of his freedom.

"How's that Airstream of yours?" Carl asked.

"Good. We towed it a bit a while back and it did good with the wagon. I need to figure a way to put a sway bar on so maybe you could come out to the house one day and help me with it. We're going to need your welder again if that's not a problem."

"No problem at all." Carl said as Jack finally looked up from his plate of meatloaf and potatoes.

"Thing is, I don't think we'll be going anywhere anytime soon."

"Why's that?"

"We put Linda in school."

"Probably a good thing. Kids need school."

"I don't think she likes it much." Jack took a longer draw on his beer and tipped the glass so he could see the color of it. "Do you think Budweiser could make a stronger beer? This sort of tastes like water."

"Yeah, but it's sort of local. You have to support that." Carl said, laughing.

"St. Louis isn't local."

"No, I suppose not."

Jack thought for a moment before saying "Martha seems to think we have all this money we could just take off with the trailer and travel all over the place. Quit my job and everything. I spent most of what we had saved buying that thing."

"Do you regret it now?"

"No, no, not at all. It's been good for me if you can believe that." Jack thought Carl was hoping for a yes here because he knew Carl was thinking in a selfish way that it would be a great thing for his family to have.

"I believe it. I love my projects."

"Exactly."

For a while they ate in silence. Jack finished his beer, and the waitress came to ask after the lunch so he ordered another.

"You know we have to go back to work," Carl said.

"Of course." Jack felt his guard go up like it used to. "Do you think having kids was the best thing you've ever done?"

The waitress came, the beer glass dripping and her leaning down smartly and placing it in front of Jack. "It's one of them." Carl said, his eyes following the waitress back to the bar.

"Why would a mother treat her kid so bad then?" Jack lifted the beer up and eyed it again, wondering if he really did need another.

"You mean Linda's mom?"

"Any mother, but yeah, her."

"It's hard to know what goes on," Carl said, "you can't know the history of that family. Just like when you marry someone and you start living together and all of this odd behavior rears its ugly head. I'm consistently astonished at the strange stuff Becky does sometimes, but I do the same stuff. Just in a different way. Kids complicate that. I'm glad I don't have to deal with the bulk of their crap."

"So you're saying it wouldn't be all Clare's fault."

"I'm not saying that at all. I guess I'm just saying that there's no fault."

"I see." Jack pushed his lunch plate out of the way and moved his beer into the center of attention. "You're the sage of the prairie, you know that?"

"I'm just a mechanic at heart with a thing for metal."

"And a fine one you are."

That was the last time he drank in front of Carl. He'd noticed his eyes on him the entire lunch, which felt familiar. Instead, on the way home each night he stopped at different markets and bought two cans of beer. He alternated between Juicy Fruit or beef jerky to mask the smell. He'd drive the long way home or stop and drink them down. This thing with Clare, the worry and work of Martha, and now Linda.

Thinking about what Carl had said that day at lunch about what goes on in families made him feel terrible for not including Clare in their plans for Linda's birthday. The guardianship papers only made things worse and he hated being the center spoke of a triangular bridge between the three of them. It would have been easy enough for him to call Clare or go to her place to sign the papers. Knowing that the women were just inside when Clare came out was more than he could take. After Clare had left, he'd gone and bought a bottle of bourbon and drove it all the way back home with it on the seat next to him unopened and hid it in the garage under the work rags.

The Saturday after Linda's birthday she and Jack were outside. His garden long forgotten now was a shambles. Tomato volunteers overtook much of the northwest corner, as did some of the squash and melons; their carcasses littered the wide patch. He'd read that the temperature was about to drop and asked Linda for help in turning them into the ground so they'd mulch over before winter hardened it. They'd worked silently for an hour together when Linda plunged the pitchfork into the ground and it shook a little, its long handle sticking straight up. It was as if she'd suddenly come upon something.

"You and Martha shouldn't be stuck here because of me."

"What are you talking about?"

"All your plans. That trailer just sitting there."

"It's okay, really."

"It's my fault you and Martha aren't going anywhere."

"Don't think like that."

"I know you both like to travel."

"How would you know that? We haven't been anywhere since you've known us." Jack laughed and with the flat of his shovel smacked a particularly large pumpkin breaking it into several pieces.

"Martha told me about you and her at the train station." Linda walked over to him to make her point. "How you guys met there one day and bought tickets to St. Louis, but didn't get on the train."

"What?"

Linda said, "You met under the big clock in that huge hall."

"I've never been to Union Station."

It took a long while for both of them to let the information sink in. They were still as trees looking at each other and time passed before either of them spoke. Linda was trying to understand why Martha would make up such a story and Jack was trying to figure out a way to make the story true. In the end, they both failed. Jack leaned on the shovel for support and Linda shoved her hands so deep in her pockets her knuckles hurt.

"I've never been in Union Station," Jack finally repeated. "I couldn't tell you the first thing of what it's like inside."

"I don't understand, Jack. She took me around the whole station and pointed out all of these things and talked about those things that you and she did."

Jack hesitated and looked out over the hills beginning to gray. "I'm sure she did. She's been through there," and then he looked at Linda. "She went through there nearly twenty years ago, but she hasn't been back since."

"How do you know? Couldn't she just drive there?"

"Have you ever seen Martha drive?"

Linda recalled that she hadn't. That, in fact, any time she'd gone anywhere with the two of them Jack had driven. "No."

"She may have gone there before we got married, but that was a very long time ago and she never mentioned it but once." Jack looked back at the house and began walking to the Airstream. He motioned for Linda to follow him and when the trailer was between them and the house and hid them from view, Jack turned to Linda and said, "I'm so sorry."

"For what? Tell me for what?"

"For everything," Jack leaned against the trailer. He was tired suddenly and thinking of the bottle under the rags. "You should be home with your mother."

"But I walked all the way out here."

"Yes, but we should have driven you right back. It would have been the right thing to do." Jack looked at Linda and was trying to decide how far to go. "But Martha wanted so bad for you to stay. I guess I did too, but only for her sake. Only because she needed you to stay." He saw that Linda was confused. "You know it's coming up in a few months, a year since she lost the baby. I could sense her slipping away from me again. And it was my fault in the first place allowing her to have it, allowing her to believe in the possibility of having a baby. She never should have gotten pregnant, not with her history. But it became an obsession for her and the only thing in this world she wanted. I was foolish enough to believe that it might save her, might erase the things she's been through. I hired you on the pretext that you would be my eyes and ears while I worked. I convinced Martha that you had to be hired because she'd need help with the house, but really I needed someone here to make sure she'd be fine. I don't know what happened the night she lost the baby. I have to believe it was a natural thing, that God didn't want her to have it for some reason – or that maybe He was just answering my prayers, because, so help me, I prayed that something would go wrong."

"That wasn't your fault," Linda said.

Jack's face ran through his emotions like weather changing.

"It is mine alone," Jack said, "Mine simply because I knew. I never met Martha at the train station. I met her in the West Bottoms where I was camping along the river, near the stockyards and railroad. A bunch of us had moved in there after the '51 flood. All those businesses were ruined for years and I had been working down there building boats and anything else I could so it was like home to me. And I was drinking. And it was costing me more than I could make in a day. I saw Martha, she was so beautiful, on a day so fine, I just up and quit the drinking because I knew she would never have me in the kind of shape I was. She was working a pick line, mindless work you know, but I think she was doing it because it was about the only thing she could focus on. Maybe I shouldn't be telling you all this, but maybe it's your right to know now." Jack walked around the corner of the Airstream and looked towards the house and came back.

He had stopped so Linda prodded him on, "So why the made up story at the station?"

Jack looked off across the hills and said, "She was sent away by her parents, so whatever she told you about them probably wasn't true either. They didn't want her because she was damaged goods. So they sent her away to live with some family Aunt and Martha just up and left one night, hopped on a train that ended up in Kansas City. But you see, all of this could not be true either, except the only thing that makes it true is the ticket she's kept all these years of that train ride."

"She told me you drove up to see her parents after you got married."

"It's true we drove up there, but we never saw them. We drove three days to get there, but Martha couldn't, at the last, bring herself to knock on their door. The only way I knew of the truth of their existence was looking in the phone book and seeing their name." Jack took her hand. "You must know your mother loves you. Whatever she did that night, of course, wasn't right, but it wasn't nearly so bad as the possibility of her turning you out. Think about it. Why did your father marry your mother?"

"I'm not sure," Linda said, "I'm not sure at all."

"I don't know much about your dad, but I do know your mother took good care of him all those years when she could have had something more." Jack waited on Linda to see if his point was taken.

Jack could tell that the last angered Linda slightly, and she looked hard at Jack "Why all the journals, Jack? Why do you write in them so much?"

Jack thought for a moment, then said, "I could ask you why the jazz records, why play them over and over?"

"How come you keep them in plain view of Martha, or me for that matter."

"Why play your records incessantly in front of your mother?"

In a long slow realization, tears began to roll quietly down Linda's cheeks. Jack took his thumb and wiped them away. He didn't mean to challenge her, but it was there and they were the same thing. Both of them were making their own little statements, their stand on things. The sun slipped behind the west hills. The air had turned icy. Linda wrapped her arms around herself.

"You're getting cold." Jack said, "Do you want to go in?"

"Not yet. It's just that we stopped working."

Jack walked over to collect the shovel and pitchfork and Linda followed. He felt sorry for Linda and a kinship in some respects. They were partners in keeping Martha afloat, it seemed, but from different angles.

"What will you do?" Linda asked.

"About what?" Jack said, stalling. He knew what the question was about, but he hadn't decided a course of action and it was too much to work through.

"Will you ask her about the station?"

"Would it make a difference?"

Linda hesitated. "Yes. It might help her."

Jack moved off to a corner of the garden to think a while. He had done it. He had tried so hard this past year to keep Martha from grief and he was worn out. A part of him thought to take Linda back to her mother tonight and just explain things to Martha. But she would know something was wrong if Linda went in to get her things. There would be a scene. As it was, they had no business being her guardians, and he could tell Clare wasn't convinced that what she was doing was right. Her signing the papers over the weekend and reluctance to leave made it clear to him that it would only be a matter of time before it turned ugly. She'd enlist the help of Stuart perhaps, check in at the school, and make it more difficult to bring Linda home if she handled it wrong. Keeping Linda there might possibly be the worst thing he could do now. He'd felt Martha slipping away and tonight was proof. If he took Linda back to her home, he'd hook the Airstream up to the Ford and they'd be off by the end of the week. It'd take her mind off losing Linda, not to mention the baby's loss, and they'd be doing the one thing they both wanted. He'd take off from work, use the remaining vacation days and keep her away as long as possible. They'd go south towards warmth. He stole a glance at Linda who sat on top of one of the pumpkins and watched him work. Is there a penny for her thoughts? When he saw that she was looking at him, wondering why he'd walked away, he walked back to her.

"I have to take you home tonight."

"I can't go," she said.

"It'll be just fine, I promise." Jack lowered down on his haunches and looked up trying to read her face.

"Then why did you have me stay here in the first place? Why did you push me back into school?"

"It seemed the right thing for both you and Martha. But, you see, the only thing it's done is made things worse. Martha is not dealing with what she has to and you are in the middle of all of it. We have no right, really, to keep you here."

"But I want to be here. I know Martha is having troubles. I see the thing she does touching her neck all the time, the way she goes all quiet. I know how hard she took the baby's loss. You did too.

"Yes."

"I was here through all of it."

"Yes, and you helped us enormously. You will never know how much it meant to us, but there are much deeper things and until tonight, I didn't realize they'd come back to the surface and now I'm worried about having you here."

"Don't worry so much about me." Linda said. Did she not want to risk going home? Was she ready to face her mother, though Jack was hoping that she was beginning to see just how hard it might have been for her this past year. Jack was part of that. "Just let me stay. You'll see. I can help you through whatever happens. I can do it." Linda stood. She shivered with cold.

Jack was at a loss. To allow it or not seemed beside the point suddenly. It wasn't Linda who was stuck in the middle, it was he and he'd clearly put himself there. Night was coming on.

"I need to take the tools back to the garage. Why don't you go on inside. You're cold. We can finish this up another time." Jack pulled the pitchfork from the ground, gathered the shovel and rake, and said, "We'll figure out what to do."

"I won't bring what we talked about up to Martha."

"I expect I need to do that." Jack let out a little exasperated laugh tinged with sadness and disappeared into the dark garage where he fumbled around for the bottle of bourbon and found it swathed in rags, comfortable to the touch, and felt the ache of the amber liquid that could soothe so much, but he carried the bottle from the garage and threw it out as far as he possibly could into the night, past the turned up garden, and listened for shattering glass.

Surfaces

Martha spent the afternoon crafting a tuna bake, which was now cooking in the oven. Cans of tuna, cream of chicken soup and French fried onions littered the counter. Her problem with cooking was cleaning.

What should have taken her fifteen minutes: grating cheese, opening cans, measuring amounts and selecting the right pot to put it all in, had, in fact, taken over an hour, and she couldn't quite place where all those minutes went. She'd caught herself not knowing where the time had gone to in the past weeks and was attributing it to the coming anniversary, which she was trying to keep at bay.

Linda had been a big help with that. Only when she was away at school, and Jack at work, did she lose herself. Since the trip to the train station, even when all of them were in the house, she caught herself staring off into space. She told herself that perhaps anyone in her situation would be subject to 'time lapses' as she called them. She'd told herself, 'I just had a time lapse, that's all.' Her whole body seemed to heat up during them, and she found that the back of her neck felt slightly damp.

When Linda came in it snapped her out of a 'time lapse.' Linda didn't say anything, but rather avoided looking at Martha and went off into her room as quickly as possible. Martha sensed a change in her. She was going to call after her, but decided against it.

A few minutes later Jack stamped his feet outside the kitchen door. There were the few moments as he removed his boots, then the door swung open. A cold blast of wind followed him through as it had Linda moments ago. Jack stood and looked at Martha in a strange way – it seemed quite vacant as if he didn't register that she was standing in front of him. Martha couldn't decipher the feeling or intent behind it. With this and Linda sweeping by, it seemed like a sudden shift of weight in the house.

"What's the matter, honey?" Martha asked.

Jack absently said to her, "Nothing, just um nothing."

"Are you sure? Because Linda just walked through here without a word; not a hello or anything."

"Hmmm."

"Did something happen outside?"

"We turned a few pumpkins over." Jack tried his best to lighten the conversation, but his voice ended on a down note and Martha picked up on it.

"Linda seemed a bit sad."

"Really?".

"Is she missing her mother?"

"Well, I expect so. I think it might be starting to weigh heavy on her," Jack said. Martha thought it might be a response of what he wanted for Linda, not what he knew she was feeling.

Martha turned away from Jack to check on the casserole and buy some time. She peered inside the oven and felt the heat waves wash over her face. The casserole bubbled around the rim; the smell of cream and tuna hit her in an unpleasant way. Maybe she'd made a mistake. Underneath her ridiculous thoughts on dinner, panic, which she'd buried for some months, in fact, had nearly forgotten its sensation, began taking hold. To her, it was an unraveling, not unlike how a diver might feel if they were in the middle of their approach and realized they were going to miss the board's end; the careful façade of control a diver creates suddenly vanishes and they are left tumbling in mid-air. When she stood up, she was hesitant to face Jack.

After all these years, he knew the signs of her letting go.

"Is she leaving?" Martha asked.

"No, not yet."

Martha circled around the small square of kitchen. "She can't leave."

"She doesn't want to."

"But you want her to, don't you?"

"I think it'd be best for her… and for Clare in the long run, don't you think? She's had time to think about things."

Martha began to unravel. "What am I going to do?" Martha said, as her face crumpled.

"We'll leave," Jack said, going to her, "We'll take the trailer and go south where it'll be warm."

"We can't leave Linda here alone." Martha searched for confirmation from Jack that she would go with them.

"Honey, I," Jack stammered. "Honey, don't you think…"

"Linda shouldn't be left alone again."

"Martha," Jack took hold of her shoulder, "Linda will be just fine." He said, forcefully, "are you sure it's not you who's afraid of being left alone?"

Martha reeled around and broke away from Jack. She wanted to leave the kitchen, but he was in her way. She turned at the sink to him and stopped. "I have been alone all of these years, Jack. You go to work everyday. When you are here that's the only time I know someone is here, but even then you find ways of leaving me alone when you're home – all those hours in the garden, the new trailer, working on your cars with Carl. I sit here alone in this kitchen so much."

It was clear to Martha that he'd never thought of it that way. "Why did you tell Linda that you and I met at Union Station? You knew it wasn't true. Do you know why you took her there?"

"Because it's true." Martha said. "Because that's the first thing I saw of Kansas City – the very first. And you were the second thing. I remember us meeting there under the clock."

"We never did that, Martha. You might have seen others there, but it was never us."

"I came by train, you were waiting for me. We met there."

"We met in the bottoms. You were getting off work. I saw you. You may be confused because of all the train tracks there, but they were only for the stockyards. You remember them? But they were mostly unused after the flood. You and I, we were just working down there and I saw you. You were so beautiful."

"I was?"

"Yes." Jack said, moving in closer to her. "You were the most beautiful woman I'd ever seen. You remember don't you? You were standing on the corner and I was coming out of the store."

"You followed me." Martha stepped back.

"That's right."

"It wasn't the station. The station was too far away. But, oh, how I wish it were." Martha leaned against the sink.

"It would have been a better memory than what really happened."

"The clock said five-fifteen. I remember it. Five-fifteen. I came out of the doors with all those people from the train, and the clock said five-fifteen. And I noted the time in my head because that's when I knew I was safe and no one could send me off, or put me away or take anything away from me again."

"You were young."

"She would have been Linda's age by now."

"I know."

"I wanted another baby."

"Yes, and we tried."

"But you didn't really want it, did you?"

"Not at first. I didn't think we should have one." Jack wanted to snatch the last bit back, but now it was out there. "I almost lost you when the baby was gone and my worst fears came true."

"Why is everything taken from me?" Martha searched Jack's eyes.

"I can't answer that. But I'm still here." Jack took Martha in his arms and in his mind hated her parents, hated that they'd sent her away for becoming pregnant, that what they did set her adrift. It took so long for Martha to tell the whole story to him, and she never quite exactly told him, but he'd pieced it together over the years. The links to the puzzle were extracted from her on their trip to Martha's home to make peace with her parents so that by the time they arrived, he was glad that she couldn't bring herself to knock on their door.

"Linda could be ours, you know."

"Linda can never be ours. You must know that deep down."

"But she came all the way out here."

"She had nowhere else to go." Jack tried to make her focus on this, the last attempt to try and make her understand. "I don't know how else to say it, but she isn't ours to keep."

Linda stood at the kitchen doorway. She saw the end of the conversation, and heard the rest from the hallway. Her understanding of what transpired sat just out of reach except for the fact that Martha lost two children, and that losing her would be unbearable. This revelation and the last year, and all that had happened broke through Linda and stirred a deep well of love. The year's accumulation of fact, Martha's losses, and the one thing she clung to that gave her life meaning disappeared while Martha lay alone in the dark waiting for Linda and her mother to find her, nearly wasted away, losing her child. Martha was just holding on. Linda understood it. She felt it like a discordant note.

When Martha saw Linda in the doorway, all of her memories came flooding back like passing window frames: her lost babies, her family, the lost boy in the lake, the Bottoms, and all the years alone.

Outside, a boot of cold descended on Olathe. The temperature plummeted. Ice formed around the window edges. The house chilled.

The three of them stood in the kitchen together. None of them knew what to say, and they all waited for the other to speak. Finally, Martha moved away from Jack and went to the oven. She pulled the casserole out. Jack got plates and silverware and Linda filled glasses with water. Each of them went to the table carrying something. They ate in silence. Afterwards, they deposited the dishes in the sink and Linda went to her room, Martha to the bedroom and Jack turned the heat lower in the house and went out to the garage.

Linda slipped the record out of the sleeve from "Everybody Digs Bill Evans" and placed it on the turntable. She put the needle down at the start of Peace Piece and lay down on the carpet to listen.

Martha heard the slow piano chords through the wall, the notes with so much breathing space between, singular notes posited over a repeating pattern. Wonderful, she thought, how Linda's father left such a lovely gift to her as this.

Martha dressed for bed and slowly brushed her hair. She took a long look in the mirror and then went into the bedroom, turned the sheets down and climbed in to wait for Jack. An hour passed. She heard him close the kitchen door, walk down the hall and pause at Linda's room. She was still playing the same record over and over. He came in, undressed and climbed into their bed. Martha turned to him, kissed him lightly, and then turned away. He pulled Martha to him, into his body as tight as possible, and went to sleep. Martha lay awake until his light snores took hold and slipped from his arms, his warmth, and the bed. She went into the bathroom, drew a glass of water, and took the pain and sleeping pills she'd gathered over the past year one at a time until they were gone.

In her nightdress, she moved silently down the hall, past the quiet of Linda's room and out into the cold night. The moon had come up and given the Airstream a clear blue sheen. She stopped just in front and ran her fingers lightly over its surface. Just like this. He felt just like this. Then she went into the trailer, pulled a blanket from under the settee, lay down and waited for sleep.

Jack woke from something he felt missing. He reached across the bed for Martha, lifted his head and saw it empty. He whispered, "Martha?" and then lifted himself up, and switched on the lamplight. He listened for any sort of sound in the house. Up and down the hall, he went, checking all the rooms and then the bathroom where he saw the empty vials, turned, and on a dead run ran out of the house to the Airstream.

The oval door swung on its hinges. He stepped up into the trailer and saw Martha's shape under blankets and shouted at her. There was no response. He couldn't see her skin's color, but he felt her loss of temperature, lifted her up and carried her out of the trailer and back in the house to warmth.

He carried her across the kitchen to the cupboard with the hydrogen peroxide and baking soda and mixed it with water. He held her upright and made her drink, which was the only thing he thought to do.

He poured it in her mouth, pulled back her head and hoped it went down her throat. In the moments of sheer terror, between the liquid, and Martha's first reaction of a cough, he felt himself slipping away. What if this is what she wanted, after all? What if her whole life was about this desperate measure?

The silence was terrible.

But then the cough, and then Martha doubling over against the sink and letting everything she swallowed empty out of her. She slumped into Jack's arms, which held her head up and he pushed his chest out to catch her shoulders sliding down. As he held her, he called for police, who called for an ambulance. He picked her up and made her walk around and around the house.

"You are going to live, Martha," he said, shuffling her feet, "by God, you are going to live. We have places to go and see. Beautiful places. All the mountains, the Great Plains, we'll ride the rails across rivers. You have to stay with me. I don't want to be with anyone else."

Jack felt her struggling hard against sleep and kept taking her to the sink, bringing water to her lips, making her drink. He had no idea what to do, except what he thought he should. In the half hour it took for the ambulance to arrive, grace and love returned to him in the opening of her eyes to see him, only him, holding on to the one thing that mattered.

Days later, with Martha in hospital again under observation, and Jack wandering aimlessly around the house spending long hours with Carl in the garage, Linda called her Mother who answered on the second ring.

"I thought you should know something." Linda said, wondering if she'd done the right thing calling her just now.

"It's so good to hear your voice." Clare said, her own up a notch with hurry in it. "What is it? Are you okay?"

"Martha is back in the hospital. I thought you should know. I'm not coming home. I need to see Jack through for a bit."

This was a lot to take in for Clare took a few moments before she spoke. "I will wait. I'm curious to know what happened, but that can wait, too. I'm sorry for Jack. He does seem to be a good man."

"He is."

"Can I bring you two out anything? Food? Anything?"

"We're fine. We've got more than enough. His friends at work have brought plenty. I just thought you should know."

Clare quickly said, "Honey?"

"Yes?"

"I'm so sorry. For everything."

Linda hesitated before saying to her mother, "I'll talk to you in a few days."

A week after the call to her mother, Jack came into her room and said, "I want to show you something."

Linda got up off the floor where she'd been reading and followed him outside. She saw the Ford backed up to the front of the Airstream.

"Carl helped me put the sway bar on. He did a smart job of it." Jack stared at this work a moment and said, "I want to see if it works. Will you help me hitch the trailer to the wagon?"

"Sure."

"Okay, I need you to back up the car just slightly until the hitch is right over the ball here." Jack pointed to a silver ball protruding from the rear of the wagon and looked up at Linda. "See. Think you can do it?"

"Of course." Linda went to the car and climbed in. She watched for Jack's hand in the rearview mirror and inched back accordingly.

"That's it!" He shouted. "Okay, come back here a moment and let me show you this." Linda went behind the car and watched as Jack demonstrated how the hitch worked by cranking on a handle that lowered it onto the ball while holding a lever in until it snapped in place. "Did you see how that worked? We just had to get it into position and lower it down. Easy as pie. But then you have to attach this wire here, see, so that it works the rear end lights on the trailer." Linda watched him take a black-corded plug and put it into a socket just under the trailer's front lip.

"Are you going somewhere?"

Jack stood up and brushed the dirt off his knee. "No."

"Are you selling the Airstream then?"

"I've thought about it awfully hard. Why don't we take it out to see if the sway bar helps some. Do you mind driving?" Jack went to the passenger side door and looked back. Linda, slightly confused as to why Jack didn't want to test it himself, hadn't moved. "C'mon, let's give it a try."

Linda climbed back into the driver's side.

Jack said, "Okay, now, go slow up the drive."

Linda felt the trailer's weight lurch forward against the wagons' back and then felt it pull as the car moved forward. They crested the drive and stopped to wait for cars passing on the road before she pulled out. Once they got up to speed, the wagon pulled the Airstream easily.

"I think it feels pretty solid, don't you?"

"Yes, but don't you want to try it?"

"No." Jack said, flatly.

"Where are we going?" Linda asked.

Jack thought for a moment and couldn't come up with any sort of destination and said, "I don't really know. Why don't you just go wherever you want," Jack added and settled back in his seat.

"Are you sure?"

"We've got plenty of gas."

Linda drove southwest and ended up on highway 50. "How about Wichita?" she finally asked after seeing a sign that read Emporia 82 miles and Wichita 127.

"Sounds about perfect."

In the days after Martha was found in the Airstream, Linda did a fair amount of driving with Jack to and from the hospital. She waited in the car or in the lobby most days while they visited. Along the way he quizzed her about traffic signs and signals, drinking while driving, parts of the car, the ten two hand position. It was all so comical to Linda, but it was something Jack wanted to do for her. A few days before Martha was to return home, Jack took her to the DMV and she got her license, him signing the consent as her father, Mr. Wallich. They never bothered to look at his identification. She wondered why he took such interest, but attributed it to the fact that he needed something to do or he'd be worse off than he was.

She knew he wasn't sleeping. She also noted that he didn't step into the trailer for days afterwards and avoided it altogether. Once Carl started coming over nights after work, Jack seemed to lighten some. She also saw that Carl spent some time sizing the trailer up and walking around it several times without ever going inside out of deference to Jack.

It was a surprise then when Jack brought her outside to hitch up the trailer. Now they were passing through Emporia, through its downtown, stopping at red lights and crosswalks on their way to Wichita.

"I think we're good." Jack said. "Why don't we make a turn and head back home."

"Are you sure?"

"Yes. I think you've done great." Linda laughed and looked over at Jack who reached into the glove compartment and pulled out an envelope. "Why don't you pull over there," he said and pointed to an open curb. She saw it and negotiated her way over angling both the wagon and the trailer as close to the curb as possible. She turned the car engine off and asked, "How was that?"

"You're already an expert," Jack said and smiled, shifting toward Linda in his seat. He held the envelope up. "This holds the registrations for both the car and Airstream. I want you to have them. It also contains money to see you through for several months and you can always call me to ask for more. You will have to square all of this with your mother somehow, but I'm sure you will."

Linda was stunned. "But Carl wanted this."

"He did. But it's mine to give to you."

"I don't know what to say."

"I can't look out the window everyday and see the trailer." Jack's eyes rimmed with tears. "And I expect you don't want to go home and live with your mother." He hesitated before going on, "Martha doesn't want to see it before she returns and when she was young, she made her choice to leave her home when she did. I think you'd like a way to make that choice as well. You can't stay with us much longer. It's not good for you or Martha and me. We need to find our own way." Jack waited for Linda to say something.

"I wouldn't know where to go."

"You'll find somewhere to be," Jack said.

The next day, Jack finally went inside the Airstream to show Linda how everything worked. She waited to be called so he could have a moment to himself. When he did call for her, he took her hand and helped her up the step. She could see the pain on his face, but he immediately launched into the details of the plumbing, the electrical and how the appliances worked. In a half hour, her head swam with information and Jack marked the most important parts in the manuals. He wrote emergency numbers for work, Airstream dealers, and his home phone across the top. Martha had outfitted the trailer well with pots and pans, kitchen items, a first aid kit, flashlights, batteries, towels and linens. They opened every drawer and took its inventory. Jack was surprised.

He hadn't realized just how close he and Martha were to leaving until he'd seen all of the work she'd done. Every so often, he'd stop and stare at something, forget Linda was there, and then pull himself back from his thoughts and carry on with Linda's tutorial.

In the evenings, they researched camps and incorporated the work he and Martha had done. They gathered photos and made more notes in one of his black journaling notebooks. They worked late into the night.

Finally, there was nothing left for Jack to tell Linda. They drove to her school and checked her out telling the registrar that she was moving out of state. He made Linda promise to finish school someday, which she gave to him. On the way home, Jack was very quiet and kept turning away to watch the passing land.

So much had happened. He returned to the moment he'd first seen Martha, her shape in the sun's reflection off the shop window and her turning, her hair swinging across her face, her eyes glinting and catching his. Love does happen like this, he remembered thinking, love like a train arriving home. Every love waiting for the moment they step off, turn and find a clock to record the moment. And all the years since, all the problems that ensued will be forgotten except that one moment, when his world changed and he wanted to be a good man.

"You know, I've always wanted children." Jack said, "Always wanted a boy and girl."

Linda was surprised to hear it, but was glad. "You have me," she said, "and you still have time. You and Martha taught me so much, " Linda said, and overcome with her own kind of grief reached over and took his hand. "You both saved my life."

"I'm glad of it," Jack said, "but I expect it's time for you to go."

When they got home, Linda went into the house to collect her things. She removed the Bill Evans record from the turntable, sleeved it, and took it into Jack and Martha's bedroom and placed it on his pillow. When she went outside, Jack was polishing the Airstream one last time, removing the accumulated dust. He heard her behind him and turned and smiled as if he'd been caught.

"You'll have to find something else to do," Linda said and laughed.

"I expect so."

She went inside the trailer and stowed her things and came back out to find Jack waiting for her.

"I'd go south to escape the weather," he offered, "but it's up to you now."

"I've had enough of cold," Linda said, and walked up to Jack who took her in his arms.

"I'll always be here."

"And I'll send you postcards from everywhere."

Leaving

Jack spent the morning of Clare's hospital release turning the soil in the garden one last time. He closed down the house, pulled all the draperies, gave a house key to Carl, who was waiting in the driveway now, trunk raised, waiting to accept the luggage.

Jack had packed his suitcase, then Martha's. He'd packed for summer and winter – not knowing how long they'd be gone.

Outside, Jack handed the suitcases to Carl, who swung them up and into the trunk.

"Don't forget to show Bill and Susan around when they come." Jack had rented the house to a young couple from Utah; the husband having accepted a job recently and needed a place in a hurry.

"I've already spoken to them." Carl said, turning the ignition "Are you sure you're doing the right thing?"

The car roared to life and they both looked at each other and smiled.

"You've added the new manifold," Jack said.

"I did." Carl said, and laughed. "After hours, of course."

"Of course," Jack slapped the dashboard, "Let's see how she sounds out there."

When they arrived at the hospital, Jack found Martha, light streaming through the picture glass, standing in the hallway outside her room. She had a small bag.

"You are packing light, my dear."

"I'm done here," she said.

"I'm glad of that," Jack said, and took her lightly by the elbow and guided her out.

Carl drove them the few short miles to Union Station, parked the car along the near empty loading zone. The building's gray granite loomed like a cliff. It still maintained its majesty – all its history encased in it from another age.

Carl lifted the bags from the trunk as Jack guided Martha out of her seat. "You two stay safe and let us know where you are on occasion." Jack nodded and took the bags from Carl.

"My parent's cabin is waiting for us." Martha said, "I expect we'll be there for some time."

"You have the rest of summer, I suppose."

"It's best when the snows come," Martha said, "It gives you time for repair."

"I expect so," Carl said.

Martha laughed, "You picked that saying up from Jack." She turned toward the monolithic station, and then said to Jack, "I believe it's five-fifteen. We should be going."

Jack shook Carl's hand. "Thanks for the lift," he said, and nodded toward the car. "She sounds beautiful."

When Clare put down the receiver after Linda's call, her head was so full of thoughts that she had to go outside for air. She was coming home. She knew it would happen soon enough. She'd told Stuart as much. She'd said to him, "It's a matter of time, you know, they won't want to keep her. They have enough going on in their lives..." She'd prattled on so much about all the reasons why Linda would come up that walk one day that Stuart finally had to tell her to stop. He didn't want her expectations to get the best of her, he told her, and frankly, he was tired of it.

But they both had their troubles. He with his father, and she with her daughter, which evened them out enough so that when they were alone together, they exhausted all their frustrations in the first hour and learned to enjoy having each other for company.

Clare couldn't find a soul outside to tell them the good news, so she sat on the stoop and smoked her Pall Malls one after another to calm herself. Finally, Mrs. Adderley came out of her house shouldering a sweater on over her bony shape. Having watched Clare just sitting there for over an hour was too much for her curiosity.

"Clare, is there something wrong? She asked, "I've been spying on you far too long."

They both laughed and then Clare said joyfully, "Linda is coming home."

"That's wonderful news, isn't it?"

"Yes, it is." Clare said, smiling broadly. "It's the best news."

"Well, then," Mrs. Adderley continued, "The neighborhood will take some shape again, what with Linda coming home and new neighbors moving in next door."

"It's been quite a year." Clare said, stamping out a cigarette on the concrete step adding to a number of small black buttons of ash.

"You should go inside and get a sweater, you know. And you need some pumpkins! Look at all the pumpkins on the street and your house doesn't have a single one! I could get Mr. Adderley to carve you up one or two."

To appease her, Clare said, "That would be nice."

Mrs. Adderley, now with another mission, turned to go. "It's too cold to be outside. I'm so glad to hear Linda's coming home. We missed her!"

Clare watched Mrs. Adderley walk back across the street. She waited to see that she got inside, and then turned to go into her own home. She went to Linda's room and turned on the light. Maybe it was time to freshen it up with new paint, curtains, and a new bedspread. It was far too young for her now. But she'd wait and let her daughter choose anything she wanted.

She worried about how to tell Linda about Stuart, whether they'd get along. They had talked about him moving in with her or she with him. His house was larger given the converted basement he'd done up for his father. They'd talk about a situation for Linda who, most likely would be gone in a couple of years anyway living on her own, hopefully with a good job or at school. It certainly would save them both the needed money and with Linda coming home, and the income from Jack most likely running out, it was sure to force a decision.

During the next several days, she told Stuart everything she knew about her daughter, showed him her pictures, the scrapbook she kept. She told him about the night her husband died and everything after. She wanted him to have the whole story. And every day, she went to work and came home to the house and cleaned it top to bottom. She fixed up the backyard like it was when her husband was alive. She cut the laurel back between the old Miller house and theirs. The idea of a new family being born fixated her so completely that, at times, she thought that Stuart might have believed she'd lost her mind. But he reveled in watching her work, become happy again, and he fell in love enough to decide that he'd make her his own very soon.

Mostly, Clare counted down the hours until Linda came home.

On a Friday evening, the sun still at enough of an angle to rake the streets, a bright, shining light flashed through Clare's house. It drew her to the window where she recognized the Ford wagon and trailer. Her whole heart thumped like thunder. Inside the car was Linda. She was surprised to see her alone, expecting Jack to at least be in the passenger seat. But it was only Linda who emerged, hesitating in the driver's seat while she looked up at the house. Clare went to the door, opened it and went out on the stoop. Her hand came to her mouth and her eyes were so full she could barely see her way down the steps.

Linda came around the front of the car and met her mother halfway from the curb. Time passed before Clare said, "I'm so glad you came home."

Linda didn't say anything, and just stared at her mother. Finally, she said, "You've changed. You look different."

"I do?" Clare asked.

"Yes... happy."

"Hmmm." Clare said, "I'm glad to see you." Clare shyly took her daughter's hand and lightly squeezed it as if it were a thing she couldn't have. She looked hard at Linda and then over her shoulder at the Airstream. "You're not staying."

"No."

Linda remembered what Jack had said about her mother, how hard it was for her, and all her disappointments. And whether she believed him and wanted to let her mother off the hook was of no importance. Before Clare could react, Linda held her mother as hard as she could and said, "You were a good mother."

"No," Clare whispered, "No, I wasn't."

"Yes," said Linda, and looked into her mother's eyes, "Yes, you were."

Stuart, who watched from the window, came out of the house and down into the front yard where the two women were. Clare introduced him and Linda smiled and shook his hand. She told them about Martha and the week that followed. How Jack came to give her the Airstream. She offered up the idea of a weekly call. They would see each other again soon she promised; there would be a time that her mother could join her in some far place. They both recognized a change in each other that went beyond time, beyond the events that brought them there.

After awhile, they'd all said everything they could. The sun was low in the sky as Clare followed her daughter to the car where she climbed in.

"I have to go," Linda said.

Clare backed away from the passenger window and bravely said, "I know."

Linda smiled. She held her eyes on her mother as long as she could, and she reached out her hand, tentatively, as if it were the last time, and said. "I'm going streaming."

A young woman wearing a cardigan is driving a Ford Country Squire pulling an Airstream trailer. Her sweater is missing a button two down from the top. She'll find a needle and thread soon enough, but she's put the button in her pocket for repair. Winter is coming on. A cold wind through the dry leaves makes them tumble down like confetti. It is near dark. She'll drive south through the night. When day breaks, she will be somewhere else. She hasn't made up her mind as to where to go, but if you were looking down on the streets, on the highways, on the endless rivers running in all directions, you'd know by the way she holds her head, or the purpose in her eyes, that she'll find a direction and follow it.

Acknowledgements

Thanks go to Elizabeth Cox for her belief in the story, her dedication as a teacher, and her encouragement. To Doug Bauer who sent me down the right road. Jill McCorkle for her sound advice. To Rebecca Evarts for sharing her insights, and to the community of writers and teachers at Bennington College so many years ago.

Thanks to readers of early drafts, Adine Maron, Elena Schabarum, Tammy Frank, Roberta Johnson, and especially Karen Fortenberry, for their insights and friendship.

My thanks to my editor, Amberly Finarelli, who took great care in guiding this story forward.

To Bob Sutryk for showing me around Kansas City, providing a place to stay, taking pictures when I asked for them, and for being such a dear friend all these years.

Finally, to my Grandmother, whose life has inspired mine.

Made in the USA
Columbia, SC
29 May 2018